Infuriated by her disobedience, Jasper followed the governess. "Mrs. Radcliffe!"

Mrs. Sophie Radcliffe finally stopped, but urged the children to continue into the long gallery without her. They looked back, slightly bewildered, but then she closed the door on them and turned to face him. "Yes, my lord?"

"What do you think you are doing down here? I gave strict instructions that all staff are to remain in other parts of the palace."

"You gave instruction to the palace servants. That is true. However, as the butler pointed out, I am not in the Duke of Ravenswood's employ, but his brother's," she said with a haughty tilt of her head. "I do as he says.

Love and Other Disasters

HEATHER BOYD

CHAPTER ONE

"JASPER," the Duke of Ravenswood said slowly. "London will have to wait till next season. I need you to stay here for the summer."

"What? Why?" Jasper Sweet, third son of the late Duke of Ravenswood, brother to the current duke, couldn't be more surprised by this unexpected order.

"Someone must keep an eye on things. Unfortunately, Nash and I are committed to this house party I promised to attend," Ravenswood murmured, looking grim, and then shrugged. "And Stratford has already promised himself to visit Aston. I'll need you here for the entire summer."

"Oh," Jasper said, utterly surprised at the duke's sudden request.

For years, Jasper had happily absented himself from the estate and reveled in the delights of

London, seeking pleasure and fulfillment, often in the worst places. Mostly to irritate his late and hardly missed sire. London had become home. A place where men like him gathered to be at their ease. Jasper wasn't truly needed at the Ravenswood estate. At least, he never had been until tonight's pronouncement.

Jasper had once had lots of plans for this summer. Plans for the money he should have inherited but had gifted to his brother instead. He'd made the necessary adjustments without rancor or regret. Yet now it seemed his adjustments were still not enough. He sighed heavily, imagining an endless summer of boredom ahead of him.

Yes, the delights of London could and seemingly must wait. Ravenswood was never left unattended to by family.

Yet Jasper had only just returned to the estate after emptying Freemont Villa of his possessions ahead of the sale of the place. He'd planned not to unpack and head toward London immediately.

"What am I to do with myself here?"

"I have drawn up a list of the most pressing matters that require oversight," Nash said, coming forward to hand it to him. "There are other matters that I shall not burden you with. They can wait until our return. I'm sure you'll find them all tedious."

Nash had so little idea of what Jasper found

tedious. His lack of faith was as apparent as their father's had always been. Father had excluded Jasper from serious discussions or sent him away whenever there was a problem on the estate to be solved. Yet, he was just as capable as his brothers.

Jasper had always been told that as a third son, he would never be important. For a time in his younger life, he'd lived up to that prediction. However, he'd too much intelligence to not make some effort to improve himself. He'd spent years visiting friends' estates, drinking away his days and nights. However, that did not mean he'd not had his eye on the future, too. He had studied the activities of other families and every farm under their management, comparing the differences and successes.

However, to his family, until now, he'd pretended indifference to all that. But he was probably as well versed in land management as the duke and Nash. A fact of which his late father could never believe him capable, hence his disinterest in providing his third son much beyond a basic education. Jasper had to direct his own learning from the age of twelve, when his older brothers had both departed for Cambridge and Father had declared tutors unnecessary.

With Father gone now, was there any point pretending he didn't know a fallow field from one bursting with a harvest-ready crop? He pulled a face.

Nash immediately turned to the duke. "Perhaps I should stay."

"No," the duke said. "I need you there by my side, distracting everyone from what I'm really there for."

The new Duke of Ravenswood was on his way to claim a bride and not just any woman would do. Lady Stephanie Kent had already been chosen for the honor. She was the right age, had impeccable connections, and most importantly of all...she had pots of money to bring to the union. That, however, did not make her a particularly nice woman. Jasper was extremely glad the pair had not asked him to accompany them.

Jasper exhaled as Nash finally gave in to the duke's decision. "Very well. I will remain behind."

"Good." Ravenswood beamed at him. "Think of it as some well-deserved relaxation in readiness for the coming season. Your return to Town, with money in your pockets then, is sure to be vastly more satisfying than pinching every penny and trying to hide that fact."

Jasper nodded in agreement. He had no money because he'd loaned it all to save Ravenswood, just as they all had. "It better be."

Jasper had had plans for that money, and the

inheritance he'd long hoped for, too. Father had bled the estate dry. The newly adopted Sweet brother family motto was *sink or swim together*, but it seemed they were going their separate ways for the summer.

The duke winced. "I'd gladly remain behind with you if I could."

Nash glared. "That is because you're still fighting your fate. Your intended bride knows you're coming."

"She's not my intended yet," the duke said quietly.

"She must be by the end of the visit," Nash reminded the duke somewhat unkindly.

Ravenswood looked away; his expression troubled. Clearly, Ravenswood had hoped there might yet be an alternative to marrying Lady Stephanie Kent. Jasper loathed the woman, but she had the money to save Ravenswood from crippling debt and the humiliation of society finding out about their precarious state. Father had likely planned all along for his recalcitrant son to come to heel and marry the woman he'd always favored. Ravenswood had not done their father's bidding in the beginning, to marry the woman he'd chosen as the next duchess, but it was inevitable that in death, he'd get his wish.

The new duke was not reconciled to it yet, though.

Ravenswood straightened his shoulders. "We should rejoin the others."

"Might as well," Jasper agreed. Unfortunately, the others he referred to amounted to two relations and a dull governess who kept appearing at the dining table. Poor company indeed, for a discerning bachelor like himself.

They left the smoking room together, strolling the shadowed halls of Ravenswood with unhurried intention. Where once they might have moved as silently as possible, now they strode boldly about Ravenswood's carved wood-paneled halls. Masters of this domain at last.

Jasper took great delight in owning, in a fashion, a tiny portion of the estate his brother had inherited. He'd given over all of his fortune to his eldest brother by way of a loan in order to save the estate. It was all nicely legal and one day that money would return to him with interest paid. In the meantime, he'd been told to make himself at home, and he certainly intended to do just that.

The duke led the way into the drawing room, throwing open the doors and catching the occupants by surprise. The ladies—Lady Win Sweet and Mrs. Amity Crawford—were not alone anymore. Stratford Sweet, their younger and newly married brother, was draped over his wife's shoulder, though Win did not seem to mind him doing so. Roman Crawford, husband of their cousin

Amity, was acting with slightly more dignity. He was merely holding his wife's hand.

"I thought you'd gone out," Jasper said to them.

"We're just returned," Crawford promised. "Fetched that half barrel of rum Uncle Henry had hidden under his old bed quicker than expected. I shall offer him a replacement when we see him. He left a few other things behind of value that I cannot in good conscience keep about and plan to return."

Crawford was a good man and unfailingly honest. But Jasper was glad Crawford and his wife would quit their newly purchased estate, and the district, to visit his family soon. He wouldn't be much of a companion during the summer anyway as he had a wife to amuse these days.

He looked about the room and then breathed a sigh of relief. The governess Nash had hired, who kept turning up for every family dinner lately, must have scurried off to bed. Probably for the best. Mrs. Sophie Radcliffe was deficient in good humor. He'd never met a woman who irritated him as much. Radcliffe's disapproving expression whenever they met spoke volumes of her true feelings about his presence. With her gone from the drawing room, Jasper could at least spend the night drinking rum in peace. This was to be his last evening amid family for quite a while, after all. The duke and Nash would go to secure a wealthy duchess and Stratford and his bride were leaving too. By tomorrow's luncheon, he'd be all alone.

What the devil was he going to do to amuse himself here for so many months?

Jasper collected a glass of rum, downed it, refilled the glass, and backed straight toward his favorite chair to sip the rest and think.

He heard a woman's squeak of protest as he dropped blindly into the chair and landed where he ought never want to be—on the governess' lap.

"Bloody hell!" Jasper cursed as he scrambled up and spun to face Radcliffe. "What the devil are you doing sitting in my chair?"

"I was here first." The governess fanned herself vigorously. "Minding my own business until you came to squash me."

Mrs. Sophie Radcliffe, a plain woman in an even plainer gown, who spent her time ordering other people's children about, always spoke to him in a way that suggested it was beneath her dignity. She was prickly, disagreeable, and as prim as they come. Traits that instantly repelled Jasper and yet challenged him to needle her. She sat in his favorite chair, thin fingers holding a faded shawl clutched tight about her shoulders, a few strands of her hair falling out of an inelegant bun as usual, and simply stared at Jasper...obviously waiting for him to remember his manners and apologize.

However, around Sophie Radcliffe, he'd not the slightest urge to be at all gentlemanly. She brought out every instinct in him to do his worst and drive her away from Ravenswood Palace. The last governess had been much older, but her presence had never bothered him in the least. Only this one seemed to get under his skin. "I would never squash a *lady*."

"But you would a governess?"

He remembered his rum and took a sip before answering. "I have never given governesses much thought. One way or the other."

Her eyes narrowed. "I'm sure you've many other more important interests. It's clear they were on your mind tonight instead of watching where you were going."

"Is there a problem?" Nash asked, suddenly beside Jasper and frowning as he glanced at each of them.

"No." Jasper did not bother to explain the conversation to his brother. Nash had become too defensive of the woman he'd hired lately for his taste. It was entirely Nash's idea to bring the governess out of the nursery so often of late, too. No one else thought of it or her.

Mrs. Radcliffe offered Nash a warm smile.

"Everything is perfect, thank you. I was just telling Lord Jasper about your sons' many accomplishments. They are so clever. Such perfect little gentlemen. Excellent manners. They must get that from their father."

She smiled and blathered on a bit more and Jasper tuned her words out, to watch his brother lap up every bit of praise she uttered for his offspring, including the oft-repeated hope that Nash would visit the nursery to say good night to them.

"Perhaps. Do excuse me," Nash murmured, but likely would not oblige her in that, of course. Nash stayed well clear of the third floor, and his children.

Nash went away, back to the duke's conversation and the rum, and Mrs. Radcliffe's smile dropped from her face immediately. She turned colder eyes on him. "I am still waiting for an apology."

"Everyone knows that is my seat," Jasper protested.

The governess' eyes widened, and she examined the chair she was sitting on with exaggerated interest. "I do not see your name engraved on it. You ought to get a little plaque affixed to the headrest, perhaps. Something of substance to declare your superior ownership. The children are fortunate to have their names on their door already. You should ask your brother for the same."

Jasper scowled at the suggestion he was being childish about the chair, but everyone ought to know by now that he always sat there after dinner. Radcliffe was not above reminding him subtly that he was not the duke, too. Some governesses were said to never speak their minds, let alone attempt to say anything provocative. Trust Nash to have hired the one woman with a wealth of opinions she only cared to share with Jasper.

In fact, to everyone else, Sophie Radcliffe was perfectly civil. Not even Stratford's endless chatter seemed to get on her nerves.

He was composing a suitable response to ensure he got in the last word tonight when a hand settled on his shoulder. *Stratford, of course.* Stratford knew the latest governess got on his nerves and had taken an interest in keeping them apart, or at least civil of late. Jasper scowled at his brother for the interruption.

Stratford merely grinned at him. "You know, you're becoming as blind as me. I almost never see what's right in front of me. Just ask my wife."

"She was behind me," Jasper ground out. "I don't have eyes in the back of my head."

"Poor Mrs. Radcliffe," Stratford said solicitously to the governess. "Assaulted by my brother's backside so early in the evening. You must be so traumatized by the ordeal. I shall fetch you a glass of sherry to cheer you up."

Jasper caught his brother's arm before he could rush off. "Have I ever told you that you talk too much?"

"Frequently," Stratford answered, grinning stupidly. "It's my most endearing quality."

Jasper released his sibling's arm with a fond laugh. He found it impossible to keep a bad mood around his younger brother, and Stratford likely knew that, too.

The governess cleared her throat. "Never fear, Lord Stratford. I will swiftly recover once your brother finds his misplaced manners," she vowed, giving him a look that said, *oh just get it over with.* "Perhaps if he has a moment to gather his thoughts, he could compose one while you fetch me that drink you promised."

Jasper scowled at the governess. Who was she to order his brother, a lord, away?

But Radcliffe ignored him and had her lips pressed together tightly again in the way she always seemed to. A pity she couldn't find even Stratford amusing, because she was vastly improved in looks whenever she smiled. Jasper had seen her laugh once with his brother's children. The transformation had been an utter shock. She had looked lovely and almost enticing for an entire minute. Yet carefree laughter was reserved only for her young charges.

Stratford mumbled something unintelligible

and went off to fetch her the drink.

Jasper inclined his head to the governess. "Forgive my carelessness tonight, Mrs. Radcliffe. Perhaps you would be more comfortable, closer to the warmth of the fireplace. Perhaps I could fetch a blanket for your knees, too."

Sophie was older than him by a few months. A fact he enjoyed dropping into their little skirmishes from time to time.

She ignored his suggestion and clasped her hands primly in her lap. "Having just escaped the heat, I've no desire to return to it. I assure you my *old* bones are perfectly comfortable here and you should think nothing about warming them. After all, I'm only a governess. I truly should be with the children every moment of my employment."

"On that, we agree."

"Yes, it has always been clear what you think of governesses, and me in particular," she murmured, and then smothered a laugh as she turned her face away. "I'm sure you'll find better company on the other side of the room."

He thought so too, but Jasper stared at the woman until she slowly looked up at him again. The remnants of her amusement slowly dimmed from her eyes, and she pressed her lips together tightly again.

He hated that the damn woman could read his mind. Not for the first time did he find himself in a battle of wills as to who would look away first. Radcliffe was always rather determined to outlast him. It was further confirmation that the woman was a problem when Jasper was the one to blink first.

But she'd agreed with everything Jasper had been thinking and saying for months. A governess ought to be with her charges and not partaking of the splendor of the drawing room with her employer's family. It was Nash who kept insisting Radcliffe must dine with them and not even the duke could persuade him otherwise.

When nothing witty or cutting occurred to him to say next, he resigned himself to not having gotten out the last word. Jasper turned on his heel and returned to his brothers. He made sure not to face the governess directly. He did not want to spend the last night they would all be together, reminded that the governess had gotten under his skin again.

Jasper addressed the duke. "Any news on our cousin's whereabouts?"

"I can only assume you mean Cousin George?"

"Indeed."

"No sight of him since he was routed from the London townhouse by us," Amity said. "But of his wife, I've heard much that troubles me. Melody has left for the continent."

Jasper grinned. He had no love for Melody Sweet, Cousin George's terrible wife, either. "Good riddance!"

"She is said to be traveling with her elderly father, but of George, there is no word if he accompanied them," Amity said, looking worried. "They had a terrible fight the night we retook possession of the London townhouse, and I fear a permanent separation has ensued."

"I tell you again it was not our fault. The lies about his situation and ownership of your property were of your brother's making," Crawford murmured as he patted his wife's hand. "He ought to have been honest with his wife about how desperately his finances depended on the charity of others. Namely, you and the late duke." Crawford looked among them. "George is not in the usual places he'd haunt in London; of that I know for a fact. My associates, many of his former friends, have not seen hide nor hair of him anywhere. Their debts remain unsettled, too."

"He'll return, meaner than ever, no doubt," Nash warned, grimacing at the prospect. "George will allow no one to feel themselves relieved of his company forever."

"Our cousin is a recurring pestilence," Stratford supplied cheerfully, joining the conversation. Stratford laughed and turned to his wife. "Should we care for a drink, my dear?"

"I thought you'd never suggest it," Win answered sweetly and pulled her husband away.

"Jasper?"

Jasper shook his head. "I have enough."

Stratford tripped after Win all the way to the rum barrel, where he poured two glasses, and handed over one to his wife with a grand flourish. Win downed the lot in one long gulp and then met her husband's gaze, eyes flashing with a challenge. Stratford attempted to follow her example, but it was well known he wasn't much fond of rum. Stratford choked it down eventually, but he spluttered afterward, and his face slowly turned red.

Win merely chuckled softly, poured herself another drink, and proved for a second time she was more accustomed to the burn of rum down her throat than her husband would ever be.

Jasper did not understand the appeal of the woman his brother had married. Win Sweet was unusual. Utterly dry sense of humor. Dull, except on rare occasions like tonight, when he caught her looking at his brother a certain way—challenging him to keep up with her.

Win was an odd duck in other ways, too. She wasn't particularly feminine, in his opinion. She did not glide, but strode boldly about the estate. As far as he knew, Win did not embroider, paint watercolors, or even play a musical instrument. It seemed she possessed none of the usual female accomplishments gentlemen were said to favor when choosing a wife. Win also exhibited a careless disinterest for fashion that society women seemed to believe important and seemed only to care for Stratford's conversation. Which was lucky indeed, because her husband talked a great deal!

Win jostled with Stratford as if they were a pair of old friends out for a night of fun in a tavern on their way to a chaise lounge they could share. The pair were always joking together, whispering, and Jasper suddenly felt the suspicion that he had been left out of some great secret of some kind. He dismissed the idea as a foolish fancy on his part, as he always did. Stratford hadn't been able to keep a secret in his entire life so there was obviously nothing important to be shared.

Everything was changing in the family, though. His youngest brother had married, mostly to reduce a long-standing debt. Amity, their favorite cousin, was married now, too. Nash was already married, but unhappily, and that left Jasper and the duke as the only unattached males in the room, but even Ravenswood must marry this year.

Jasper shifted in his chair, uncomfortable with the idea that soon he'd be the only bachelor left standing. It would make future dinners awk-ward and likely dull as the married couples flirted around him. He would have to find other ways to amuse himself on those nights, other than squab-bling with the governess.

He let his eyes drift about the riches of the Ravenswood estate drawing room, fighting the usual bitterness when nothing he saw here would truly be his to call his own. Not even his favorite chair.

Jasper inevitably turned his gaze that way and discovered the governess had slipped from the room unnoticed. He was surprisingly disap-pointed about that. Jasper would have liked a chance to deliver the final word before she went on her way tomorrow. She and the children were to travel with the duke and Nash to meet the fu-ture duchess. He would not have to speak with Mrs. Radcliff beyond wishing her a pleasant journey tomorrow morning.

Yet what was he to do about the coming summer?

Suffer his own company for months and go out of his mind with boredom? He'd no close ac-quaintances in the district. Most being older, married, or decidedly poor company.

But he would be comfortable for the summer and the longer he thought about it, the more he was looking forward to having the place to himself for the first time. A few months of supposed quiet was just the thing he needed before next season got underway. The estate would hardly require much of his time, and what was left could be thoroughly enjoyed.

Perhaps a friend might visit.

Perhaps he could invite one or some.

He smiled slowly as an idea took hold. He could host one of his little parties here.

The duke had not expressly forbidden Jasper companionship over the summer, had he? Jasper had responsibilities that would not be too taxing on his time. He glanced at his brothers. Nash had always disapproved of his friends and his wilder amusements, but the duke was not a saint. He was well aware that Jasper supplemented his income with gambling. Jasper could host a party, with gambling and make some money for himself and the estate. It could be a surprise windfall for them all.

However, if Jasper told his brother's what he intended to do, his older brothers would want to discuss the matter until dawn. Thankfully, he had never confessed his every waking thought to his elder siblings, or Stratford, who couldn't keep a secret to save his life. Jasper stuffed his hands under his arms to hide his excitement at hosting a party here. It was a brilliant idea. The best of his entire life, perhaps.

CHAPTER TWO

"SO, this is where you rushed off to," Mrs. Amity Crawford whispered as she slipped into the Ravenswood nursery and shut the door behind her. "I could not help but overhear your exchange with my cousin. Please, pay Lord Jasper no mind. His bark is far worse than his bite."

"I did not rush away because of him. It was time to check on the children," Sophie promised as she gently raised the blankets about Thomas Sweet's shoulders and ran a soothing hand down his back when he stirred from sleep. Lord Nash's eldest son had become dear to her during her tenure as his governess, as had the younger, more exuberant brother, Liam.

"Poor motherless, nearly forgotten lambs," Mrs. Crawford whispered, following Sophie through the room. "You've done wonders with them. Do you think they even remember their mother?"

"I try my best to keep her memory alive," Sophie promised. "But it is difficult when Lord Nash will hardly speak of her."

"You should talk to Jasper. He and Laura were childhood friends."

That surprised her. "Lord Jasper had a friend?"

Mrs. Crawford laughed softly and then shook her head. "Perhaps it might have been more than friendship if nature had taken its course. But then a marriage was arranged to Nash between their fathers and they—Jasper and Laura—became brother-in-law and sister-in-law. And now we are left with the consequences of a badly made match."

"An unhappy marriage takes two, I'm told," Sophie said.

"No. It is Nash's fault because he agreed to marry for money alone, and he told Laura so. I'm sure you'll agree that is not what a lady wants to live with for all her days."

"I'm sure it is not," Sophie said, turning toward young Liam and wishing the other woman would return to the drawing room and her family. Sophie was an orphan, and a servant here. A woman with no past and only the future she created. She'd no true understanding of the challenges the women of the *ton* faced in marriage, so it was difficult to feign sympathy for those women forced to such matches. Privately, she thought them lucky to have any chance at all to make a marriage and have somewhere to call home forever. To have a family that cared enough to consider their security.

Sophie would never be married. Had resigned herself to spinsterhood long ago. She'd had the chance of any better future taken out of her hands by a scoundrel of a man who had pretended to care for her and broken her heart. She'd learned the hard way that gentlemen routinely lied about their intentions to get their way with unprotected women like herself.

Mrs. Crawford drew close. "Ask Jasper your questions about Laura."

She winced, feeling uncomfortable. "I cannot."

"Why ever not?"

She forced a smile and shrugged. "Lord Jasper has a low opinion of servants who believe themselves deserving of his conversation."

Mrs. Crawford shook her head. "I'm sure he doesn't mean to be that off-putting."

"Oh, he means to be," Sophie replied with a soft laugh. "Of that, I'm quite certain. It's easier to talk with Lord Nash than with him."

"That does indeed sound dire." Mrs. Crawford sighed and sat down, forcing Sophie to do the same. "Perhaps it's the curse of being the third son that colors his tongue still."

Sophie settled on a wooden stool, arranging her old blue muslin skirts into unnecessarily neat folds about her legs. "What does being a third son have to do with him being rude to me at every turn?"

"The spare's spare. A forever afterthought. He had it worse than even Stratford growing up." Mrs. Crawford raised a brow as if it was all the explanation needed. When Sophie shook her head, Mrs. Crawford continued. "Jasper has spent all his life knowing he's been set to one side. Not wanted until he becomes necessary, like at dinners such as tonight. A man to make up the numbers, just as you often are, too. I cannot count the number of times he's made a new friend, only to have them set their sights on joining Ravenswood and Nash's circle of acquaintances instead."

"Oh, that's terrible," Sophie protested. "What horrible people they must be to use anyone so callously."

"Yes. It's even worse when women do it. Each eager to catch an elder brother's eye. Hoping to become the next duchess or mistress. Next season, the duke will return to Town and that will be a trying time for everyone, especially

Jasper. People will climb all over him to get to the duke's or Nash's side."

She had to admit she was glad to learn the way Lord Jasper spoke to her might have nothing to do with her at all. "Why Nash?"

"The entire world knows Nash and the duke are extremely close, and you are important to Nash as well, as governess of his children. The duke and Nash always like the same people, and you hold a special place in the family hierarchy in your own right. Perhaps greater than Jasper."

Sophie drew back, shocked by that suggestion. "I'm not like those women. I only want to speak about, and for, the children to Lord Nash. To convince their father to become more involved in their upbringing. They are so alone here."

Mrs. Crawford smiled sadly. "I felt that way before I married."

"Even without family, we can touch the lives of others and become content," she said, looking down at her faded skirts. "Even if it is only for a little while, we can choose to be happy with our lot in life."

Mrs. Crawford leaned forward. "My dear Mrs. Radcliffe. I cannot fathom the loneliness an orphan must face every day. I had a horrible brother and a large family that wanted complete control of my life. Even if they did not treat me with the kindness and understanding I hoped for, they were always there."

Sophie nodded. "One cannot miss what one never had."

Mrs. Crawford impulsively clasped Sophie's hand and squeezed it. "Well, you're with us now, and a delightful companion indeed. Do not let Jasper convince you otherwise. Besides, my cousin Nash seems determined to include you and that is all that matters."

"He's been so kind," she said, blushing in remembrance of the uncomfortable nights she'd spent at the duke's table of late. She was utterly out of her depth around the duke, and her employer, too, unless she was talking about his children. She found Lord Stratford easier to deal with, but Lord Jasper was impossible. He was determined not to like her and make her appear difficult in front of everyone. Sophie would prefer to be ignored entirely.

"Please do not make the mistake of thinking too well of my cousin Nash," Mrs. Crawford warned suddenly.

Sophie gazed at Mrs. Crawford without understanding.

"He's not for someone like you." The woman winced. "I should not like you to mistake his kindness for something greater."

Any sense of companionship with Mrs.

Crawford vanished, only to be replaced with horror at the idea of an improper relationship with her employer. "I certainly will never forget my place, madam."

"Not that I don't think well of you, you understand. Quite the opposite," Mrs. Crawford promised. "I just wanted to be certain you understand the situation."

Sophie clasped her hands tightly together in her lap, horrified by the discussion. "He's married. Indeed, he is. He has never given me any sign of... I have never encouraged him to think..."

"I'm glad. I should hate for him to betray his vows, even if his attraction to another became urgent."

Sophie stood, unsettled by any discussion of attraction. Those feelings were not to be trusted in her experience. "I would too, especially for the children's sake."

Mrs. Crawford rose as well. "I did not mean to upset you, my dear. It's just...I see how you are together and wonder if something is brewing under the surface."

"Not within me. As I told Lord Jasper earlier in the evening, I'm just a governess."

Mrs. Crawford shook her head at that. "That is not all you are, but we will speak no more on the subject since it has upset you. Perhaps when I return from my trip, you and I might discuss the topic of your future."

"My future?"

"You cannot remain a governess here forever."

"I know I cannot." Sophie lifted her chin. Her time here was defined by Lord Nash's requirements and the children's ages. "The children will not need me soon. They are so attentive to their lessons," she said, to turn their conversation to a topic close to her heart.

Mrs. Crawford nodded, and the subject of Lord Nash was dropped between them. "How do you get them to attend to their studies so well? I am ashamed to say I was an indifferent student."

She smiled. "They are agreeable children, and I praise their efforts daily."

"That is something I'm sure their grandfather, the late duke, would never have approved of. He believed in obedience or the rod. Praise was nonexistent," Mrs. Crawford said, and then shuddered as if to rid herself of an unpleasant memory. "We should return to the drawing room now."

"I should remain with the children," Sophie decided. The last thing she wanted was to be around Lord Nash after her conversation with Mrs. Crawford. She had much to think about. Her plan to bring Lord Nash and the children together more often had taken an unexpected and unwanted turn.

"The duke expects us both," Mrs. Crawford informed her in a way that suggested there could be no argument.

Resigned to a few more hours in the company of her betters, Sophie dutifully followed the woman back downstairs to the drawing room. But once Mrs. Crawford reached the room, she broke away to run to the open terrace doors and looked outside.

Mrs. Crawford laughed, beckoned Sophie to join her, and then disappeared into the darkness beyond. Sophie followed more sedately, glancing left. Lord Jasper had retaken possession of his favorite chair while she was gone. He had papers in his hand, but did not look up to acknowledge her return to the room.

Sophie headed for the open door and looked out.

"There you are," Lord Nash said to her right, making her jump almost out of her skin. "I feared I'd have to send a servant to fetch you back. There's no problem with the children, I trust?"

"None at all." Sophie stepped outside, smiling, but added a little more distance between herself and her employer than usual. "What is going on?"

"Lawn bowls. My brother insists on a game."

The duke and his brothers had been playing the game every day this week. The boys and herself had watched from the nursery windows between lessons but had not been invited to join them even once. "But it's nighttime."

"Therein lies the challenge of making a decent shot," Lord Jasper drawled, as he suddenly appeared on her other side. He gestured out to the lawn. "We were waiting for you."

"Yes, we were," Lord Nash announced, offering his arm.

Sophie could not take Lord Nash's arm. "I would enjoy watching."

"No, no. You will play," Lord Nash decided.

Lord Jasper agreed with him, too, which surprised her. "I'll partner Mrs. Radcliffe. You partner Ravenswood, as usual."

"Your partner is Stratford," Nash said, arm still extended to her.

"No. Not anymore. Stratford has chosen a new partner," Lord Jasper replied curtly, stepping closer to her side. "Only his wife will do for him now, you know."

Sophie winced. Had that hurt Lord Jasper's feelings?

She glanced across the lawn, straining her eyes to see the shapes moving about in the poor light from a few lanterns. Lord Stratford and his wife appeared to be wrestling over ownership of the little round balls they were to play with. They were a competitive couple. She knew enough about high society to realize Lady Win Sweet was more than a little rough around the edges.

Sophie liked Lady Win. She was interesting. The maids whispered of her habit of secretly wearing a pair of men's breeches under her finery. She also made Lord Stratford vastly happy, even when she triumphed in their many inconsequential competitions. She kept him in line and even on time for dinner. Everyone thought it a miracle.

Nash caught her eye. "Perhaps the lady should be the one to choose her partner?"

With Mrs. Crawford's warning about Lord Nash's interest still ringing in her ears, it was a straightforward decision to choose Lord Jasper as her partner in the game. She would not encourage a married man, and Lord Jasper, a rake, had already proved to have no interest in her. For a change, Lord Jasper was a safer choice. "I could not deny the duke his preferred partner," she told Lord Nash.

"As you wish," he replied, but his tone suggested he was not disappointed with her decision. However, he had to accept it. He was too much of a gentleman not to.

Sophie squared her shoulders. "Might someone explain the rules?"

Lord Nash tried to explain, but he did so in a way that utterly confused her by the end. Eventually, he stopped talking and Sophie could only nod. But she still did not know what she was meant to do.

Eventually Lord Nash was called for, and he bowed and departed, hurrying over to the duke, who was directing servants to set out more torches around the pitch.

She glanced up at Lord Jasper apologetically. "I must warn you I've never played before."

"Something tells me you'll do admirably despite my brother's baffling instructions," Lord Jasper drawled. "All you have to think about is the little ball at the end. Imagine it as someone you know. In your case, I suggest it is someone you truly despise."

One person immediately sprang to mind. "Very well. But why someone I despise?"

"Women are emotional creatures," Lord Jasper explained, leaning a little closer. "Emotions guide your actions in everything."

Now that was unfair. However, armed now with a little of his history, she could almost forgive his low opinion of some women. She tempered her reply to be less caustic than it might have been. "How do you know that is true for me?"

He gave her a look and went on as if the answer was self-explanatory. "Now. You want to get your ball close to that little one. Think of it as a battle. It must stop near enough that if it was your enemy, you could stab it. Close means we win."

She couldn't help it. She laughed. "That is an unusual way to explain a game of skill."

"And of cunning," he warned. "Play to win, Mrs. Radcliffe. If you dare."

Sophie gulped. Winning wasn't her strong point, but Jasper was clearly competitive. She would do her best not to be a complete disappointment to him.

She followed him and went where told to await her turn. She studied the other players' techniques carefully while testing the weight of the bowl in her hand. Lord Jasper was an excellent player. His bowl came to rest less than three inches from the smaller ball. Much closer than any of his brothers had managed so far. She saw him hide his elation and pride in that achievement, though.

The spare's spare. His achievements dismissed as unimportant. Sophie clapped for him, but he scowled at her.

When it was her turn, Sophie tested the weight of the ball in her hand again. It had a comforting weight, and she easily imagined the person she despised at the end of the green stretch of lawn, as Lord Jasper had suggested she do. She stepped up to the designated spot, but Lord Jasper was by her side in an instant, taking up her hand holding the bowl a different way.

"Turn it like so," he told her, turning the ball on her palm with careful fingers until it was properly aligned to his liking. "Remember to bend your knees as you step forward and think vindictive thoughts. Shouldn't be hard for someone like you."

With that remark ringing in her ears, any sympathy for his situation as third son diminished markedly. She had done nothing to Lord Jasper besides speak her mind when he put her down. He had no other cause to think ill of her, unless he, too, suspected she was interested in capturing his older brother's affections. Lord Nash had been determined to have her as his partner, but so had Lord Jasper.

Sophie stepped up to the designated spot, frustrated by all men yet again. She should not be playing games with her employer and his family as if she were one of them.

Sophie had made that mistake before.

She took aim and pictured the man who'd lied about loving her standing over the little ball. The man who had taken her innocence and then tossed her away like garbage. Lied and deceived his way under her skirts with promises of a happy forever.

Unfortunately, Sophie had underestimated the depths of her remaining rage for that man as she flung the bowl from her hand. The bowl sped past the smaller one and promptly disappeared into the darkness amid hoots of laughter from the other players. When Lord Jasper cursed roundly, Sophie hitched up her skirts to bolt into the dark after the bowl, her face flaming with embarrassment and wishing to disappear forever into the darkness, too.

CHAPTER THREE

"WOULD you just get in the damn carriage and go," Jasper demanded of his younger brother, Stratford, pushing him toward the open carriage door. Stratford had his lady waiting inside, and Win appeared to be growing impatient with her husband's dawdling and babble too.

"We could stay," Stratford offered, turning back again.

"For heaven's sake, and do what? Till the fields yourself? If we are to have a better next year, it will not be through everyone staying behind to watch others at work. Go visit Aston, paint a portrait of him," Jasper demanded with a laugh, then lowered his voice. "We cannot afford the expense of you home for the summer."

That wasn't strictly true, but it was a useful suggestion to throw out.

"We don't eat that much," Win grumbled just loud enough that Jasper heard her.

"But your husband eats enough for six," Jasper informed his sister-in-law with a shrug. "I'm staying to make sure the right things are getting done and our brother is free to make his proposal. You go off and enjoy a proper honeymoon. Enjoy yourself and each other and, for heaven's sake, do not fall out with your host, Aston. We cannot afford him to conjure up any reason to call in the remaining debt."

"I'll try not to," Stratford promised solemnly, to which Win laughed. But then a bright smile flooded his face. "Try not to miss me."

Jasper rolled his eyes. "I cannot miss you if you don't leave."

Stratford suddenly pulled Jasper into a fierce embrace. "Be good, brother."

"Ha," he snorted, shoving his brother away. "That's not my motto."

"I know," Stratford said, grinning. "It's never get caught enjoying yourself too much."

"Exactly." Having fun had not exactly been encouraged by his family. From an early age, he'd learned to enjoy any pleasures in life quietly. But things were different, his father dead, his brother now the duke. Jasper had awoken this morning knowing he could live a little more loudly. "Get out of here," he urged, shoving Stratford into the carriage. He'd already said a prolonged goodbye to everyone else who mattered. "Have a pleasant journey, both of you."

Stratford finally sat himself down beside his patient bride. Jasper waved them off and then turned back to the steps as soon as the carriage moved. "I thought they'd never go," he complained to his older brothers, who had wisely chosen to remain at the top of the stairs.

"Stratford has always enjoyed making us all stand about to wave him off," Nash noted sourly.

"It makes him feel loved," the Duke of Ravenswood said. "Now it's our turn to bid you adieu, Jasper."

Jasper barely kept himself from shouting with glee. He had so much to accomplish today. "The carriage should be here at any moment," he promised, hoping his jubilance was safely hidden.

The duke adjusted his gloves. "I am sorry about this."

"I understand and know what to do," Jasper replied. "See off as many of the servants who want to go to visit their relatives and ensure as many of the items on Nash's list are taken care of before your return."

Ravenswood nodded. "Send word if there are serious problems."

Jasper didn't expect there could be but nodded. "The carriages for the servants leaving will be drawn up here shortly after yours departs. I hear from Seymour that they are all quite excited about having an unexpected holiday."

"Good," the duke said, but he looked pained as he glanced about. His reluctance to leave was palpable.

Jasper clasped him on the shoulder as the ducal traveling carriage came into view. "I promise to return the estate to you without a scratch at the end of summer."

"Was there ever a reason to suspect Ravenswood wouldn't be safe in your hands?" the duke asked, looking serious for a moment. "I know you always do the right thing."

Jasper winced inwardly and turned his gaze on Nash, who had made a sound of disagreement. "Pity someone else doesn't share that opinion."

The duke punched Nash's shoulder. "It's in his nature to worry about how you'll fill your days."

Jasper put his hands on his hips. "I am not a child."

"Well, we all know what you'd rather be doing for the summer," Nash said with a disapproving look in his direction. "Ravenswood will be quiet for someone who prefers the bustle and wild parties of London."

"A wild party is just what you need, too. Might make you happier."

"It would not do that," Nash answered, his expression turning grim.

At that moment, Jasper realized there was an absence on the stairs. "I wonder what is keeping the children."

"They are staying here," the duke informed him, adjusting his cuffs.

Jasper's jaw dropped open in shock and disbelief. Nash's children could not stay. Certainly not the governess with them, as well. "I thought you said she was going with you. That they were all going with you for a holiday?"

"'Tis not the right occasion to foist so many onto our hosts, and Nash agrees with me," the duke said, looking suspiciously pleased with himself about that.

"There is still time for them to join you," Jasper urged. "I could have them and their luggage sent along after if you like."

The duke shook his head firmly. "No, they stay here for the summer. It is less disruptive to their schedule."

Nash and his rules and schedule for the children were fixed in stone, but even he did not seem pleased with the duke's decision right now.

How unusual of him.

But clearly, the matter had been discussed

while Jasper had not been around. And Jasper would get nowhere arguing with the duke that the children should go with their father. To complain might draw unwanted attention to the fact he wanted them gone, too.

He shrugged the problem away as the carriage drew up before them. "Well, it's decided then."

Nash stopped in front of him. "When it comes to the children, Radcliffe is to be trusted entirely, you understand," he warned. "You should have no need to bother her at all. If you do see her, convey my satisfaction in her employment and my ongoing trust," Nash offered as a parting remark before entering the carriage.

The duke turned his back on the carriage. "Speaking of the governess, see that the bowl she flung into the dark last night is recovered, and..." The duke bowed his head, leaning closer. "If Nash's wife returns while we are gone, send word immediately," he whispered.

Jasper gasped softly. "Is that likely?"

"Who knows what Laura will do, but I hope we will see her again. Make certain she knows she is welcome," Ravenswood insisted. "We cannot afford another scandal in the family this year."

"It's the same scandal as ever," Jasper reminded the duke. Nash's wife had abandoned the marriage years ago and gossip about her desertion refused to fade.

The duke pursed his lips, eyes glancing up at the facade of Ravenswood briefly. "I mean the fresh scandal that looms over us."

Jasper frowned. "What scandal?"

"You saw it last night. I gather you've suspected for some time."

"Saw what?"

The duke glanced at the carriage. "Nash is too interested in the governess for my liking. I would hate to dismiss Radcliffe, but I will if it becomes necessary."

Then he was gone, stepping into the carriage and leaving Jasper reeling on the front steps of Ravenswood Palace.

Jasper had seen nothing of any impropriety between his brother and the governess last night. Just the usual Nash attempting to exert his authority on yet another matter. Last night, when Nash had almost refused to yield to Jasper's claim on the governess as his partner in the game, he'd thought nothing much of it. But now, had last night revealed a hint of possessiveness on his brother's part?

Nash had always partnered the duke. Jasper and Stratford played on the same side. It had been that way since they were boys. But Stratford had a wife now, and since he preferred Win's company to Jasper's lately, Jasper had assumed he'd take on the role of umpire more often. But with the governess there, unattached, he'd seen a way to be part of the game again.

He kept his eyes on the departing carriage. At dinners of late, the duke had stuck him with the governess' company almost every time, and he'd thought that simply unfair. Had the duke done it on purpose? And what of Ravenswood's decision to leave the children behind? Might that have been purely to keep Nash and the governess apart? To prevent a scandalous alliance forming at the worst possible time?

Now he truly grimaced. Sophie Radcliffe was an adequate governess for a pair of boys, but nothing else about her should have drawn Nash's interest.

Jasper stood on the drive, watching the carriage make its slow disappearance. Was Ravenswood leaving behind the governess and hoping upon his return, any infatuation Nash may have would be entirely forgotten? Snuffed by a prolonged separation of some months. But the duke was also leaving behind the hope for the return of their first sister-in-law, too. It was more complications than Jasper had counted on for the summer months, but he would deal with one and all, he supposed.

Starting with the governess and any *feelings* she might have developed for Nash.

The isolation of Ravenswood this summer would show her how truly unnecessary her company really was. He slowly grinned as he imagined her boredom and potential frustration at being left behind.

Too bad. Now she would know how Jasper had always felt.

He started up the stairs. There was so much to do and little need for delicacy. Ravenswood was about to become a temporary gambling hell for a dozen or so rakes and scoundrels barred from the usual venues in London. He'd spent the night making plans and considering who to invite. It could only be friends with deep pockets, questionable reputations, and a growing appreciation for the finer things in life. Things their new money could not buy them unless they married into the *ton*. A gentleman needed impeccable connections or someone to vouch for them if they wanted to get ahead in society.

Jasper intended to do that for them next season. But in the meantime, he could give them a taste of what was missing from their lives—for a price. He was a duke's younger brother and well versed in experiences and information they'd never dreamed existed.

His friends could expect high-stakes gambling and some losses at a house party Jasper hosted here at Ravenswood. And those losses would add up and refill Jasper's empty pockets each day of the house party. The event would be by invitation only, for those who would pay a fee to walk these hallowed halls for a week or two and pretend they belonged here. They would become the envy of society. His monied friends were bound to accept such a unique invitation to join him for fun and scandalous games.

He strolled the entrance hall, skirting chattering servants lining up in wait for the carriages that would take them on their holidays. Those who were staying were helping round everyone up, so no stragglers were accidentally left behind.

The butler drew him aside, his face clouded with worry. "Lord Nash's children did not go with him."

Jasper had spoken to the butler about his intentions first thing that morning. He had agreed that the duke should not be bothered with the details. "Yes, I was just made aware of that. It doesn't change my plans."

"What about Mrs. Radcliffe?"

Yes, a governess who might fancy his older brother sweeping her off her feet and into his bed. He grimaced at that image. The governess was a thorny issue indeed. She would disapprove of the party he had planned, but she also needed to be diverted from any interest she might have in Nash. Jasper was just the man to make her see how ill-suited she was to remaining in their society. Nash, too, would need a similar diversion, but that was the duke's problem to deal with while they were away. If Nash was lonely, the duke would steer some equally lonely widow or bored wife into his bed and absolve him of any guilt over it later. Anything to avoid a scandal involving a governess.

Until now, Jasper had actually believed his brother was incapable of infidelity. But with a governess always under his nose, encouraging him to visit the nursery at night, there was only so long Nash might resist his misplaced lust.

"I'll deal with the governess later," Jasper promised. Although the butler appeared worried, Jasper offered him a reassuring smile as Cook bustled up to them wearing a ridiculously ugly bonnet.

Jasper liked Mrs. Derry, and she liked him. "Are you sure you don't want me to stay?"

Although he would miss her cooking, he'd rather not have her remain. "Derry, do you think the duke will offer this boon again? Once he marries, these decisions will be out of his hands, and who knows what the new duchess will do with you all."

She frowned.

"Duchess' have replaced entire household staff on a whim," he warned, watching as the cook and others standing near grew pale. "My mother did several times in her life. Yes, indeed. We'll all be dancing to a different tune when the next duchess is installed at Ravenswood. Even me. Best we make the most of it."

Jasper certainly would. He suspected he would be elsewhere a great deal when the new duchess was installed in Ravenswood Palace. The only reason to remain in close proximity to a married elder brother was the money he'd invested in the estate's future and the family. Once that was repaid, he'd slip away back to London where he belonged.

He glanced around impatiently. It was imperative to get any respectable servants away today. Only then could he begin preparations for the party. A great many changes—removals—needed to be made before the palace was fit for his guests. Precious items must be locked away; private rooms, like the duke's chambers and study, covered up and locked as planned.

Once that was set in motion, he would decide what to do with the governess. Which reminded him that there was a bowl to be found somewhere out there in the vast garden and returned to the set as well. He wondered who she'd been thinking of. He'd been able to see her expression as she'd released the bowl, and he was reluctantly impressed.

From that one look on her face, Jasper concluded that there was someone in the world Sophie Radcliffe hated. It shouldn't have anything to do with him. Jasper had only lashed her with a dozen subtle and not-so-subtle insults over the past months. He was curious to know who in her past had ever done her so wrong.

Could that information be used to make her quit her employment before Nash returned? Or at the very least, sour Nash's interest in her later? Only time would tell.

CHAPTER FOUR

A PAIR of tiny hands covered Sophie's eyes and a young boy giggled in her ear. "Guess who?"

Sophie acted as if she'd been surprised by her youngest charge, Liam, sneaking up on her, but she'd heard him tiptoeing across the hardwood floor, as he had every morning for months. "Is it the butler?"

"No," the child of four protested.

She slapped her hands over his tiny ones where they rested on her face and held them there. "Is it the boot boy?"

"No! It's me, silly," the boy said, wrenching his hands from under hers and then dropping into her lap. The boy did that every morning, too.

Sophie gathered him up in a hug. "Oh, it is Liam! I never would have guessed."

"I tricked you again!"

"You did indeed. Good morning, young man. How are you today?"

"I am well indeed, thank you," he promised, switching from playful to solemn in an instant and reminding her of his father. He'd been quiet, unusually so, when she'd first arrived at the estate to be his governess. She never wanted his playfulness to disappear.

Sophie tickled him under the arms, which made him laugh and squirm to get off her lap, and she set him on his feet with a fond smile. "Where might your brother Thomas be?"

"He is watching Papa."

"Oh, is he now," Sophie said, and grinned. Seven-year-old Thomas Sweet was an independent, inquisitive young man. He often rose early, usually asked permission before setting off to explore the grand Ravenswood Palace, but he only ever ventured to the limits of their domain, mostly in search of a glimpse of his always-busy Papa. "Well, why don't we see if we can find him? It's almost time for your breakfast and lessons begin soon after."

Lord Nash was like most fathers she'd ever met. He claimed he wanted the best for his sons, yet he kept himself at arm's length from them. Lord Nash met with them but once a week, unless she could engineer other encounters between them. Of course, now that she knew what Mrs.

Crawford feared to be happening between them, Sophie should not encourage her employer at all.

She caught Liam's hand in hers, and they went in search of Thomas together. Liam was silent as he drew her toward the front of Ravenswood Palace, to the windows that looked over the front drive.

Thomas had his nose pressed to the window glass, looking out at the gravel drive below and gardens beyond. "Uncle Stratford has gone away with his new wife," Thomas told them without turning. "But Uncle's carriage is now in its place."

Sophie joined him and looked out. The duke's gleaming traveling carriage and team of six fine black horses with liveried grooms stood about in wait for a journey of some kind. She drew back from the windows, confused. She'd heard nothing of Ravenswood planning to visit anyone last night. They were all to leave the estate for a house party at the end of the week. She'd not told the children that yet. She'd planned to surprise them with the news the night before.

Liam tugged on her sleeve. "Are you sad Papa is going away too, Radcliffe?"

"I'm sure it's nothing like that," she promised. "I'm sure he's simply seeing the duke off or making an early-morning call to one of the neigh-boring properties."

But her heart sank a little as she watched the activity below continue and many trunks were loaded. The duke must be going, but was Lord Nash too?

She pressed her lips together tightly, hoping that was not the case. The boys always got a little down in the dumps when they were left behind.

She drew the boys against her side as their father and the duke stood below on the stairs, talking. Sophie kept out of sight, but the boys had no hesitation to peer down at their elders. There seemed some rush about this early-morning jaunt, but only the duke looked up to the palace facade as Lord Nash disappeared inside the waiting conveyance—and then the duke followed, his greatcoat swirling about his legs.

Lord Jasper remained behind on the steps to wave them goodbye. The children leaned a little harder against her as the carriage took off and started its slow turn before it picked up speed. "Where is Papa going?"

"I'm sorry, but I don't know," she said, smoothing her hands over their hair. Sophie stood at the window, watching the conveyance go on its way without them with a conflicted heart. She hoped Lord Nash's journey would be of short duration, yet the number of trunks loaded on top suggested the pair would be gone for some time. That was confusing but a relief in a way. If he was gone, she'd not have to confront Mrs. Crawford's suspicions.

Sophie shook her head. Lord Nash ought to have told the boys he was going away, but what could a governess do about it? Nothing. Sophie could not make him show his love for his children. She had tried so often to increase his interest to no avail.

She hugged the boys ineffectually, knowing a governesses affection wasn't what they really needed. A governess was not family. It was the love of their father, uncles, aunt, and cousins—and most important of all, their absent mother—that they needed more.

The boys turned away from the window of their own accord, but Sophie could see their disappointment clear as day as she followed them. She wished their father was still here to glimpse the damage he could inflict so carelessly on his sweet children. It wasn't her place to berate an employer for his lapses, but not for the first time did she wish she could knock some sense into Lord Nash's head.

She followed the boys back to the nursery, a little sad that they went directly to their desks without being told to do so. Liam picked up his slate and chalk, Thomas took up his quill and papers and bent his head to his lessons. Their penmanship was coming along nicely for their respective ages, but there was more to life than study and Lord Nash's strict schedule for them. There was fun and friendship and family love. Sophie sighed heavily again. She knew little of family love herself, being an orphan, but she'd seen it with others, glimpsed it last night with the duke's family, and knew what was missing from the boys' lives...and hers, too.

That, of course, changed nothing.

Sophie sat by the window as the children worked silently, continuing a lesson they had begun the previous day. They only stopped when a footman arrived, not the usual one though, carrying their breakfast on a large silver tray. "Bread to be toasted and porridge, my lords," the man announced to the children.

"Is there a note or letter for me?"

"No, Mrs. Radcliffe."

The boys descended on the food, and Sophie worried as she helped with their breakfast. She'd hoped Lord Nash might have left her a message, and had also been longing for a letter from friends in London. It had been many months since she'd had news of them and she was becoming worried that she'd been forgotten.

She glanced up as another servant burst into the nursery. Not the normal nursery maid, Jess, but a recent arrival from a distant estate. "Yes?"

The woman dipped a clumsy curtsey to her.

"Mr. Seymour sent me to help you." The woman announced her name as Kate. "I'm to fill in for Jess."

Sophie frowned at the woman. "Where is Jess?"

"Already gone, Mrs. Radcliffe."

Sophie burst to her feet. "Gone where?"

"On holiday, like the others have done," she explained as she poked the fire into greater life.

Sophie blinked. "Holiday? What holiday?"

"I don't know too much about it, I'm afraid." The woman shrugged and wiped her soot-covered fingers on a dirty rag. "His Grace has given many of the women, and a few of the footmen, leave to visit their families for the summer. Everyone is so excited to be on their way."

Sophie drew closer to Kate. "But you didn't go with them?"

"No, madam. I'm an orphan, and I had no one to visit. I like it here though. Did no one tell you about it?"

Sophie pursed her lips. "No. They did not."

"How strange."

"Yes, it is." Sophie squared her shoulders and issued instructions for what the maid should attend to in Jess' place. She seemed efficient enough and was soon done with all the tasks Sophie wanted completed.

"If there's nothing else you need, madam, I'm

to return downstairs and help in the kitchen now."

"Yes, of course. Good work and thank you."

"It's my pleasure, madam. I'll return in the afternoon for dinner, or someone else will come."

Sophie followed the maid to the door. It pained her that this maid knew more about the goings on in this place than she did. Sophie also hoped she was the type to gossip. "The children saw the duke's carriage leaving earlier. Did Lord Nash say when he would return or leave any message for his sons?"

"No message I've heard about, but His Grace was in a rush, and they say he'll be away for weeks and weeks."

She blinked in surprise to hear that. How could they be gone for weeks and weeks when Sophie and the children were supposed to be going on a journey with them later in *this* week? "Do you know where they've gone?"

"Don't know that I heard that, madam. The butler likely knows. I could ask him for you. At least Lord Jasper stayed behind. He's a handsome devil, isn't he?"

Devil indeed. A maid as pretty as Kate should not think too well of any rake. "I will ask my own questions, thank you. Hurry back to the kitchens now."

"Yes, madam."

Sophie bit her lip. So, Lord Jasper remained, but for how long? Hopefully not too long at all. It would be a horrible time if he did. Not that he'd ever come to the nursery or had any reason to. She was deeply sorry he was still here. She might have enjoyed herself more, been herself again, if he were anywhere else.

When the servants were gone again, and the food eaten, Sophie set the boys to work on their mathematics and sat herself down at the window with a heavy sigh. But there was nothing to see outside her window besides endless green gardens. No carriages or people out for a stroll. Even at the orphanage there had been something to see outside her grimy window. Sophie missed London and her friends terribly. She missed the excitement and noise so, so much.

After an hour of solitude contemplating the empty grounds around the palace, Sophie glanced around to find the butler standing at the door, watching her. She shot to her feet. "Mr. Seymour?"

"Mrs. Radcliffe." The butler remained at the door. "I trust everything is in order here?"

She hurried to meet the more senior employee at Ravenswood Palace. "Yes, sir. The children have been working diligently at their lessons this morning."

"Very good." He turned away.

"Sir," she called, hurrying out the door after him before he could disappear downstairs to his usual post. "Might we speak a moment in private?"

He looked pained but inclined his head. "Very well, but I am quite busy today."

"Of course," she said, although how busy could he be with most of the family gone away? She wet her lips before speaking softly. "Lord Nash left the estate."

"Yes. He and the duke journey to a summer house party."

Sophie gaped. "But the children were supposed to go with their father as well, but I was told the end of the week?"

"The duke's plans changed unexpectedly, and they have gone early."

"Oh," Sophie whispered. "Are we to travel there on our own later?"

"No. The children are to remain at Ravenswood for the summer, and with you."

She closed her eyes briefly, holding back a curse she shouldn't ever let the butler discover she knew. She had been looking forward to a change of scenery. "If I may also ask, why wasn't I told about the holiday everyone else seems to know about?"

Seymour sniffed. "The staff of Ravenswood were given a choice to stay or go."

"But I am a servant, too," she protested. "I would have liked a chance to return to London and visit my friends, too. They are my family."

Seymour winced. "I had assumed Lord Nash had mentioned the matter to you."

She shook her head. "Lord Nash told me nothing, sir. Not even that I should not pack up the children to attend a house party with him when he had ample opportunity last night."

The man pursed his lips momentarily and then offered her a sympathetic smile. "The household staff has been reduced by two-thirds for the summer months and consists mostly of men now. Very few female staff remain. But I assure you, the children's needs will not be neglected."

"That was not truly my concern," she blurted. "It just struck me as odd that the servants who normally came to assist them were gone without warning. A staff holiday did not occur last summer."

"Of course not. The late Duke of Ravenswood entertained lavishly last summer."

"I see, but the new duke will not do the same?"

The butler's expression soured. "Obviously not, since he will not return for months now."

Months? "I see. Well, thank you for letting me know," she said. "I assume most of the palace will be closed up then. Will the long gallery still be available for the children to play in? And the library, too?"

"That would be Lord Jasper's decision to make but I think it likely you will find less of the palace available to you and the children now," he warned. "Lord Jasper is in charge. Kindly remain upstairs with the children until told otherwise."

She grimaced inwardly at hearing that Lord Jasper would remain, and in charge, until Lord Nash returned. They did not deal well together. "But in the evenings, when the duke was not entertaining, I had permission to visit the library to peruse the shelves for new reading material for the children and myself. I must be allowed to continue their usual routine. Lord Nash would expect that of me, even if he'd not specified it before leaving. The children's outdoor games are stored in the long gallery, too. They use that room on rainy days. Perhaps Lord Jasper needs to be reminded of that?"

The butler tugged on his waistcoat, clearly bothered by her request. "Lord Jasper is extremely busy, but I will mention your concerns and send word back to you about his final decision. Remain upstairs until told otherwise."

The first time the butler had promised to pass along a concern of hers to Lord Nash, it had taken a month to get an answer back. Although the last thing she wanted to do was appeal to a rake like Lord Jasper, Sophie might have no choice but to seek him out herself. It was for the children. She would do anything to ensure their happiness. "Perhaps I could speak to Lord Jasper myself?"

The butler's smile was tight in return. "I will speak to him on your behalf, never fear."

He backed away and rushed off, leaving Sophie with no illusions that her problems would be attended to by the man soon. In fact, the butler had acted strangely today.

She glanced down the hall and wondered why he'd rushed off with so much haste. He acted as if they were on the cusp of hosting a grand party, which was hardly likely since the duke was to be gone for months.

Sophie put her hands on her hips and wandered down the hall a little further to the top of the staircase and looked down. She could see nothing and no one moving about below. How odd that the household staff was reduced so dramatically for the summer, too. She'd never heard of such a thing being done before. In a house this size, surely there was as much to do whether the family was in residence or not.

And with the household staff reduced so dramatically in number now, the butler could become so busy that he might just forget about the importance of her questions. She might wait weeks for an answer from him, and that would never do. The children could not bear to be cooped up for so long in the nursery wing alone. She could barely stand it herself.

If she did not hear about the matter in a few days, she might just have to carry on without Lord Jasper's permission altogether. A circumstance she'd only consider as a last resort.

CHAPTER FIVE

A week later

JASPER PUT his feet up on the desk. "Are we ready for my guests?"

"Yes, I believe so. The east wing has been cleared and the remaining servants not involved with the event have retired to other locations about the estate."

"Good. Good." Jasper glanced out the windows facing the rear garden and smiled. "Now, I want a pair of footmen waiting with drinks in the entrance hall from four in the afternoon today. They are to serve refreshments to my guests as soon as they arrive. No waiting to show them to their rooms first unless they specifically ask for it. After that, point them toward the long gallery, where they are to make themselves scarce until the next carriage arrives."

"Yes, my lord."

Jasper eyed the butler. Seymour was looking a little flushed today. It had been an exhausting week of setting up and putting away the most valuable heirlooms for everybody. Seymour had been in the thick of it always, but he was getting on in years. The strain of their frantic preparations these past days was showing on him finally.

No doubt the type of guest expected for his party would not appeal to him, either. He was the duke's man now, and probably should have been sent off to visit his family, along with all the others. And yet, the palace barely functioned without his steady hands on the reins, keeping the other servants in line.

"Seymour, if you do not feel up to the task, please elevate one of the younger men for the duration of the festivities."

Seymour stared at him stonily for a moment. "Do you imagine this is the first scandalous party held at Ravenswood?"

"I'm only saying..."

"Well, respectfully, my lord, perhaps you should not continue expressing that thought. Your mother held lavish entertainments and brought scandalous friends here many times while you were still safely tucked in your cradle.

There is nothing I haven't seen. Including the duchess undressed, my lord. Quite a fine sight, I might add."

Jasper laughed as the butler's cheeks grew red, but he let the comment pass. Mother had been a beauty, and Seymour had been in service here for a very long time. He was not surprised to learn the man had admired her figure, too. Jasper, though, had trouble imagining his mother misbehaving or cavorting naked anywhere. He'd never really known his mother as a woman of the world. The late Duchess of Ravenswood had no time for her sons, but she had loved her friends dearly, and they had forever been visiting each other's homes. Perhaps there was a side to his mother that should remain a secret from him, but obviously wasn't possible for the older butler. "I stand corrected."

Seymour nodded, looking pleased. "Everything at Ravenswood shall be taken care of as usual, I assure you."

He nodded. "Thank you. Listen, about keeping my brother in the dark about my little gathering..."

"What gathering?" Seymour asked, eyes twinkling. "'Twill be just another quiet summer in the countryside. Nothing to report to him. Just as there was nothing to report to your father, the late duke, about the duchess' activities, either."

Jasper grinned; glad Seymour was head of the household. He'd earn a few extra coins from Jasper when this party was over. He'd honestly expected some difficulty with the older man. However, given the butler was fully apprised of the estate's precarious financial situation by the duke himself, and Jasper's intentions was to use the money for the improvement of the estate, he readily agreed that discretion was called for. At least until later. But the party could not involve the new Duke of Ravenswood, since he was set on making a good impression to score himself a wealthy wife.

He stood and put his hands on his hips as he looked around. "Are the ladies here yet?"

"Yes, my lord. They are ensconced in the parlor adjoining the long gallery," Seymour reported. "Drinking wine and eating stew until called upon."

"Good. Remember, I want them receptive to my guests' advances, but not so influenced by an excess of spirit that they forget their role here."

"I believe the women will be capable of all you wish for," Seymour advised. "But the drink has reduced their awe of their surroundings."

"Awe?"

"They are unaccustomed to the riches that surround them," Seymour reminded him with a tight smile.

"Ah," Jasper said, then dismissed the matter. He cared not that the whores he'd hired had never been to Ravenswood Palace before, or anywhere half so grand. They only had to do what they were paid to do. Be pleasing and attentive to his friends. Distract the gamblers at the right moment, he hoped, so they would rush to finish the game in favor of other sport and play carelessly. "That will be all for now, Seymour."

The old butler went on his way, and Jasper sat back in his chair, though he could hardly settle. He was impatient for the guests to arrive and for the fun to begin. To begin to rebuild his funds, too.

Jasper's allowance had never been enough to cover all his needs, and to make up the difference, he'd always resorted to other measures to support himself. He had to make money somehow, and why not take advantage of others? He had no creative talents like Stratford. Nor could Jasper tend to the sick of high society the way Nash did, and be paid for his discretion. And, of course, he was not first-born like the new Duke of Ravenswood.

Father had refused him a commission in the army—out of spite, most likely, because he'd dared ask for it—and he was forever set on the path to be considered a useless third son. The spare's spare. A man with no prospects at all.

Yet one thing he was good at was making new

friends. He'd make a fortune as the owner of a gambling hell when he could save enough to begin such a venture in London himself.

Father would never have allowed it, and now his elder brother hadn't even the funds to consider backing him, if he'd been so inclined. Until the estate was back on its feet again, Jasper would make do.

He sat at his new desk, running his hands over the smooth mahogany surface. Since he currently owned a tiny part of Ravenswood, he had taken over this chamber for the summer. From here, he could manage the few concerns of the estate left to him and contemplate his future money-making endeavors without being spied upon.

A child's laughter broke his reverie, and he spun around to see his oldest nephew run past his open door. The younger nephew followed, then the governess a moment later, straight-backed and in an obvious hurry to catch up with her charges.

Jasper flew out of his chair and into the hall, calling after her. "What the hell do you think you're doing?"

The little woman continued on her way as if she'd not heard him.

Infuriated by her disobedience, he followed the governess. "Mrs. Radcliffe!"

Mrs. Sophie Radcliffe finally stopped, but urged the children to continue into the long gallery without her. They looked back, slightly bewildered, but then she closed the door on them and turned to face him. "Yes, my lord?"

"What do you think you are doing down here? I gave strict instructions that all staff are to remain in other parts of the palace."

"You gave instruction to the palace servants. That is true. However, as the butler pointed out, I am not in the Duke of Ravenswood's employ, but his brother's," she said with a haughty tilt of her head. "I do as he says, and at this hour, the children are to play in the long gallery for an hour and a half. It's on their schedule."

"The schedule has been set aside," Jasper ground out.

She appeared incensed by that. "May I ask why?"

"No, you may not," he replied loudly. It was quite enjoyable to deny her wishes so loudly and not care who heard. He could see it annoyed her to no end, which made him endlessly happy.

She drew a little closer, chin dropping. "I've asked to speak to you repeatedly about the restrictions you imposed upon us. The only response I received was to have my request summarily ignored."

"The new rule applies to everyone," he said,

punctuating the statement by pointing his finger at her. Her hand flew up between them and his finger stabbed her palm. "You and the children should be upstairs at all times."

Her fingers curled over his digit, and she pushed him back. "Then you should have said so from the outset, instead of failing to answer my earlier questions or even lowering yourself to speak to me," she insisted. "The children require *exercise*. To run about and play games. I will not endure them being locked up in the nursery until Lord Nash returns. Whenever that might be."

"I never said they were to be locked up, although it is not a bad idea, especially at night," he mused.

Jasper had ignored Radcliffe to prove how unimportant she was in the grand scheme of things. Her endless demands via the butler's ear had been like that of a fly trapped under glass. But today, with his fingertip trapped in her grip still, her whispers had turned into a roar he could not ignore. She was the most frustrating woman he'd ever met, and he had to do something about her.

Yet today was not the day to deal with her, or for the children to be roaming the palace. "There are entire acres of land around the palace. Take them outside if you must."

Her eyes widened. "Do you want them

playing near the drive and to see your secret guests arriving? The guests I've not been told about directly for some obscure reason that only you and the butler know? The children might believe their father has returned, and also may run off beyond my power to call them back. They do love horses and fine carriages."

Jasper narrowed his eyes on her. He heard her threat clearly. Dear God, this woman tried his patience. Was she trying to have herself dismissed?

He brightened slightly. Impertinence, outright disobedience, might be reason enough to get rid of her before Nash even came back. He might have considered it, too, if it was any other day.

But his guests were expected in the next hours, and she had to go away somewhere—anywhere else—*with* the children. Someone had to care for them and there was no better choice than Radcliffe right now. He realized then too that he would have to compromise to keep her happy and quiet. "The lawns at the rear of the palace, away from the front drive, beyond the kitchen garden walls, are where you can take the children. Please use the kitchen entrance and servants' stairs for the next few days as well. Not that I should need to explain myself to you. My guests will be here for at least a week, perhaps longer. They will not require your company or your conversation at the dining table, either."

"Good," she muttered, almost too softly to hear.

But he heard her relief, and he straightened his spine at the implied insult that she considered herself too good to sit down to dinner with him and his friends. "My friends will come in the front, use most of the lower floors and guest rooms in the east wing, and likely stroll the east-side hedged gardens and the maze, if they ever care to stretch their legs. The children are absolutely forbidden to speak to them or be seen by them. Is that understood?"

His finger was finally released. "Yes, my lord. Thank you for the explanation and concession for the children, such as it is," she said, her voice dripping with sarcasm now as she curtsied to him. "I shall endeavor to keep the children well away from your special guests in the coming days."

"And the long gallery too," Jasper added, getting cross with her snippy superior tone as he rubbed his finger against his thumb. Radcliffe clearly did not approve of anyone having the least bit of real fun, but then, she was only a governess and lacked an imagination for such amusements. He looked down his nose at her, noticing the heightened color of her cheeks from their arguing made her almost pretty. The absence of pallor suited her better. Some time spent in the outdoors might do her sour disposition the world of good. "I want them gone this minute."

"The children still need to run about today. Your father always disapproved of their noise, but I had hoped you of all people would allow them to move freely about the palace, now he is gone."

"Me, of all people?"

Her lips pursed together, and then she nodded. "I know he was not a kind or forgiving man when he was interrupted."

Jasper stiffened, unhappy to be reminded by the governess of what had occurred in his past. "Whoever told you such a thing?"

She rocked back on her heels, looking down momentarily. "While discussing activities for the children, Lord Nash has said enough to suggest he'd had an unhappy childhood. I assumed that was the case for you as well."

Well, Jasper couldn't dispute the truth of that, but he didn't want the governess' pity. Nash had been treated just as harshly as all of them, and if he'd complained to the governess, so be it. "Father cared only for himself and what he wanted."

"Yes, I had assumed as much. It explains why it is difficult for Lord Nash to return his children's attempts to know him better."

Jasper did not want to talk about his brother with the governess. Even Nash's wife had left him, and the children too, because she couldn't stand the loneliness of being married to him. Nash could never change enough, soften enough, to please his wife while their father had lived, or after. He certainly wouldn't do it for this governess. "Take the children back upstairs."

Her expression turned sweet. "After they have run about, so that they will be tired enough to sleep through anything that goes on tonight."

The long gallery was part of his plans for the evening. The space needed to be pristine. He pushed past her and entered the long gallery, which had undergone a profound change since his brother's departure. The room was more of a boudoir now than a space for taking a turn or childish games.

His nephews were at the far end, lolling about on chaise lounges, tossing fine silk pillows at each other, and eating sweets meant for others from the serving bowls. "Thomas Sweet, Liam Sweet," he bellowed. "Stop what you are doing!"

The boys spun about with wide eyes, shot to their feet, and put their hands behind their backs, rigid with fear.

Jasper, reminded of himself at that age, winced to see them that way.

"For heaven's sake, you sound as harsh as

your father was when you shout like that," Radcliffe chided as she brushed past him, bustling toward the distant end of the room, where the children seemed frozen in place.

He watched them together for a moment, Sophie reassuring them they were not truly in trouble, and then followed her more slowly, determined not to frighten the children even more than he had. Father had always barked at Jasper like that, but he'd not had someone like Sophie to hold his hand or kiss his head, either. He'd not meant to treat his nephews so meanly.

"I am not like him. I'm *not*."

Radcliffe clearly heard his promise but didn't respond as she stood looking down at the boys, who were showing her something and wearing matching worried expressions. She gathered the articles from them, then kissed them on the top of their heads again. "Thomas, take your brother to the kitchen now and ask a servant for milk and little cakes while you wait for me. I'll be along shortly."

Jasper heaved a sigh of relief to see them go. He really didn't want those children anywhere about the public rooms that day, or tonight, either.

Radcliffe spun about to face him, holding out her hands. "The children had these. I assume you know where they came from and can put them back where they belong."

Jasper looked down—and cursed as Sophie shoved two marble dildos at him.

"Dear God," he exclaimed, taking them from her immediately.

Radcliffe glanced over the room. "Now I understand why you didn't want us here. It's a room intended for wickedness and rakes," she murmured. "No wonder you're keeping secrets from me. I can't imagine Lord Nash will be pleased to learn what you're about, either."

Jasper briefly considered denying it all, but what was the point. "No, he won't be, but what I do with my friends is none of his business—or yours."

"I see. And the duke similarly is in the dark, too?"

"Yes," he admitted, wondering how much trouble she would be for him now.

She nodded slowly, eyes darting around the room. "And most of the staff members who remain know what's occurring this week."

"Yes."

Her chin lowered. "But you never thought I should be informed?"

"You were not meant to be here for this. Nash was to take you and the children away with him, but left without you all."

"Yes, without a word," she said. "I saw him leave, and that was the first I knew that the children's summer holiday was canceled."

Jasper folded his arms over his chest. "I suppose you expect me to apologize on his behalf."

"Don't bother," she replied, chin lifting. "The children never knew about the trip. I planned to surprise them the night before with the news. Lord Nash should, however, apologize to his children upon his return for failing to say goodbye."

Jasper marveled at her optimism, completely misplaced, that Nash had ever apologized to anyone. "My brother never will."

"Your brother should include his children in his life." She smiled tightly and then shook her head. "For how long must we keep out of sight of your friends?"

"A week or two."

She nodded and looked away. "A week or two and then everything can return to normal?"

"Yes." He glanced down at his hands, discovering to his shock he'd been standing about talking to the governess with dildos in his possession. He tucked them back where they had come from. "I did not know such things were out yet."

"If you had, I certainly hope you might have warned me instead of beating your chest about keeping to my prison," she retorted.

"I did not beat my chest," he hissed. "Ravenswood is not a prison either."

"I'm sure you did, and it has become so for me and the children," she countered.

"It is for your own safety, madam. My friends are a little rough around the edges."

"Well, I suppose I must forgive you then for being so beastly since it was for our protection," she whispered.

He grabbed her arm. "Now listen here, madam. I'll not put up with your impertinent tongue the way Nash has done."

She glanced up at him, her eyes full of anger. "Your brother doesn't even hear me. But you always do. Why do you care what I say or think about all this, anyway?"

"Madam, the only thing I care about is my own pleasure," he promised.

"I'm sure your appetite for pleasure is vast," she murmured, lashes fluttering and a blush forming on her cheeks. From any other woman, he'd imagine her actions were meant to entice him, but this was the governess. A prim and proper woman. A woman he should not be touching.

He released her arm with an oath. "I apologize. About the boys..."

"They are too young to understand the nature of what they were holding, never fear," she promised, with a shake of her head. "But if they ask, I know what to say."

"Do *you* even understand what those things were for?"

"Of course I do. They were instruments of pleasure. I don't see any devices of flagellation, but I'm sure they're around somewhere, too." She glanced up at him and smirked. "Are you shocked I know of such things?"

"Vastly. I expected..."

"Disgust, outrage, or for me to fall into a swoon? Or even shriek, perhaps, like some sheltered and ignorant society miss might?"

Yes, he'd expected...something more along those lines. He drew closer to the governess, looking directly at her face for possibly the first time in their acquaintance.

Sophie Radcliffe was amused with him, when normally all he noticed was the defiance and distrust in her eyes. "You're not scandalized at all, are you?"

"I should be, shouldn't I?" she laughed. "And yet, I'm not. A rake like you must always have the many and varied accessories for pleasure at a party such as this is sure to be."

Jasper was thoroughly confused now. "That was uncalled for."

"But which statement is incorrect? That you

are a rake, or that you and your friends require all the help you can get to satisfy your lovers?"

He blinked. "The latter."

She moved away, flipping up pillows to uncover one dildo after another. She stopped and looked down the length of the room at all the furniture and scattered pillows. "How lacking your friends must be in imagination to need so many implements strewn about. I assume there will be courtesans?"

He winced and hauled Sophie around so he could see her face. She seemed unperturbed by their conversation while he was struggling to keep up. "Men enjoy variety."

She seemed unconcerned that he held her and did not seek to pull away. In fact, as her eyes traveled from his chest up to his face and down again boldly, so slowly, he felt it as a caress across his body.

His breath caught. Was that anticipation in her eyes?

Her lips suddenly turned up in a smile, and he was rendered mute by expectation. He slid his hand up to her shoulder slowly as his pulse quickened. "In fact, men enjoy many forbidden things."

Her chin lifted in defiance. "Yes, I can believe that all too easily."

Jasper felt that remark like a slap, but held his

ground. He would get the last word today. He was a bachelor, a rake, and proud of it.

Yet, he had missed a great deal about the governess. There was far more to Sophie Radcliffe than met the eye. And after many months of not knowing her, it was a shock to realize she wasn't quite the prude he'd imagined. "Now that you see why I did not want you or the children in this part of the house, you should go join them."

"I've no desire to stay."

And yet she did not leave. "What is it you want me to say, Mrs. Radcliffe? I am what I am."

"You could be anything you want. You have unlimited potential."

Now that was something he'd never heard said about himself before. "Do not provoke me."

She held his gaze with a trace of bitterness. "I do nothing beyond extending you the courtesy of conversation. That is more than you have ever done for me."

He would not apologize. They simply did not get along. "Well, what are you waiting for, Radcliffe? Go!"

"I *would* go—if you could please release my arm," she said, looking down at his hand pointedly.

He was startled that he had hold of her again.

And Jasper's fingers did not seem to want to cooperate and release her at first, either. They pulled her toward him ever so slowly until that smart mouth of hers was mere inches away from his own. He could see the flare of defiance in her eyes again, and the rapid rise and fall of her breasts beneath her prim starched gown confirmed she was not unaffected by his proximity.

Jasper's gaze dropped to her lips, and they parted slightly. He could turn her head so completely that she would forget any infatuation she may have imagined she'd had for Nash. He could prove to her, too, that he required nothing but himself to please a woman in his bed. But then he'd never be rid of her.

He let her go, and Sophie Radcliffe swayed back from him, a slightly dazed expression on her face now. Her gaze dropped slowly down his body and stopped at his groin.

Her breath caught.

Jasper refused to be embarrassed that his cock had a mind of its own. He had never seduced a governess and didn't intend to start now with her. No matter the provocation. "Begone, Radcliffe."

She curtsied to him. "Enjoy your evening with your friends, my lord...and may you find someone willing to take care of that *small* matter for you?"

She swept away, chin high, shoulders back.

Jasper watched her leave, held captive by the

sway of her hips and considering a vastly different ending to their little skirmish today...at least until he heard her laugh.

He narrowed his eyes. The saucy *minx*! Sophie Radcliffe wasn't at all who she pretended to be. Nash must have no idea of the character of the woman he'd employed.

CHAPTER SIX

A SOUND JERKED Sophie out of a light doze. As had become her habit during Lord Jasper's party, she slept in the nursery with the children. Sophie lifted her head to study them in their beds across the dark room now, but she was certain they were still fast asleep.

She turned to look about the chamber, noting the position of the moonlight across the floorboards. Only half the night had passed and she closed her eyes again. It had merely been a dream.

Sophie was dozing off again when another laugh rang out, this time clearly not from the children, and it was more than one voice, too.

She groaned and sat up, pushing her blankets aside. No one should be roaming the halls of the upper floor or laughing outside the children's nursery at this time of night. She got to her feet, snatched up her robe to slip on even as she approached the door to put her ear against the wood. Definitely someone's footsteps out there.

She pursed her lips. None of the servants had reason to be moving about near the nursery at this hour, unless there was a problem that couldn't wait until morning.

Sophie quietly unlocked the door and opened it a crack to see what was going on.

Light danced along the walls of the hallway, where it should have been completely dark. She glanced over her shoulder, but thankfully the light hadn't disturbed the children yet. But it might soon enough if more people came this way. Annoyed by the disturbance, she drew her robe tighter about her, forgoing slippers due to the sound they might make on the bare floor outside. She stepped out into the hall fully and pulled the door shut behind her. "Who's there? Show yourself."

No one answered except for a burst of raucous laughter, but from further away now. A man's and a woman's laughter rang out, along with what seemed like moaning.

She grimaced and quietly secured the children's room with the key and reluctantly headed for the sound, barefooted.

The light was moving away, but she followed quietly to discover who it might have been. A woman yelped, and a rumbling male voice offered wickedness and to make use of one of the nearby guest rooms.

Sophie shook her head. Were Lord Jasper's guests allowed to wander about the palace unrestricted? Carrying candles and doing wickedness in all the rooms? Dear heavens, the place could burn down through carelessness at this rate. Where the devil was Lord Jasper to enforce a few rules on his friends?

Sophie strode boldly toward the light. Ravenswood had grown dear enough to her that she'd hate to see it in flames.

On the stairs, she encountered a couple making love to each other, apparently so drunk and lost to propriety they didn't care who saw what they were doing. A lit candlestick dangled dangerously from the man's hand, and they were leaning far enough over the railing above the entrance hall that they could fall. Sophie noted his breeches had slid down all the way to his knees, too, though he seemed not to care who might be offended by the sight.

Sophie hurried to them, blew out the candle, and hauled the pair back to safety.

"Here now!" the man cried out, protesting her rough handling and an end to his lovemaking, or perhaps to the darkness she'd plunged them all into.

The man turned squinting eyes Sophie's way. "Where did you come from?"

She ignored the question to ask her own. "Where is everyone else?"

"Downstairs." The man's lover edged closer. 'Ere now. Are you just come from someone's bed?"

"Of course not," she protested.

The woman nudged her. "Lucky you. I've had to grapple with him. I could use an extra set of hands."

"Excellent party," the man said, slurring every word. "Thought we'd look around. Want to come to bed? You're already dressed for it I see."

"No, thank you." She got a firm grip on the fellow and tugged him in the direction she wanted to go. *Downstairs.* "I need a word with Lord Jasper."

"Excellent fellow. Knows how to host a good party."

"Does he?"

"Yes, but he's not his brother of course," the man confided. "I was disappointed to learn Ravenswood was away. Remarkable businessman the duke. Savvy in a way few in his family are."

Sophie gritted her teeth to meet someone singing the duke's praises, when it was Lord Jasper he should be thanking for his invitation.

"Tug up those breeches, sir, and we'll go find your host."

Thankfully, the man complied with her request. The man put his arm around her shoulders and together, she and the other woman, maneuvered him down the stairs to the first landing. Then he stopped and pulled Sophie close. Her skin crawled. "We could all go to bed together, the four of us, make a night of it."

The other woman tried to separate them. "I thought you said you liked me best, sir."

"I do. I do," the drunken man promised her, but he cast Sophie a lascivious grin. "But the more the merrier, eh?"

The woman simpered, looking down her nose at Sophie in the somewhat brighter light of the staircase. "As you wish." But then she whispered to Sophie, "He's already paid me. You can get what's owed to you from his pockets when he nods off after."

Sophie was appalled at the suggestion she fleece a man while he slept. What sort of party was Lord Jasper hosting? Had he employed light skirts who were also thieves?

Sophie intended to usher this pair downstairs and hand them off to Lord Jasper as soon as possible. But not before she gave Lord Jasper a piece of her mind and warned him about this man. It was one thing to host a scandalous party, but quite another to permit his friends to roam any-where they cared to or be robbed blind even by people using him to reach the duke's notice.

Sophie got the pair down the stairs in one piece and then urged them towards the long gallery, where the French doors stood open to the gardens and voices could clearly be heard. Lord Jasper should be among them. Beyond the door-way, out on the lawn, were a dozen shadowy fig-ures, all hanging off each other and laughing over some ribald jest or such.

Wishing to avoid the notice of so many, she unentangled herself from the pair and sent them on their way alone. Sophie skirted the gathering, keeping to the shadows or hiding behind plants and statues in search of a certain rake she wanted a word with. But Lord Jasper seemed nowhere among the revelers as far as she could tell and she looked back at the palace. Was he being enter-tained in some dark corner of Ravenswood by a scandalous lady?

She pulled a face at the thought of inter-rupting Jasper, mid-tryst, and then scurried back inside before she was seen by his friends. But So-phie ran headlong into the butler in the hall, Sey-mour spluttered. "You should not be dressed like that," he said, his expression disapproving as he looked her up and down.

Sophie straightened her spine, ignoring her

discomfort. "I'm not down here by choice, sir. Tell me where Lord Jasper is?"

"I'm not entirely certain at the moment," the butler confessed, looking around as if Lord Jasper might be found behind a pillar or potted palm tree nearby. "The long gallery, perhaps?"

"Not that I saw just now when I was there, or in the garden." The butler's eyes bulged at her statement. "I must speak with him as soon as possible. Where did you last see him and when?"

"His study, that little room he's taken over, but that was over an hour ago now, madam."

Sophie ground her teeth. She'd no idea what little room the butler meant, but she'd no time or patience to chase Lord Jasper all over the house at this hour. She ought to go back upstairs and make sure no other guests were wandering where they ought not to be. "Very well. I want a servant posted on the second floor near the main staircase to prevent any more guests wandering up to the third floor. A pair I just encountered making love might have toppled over the balustrade to their deaths had I not been there to stop them. And when you see Lord Jasper, if you ever do before dawn, will you please inform him I need a word with him immediately?"

The butler shook his head. "It will have to wait until tomorrow."

She put her hands on her hips. "I could bring

the children downstairs, and we could all seek him out together?"

"No. That's not a good idea," the butler said, growing pale. "I will post a footman on the stairs and will speak with Lord Jasper on your behalf as soon as I lay eyes on him, but only if you promise to keep the children safely upstairs and away from all this."

Since Sophie had no intention at all of waking her charges or bringing them down into this den of iniquity, it was an easy promise to make. "Agreed, but make no mistake, I will not forget about the matter before dawn comes. I will speak with Lord Jasper tonight, whether he likes it or not."

Another set of doors burst open, and the guests from the garden tumbled inside with an overwhelming burst of raucous laughter. With them, she noted several young women. Young women she'd seen loitering about the nearest village on her infrequent shopping excursions. Women who, for a coin, would engage any gentlemen in need of release.

She blinked. Lord Jasper had brought cheap whores to Ravenswood, one of the finest houses in all of England. Had he no sense?

She had assumed he had experience in arranging events of salacious refinement, given the way he had carried on about the dildos and other things. To discover he offered his guests only base amusements no better than a dockside madam might offer a poor sailor was disappointing in the extreme. She'd thought he had some finesse and discretion, but clearly, he lacked the experience Sophie had been granted before becoming a governess.

Her friend Madam Clover would never approve. There were better ways to manage amorous men's needs. More servants, more distractions, and definitely a better class of companion than these. Women who would not think to take money into their own delicate hands. That is what the madam was for. To arrange things properly so there could be no lack of fair payment and certainly no thievery possible.

Lord Jasper needed help.

Sophie could provide that help, too.

Not that he knew that or ever should. To offer her help would undoubtedly change the way he thought of her and not for the better.

CHAPTER SEVEN

JASPER WINCED as a pair of bachelors dived onto a drawing room chaise where a local whore lay strewn, barely covered by a shabby gown. He pulled the doors shut on their antics and turned on his heel to go anywhere else. Jasper was no voyeur. He had merely provided the service of the introduction to adventurous women in need of similar delights. But tonight was turning out to be more of a challenge to keep his guests in line than the last time he'd played host.

He turned to Seymour, who'd been glued to his side for the last ten minutes. "Next?"

"Mr. Fisher has asked for a riding crop," Seymour said.

Jasper blinked. "Whatever for?"

"He seems to find particular enjoyment in flexing them, but has broken his own and a replacement, too. The young lady entertaining him indicated that he enjoys showing off his strength, such as it is."

Jasper rolled his eyes. "There are no more crops I can afford to give away. The party is meant to make money for me, not incur expenses for replacements."

"Yes, my lord," the butler agreed. "But can you afford for Fisher to leave the house party early if his needs are not met?"

"No. He's losing too well and often to let him storm off in a huff." Jasper ground his teeth. "I know, send one gardener out to the willow trees to cut and strip a dozen lengths of a size similar to the riding crops and deliver them to him. That's the best I can do."

"Very good."

Jasper was incurring a variety of costs he'd not expected hosting this little get-together at Ravenswood. A table had been unequal to the task of supporting a vigorous tupping, a set of fine wine glasses had been knocked to the ground and shattered, and other small, similar damages had occurred all over the palace.

He had been called away to the stables for only an hour and had come back to a mess he could do without. The servants had been apologetic, but they were not at fault. His guests were becoming almost too wild to be reasoned with. "Water the wine and spirits," he whispered.

"Consider it done," Seymour replied, and then cleared his throat. "There is one other matter that requires your attention."

"Yes?"

"The governess."

Jasper groaned. Sophie Radcliffe should have no further dealings with him. She should stay out of his way if she knew what was good for her, and he planned to stay well out of hers for a while, too. "The governess should be tending my brother's children."

"Yes, my lord, and I reminded her of that."

He frowned. "When?"

Seymour's expression grew sour. "When I found her downstairs earlier tonight. She is most insistent that she speak with you before dawn."

"I'm starting to think *most insistent* is her middle name," he complained. "What is she doing roaming the halls?"

"Some guests wandered upstairs, and the noise of them disturbed her." Seymour smiled slightly and then shrugged. "It is Regina."

"What?"

"The governess. Her middle name is Regina. Sophie Regina Radcliffe."

"Well, Sophie Regina Radcliffe is a pain in my backside."

"That is becoming clear, my lord," Seymour replied, nodding. "She said she was willing to seek you out downstairs herself, with the children in tow, if you did not agree to her request."

Jasper choked. "My guests do not want to see a governess and two brats looking on while they are enjoying themselves!"

"I believe she knew that when she made the offer," Seymour murmured.

Jasper ground his teeth again. "Very well. Inform her I will arrive at the nursery shortly."

Seymour nodded and went on his way again.

Jasper headed back the way he'd come, glad the evening was almost over. He went to his chambers first, slid under his bed, and deposited the funds he'd gathered tonight, winnings from the games of chance, into a secret hiding place.

He slid out again and breathed a sigh of relief, but wished the amount might have been more. Jasper calculated he'd need to arrange at least six more similar events this next year to be as successful as he wanted to be. But the slow pace of his efforts was frustrating, not to mention the pain of the cost of repairing any breakages. The recurring question about his oldest brother joining them for the party had particularly soured his mood in his friend's company, as well.

He smoothed his hair and braced himself for the coming confrontation with the governess before he trudged upstairs. He found the woman waiting in the dark hallway in her robe and night-gown, arms crossed under her breasts, feet bare. Jasper slowed his steps as he drew near—stunned. He'd never particularly found women's night attire provocative, but tonight he was forced to change his mind.

With her hair down, tumbled about her shoulders, and her bare toes peeking out from under her garments, Sophie Regina Radcliffe had turned into a siren.

He coughed into his fist, disconcerted by that discovery. "Radcliffe. You should be in bed," he said, but it came out as a growl of demand as he pictured her in *his*.

She put her hands on her hips, scowling. "What were you thinking?"

"I beg your pardon."

"Those girls downstairs are from the local village."

"So?"

"Do you not think they will tell everyone that Ravenswood has become a brothel?"

"It's not a brothel and it wouldn't be the first time scandal took place here, either. My father..."

"Your father is gone, and it's your reputation you should worry about. You hired young women to provide unlimited sex for your drunken friends. In London, or anywhere at all, this would be termed a pleasure house, but you seem to have not the faintest idea of how to go about it."

Jasper scowled. "The women were convenient."

"There are other women better suited to the party this could have been," she complained.

He scoffed. "What would a governess know about the comforts men expect at a house party?"

She shook her head. "The sensible decision would have been to invite a London madam to supply a better class of companion."

Jasper shuffled his feet because that was what he would have preferred to do, money permitting. "A London Madam would require payment up front and time to prepare. Time I did not have to spare."

She pulled a face. "Thankfully, you can easily explain away a singular event if this comes to your elder brother's attention, but if you plan to make this a regular occurrence, and I suspect you have that in mind, you cannot have those women back at Ravenswood. They have no protection, no one to look out for their welfare either. One could have died tonight, along with an idiotic drunkard who decided the staircase was a perfect place to make love. He shouldn't be here."

Jasper bristled. "Who are you to lecture me about the company I keep?"

"I'm not. I'm..." She bit her lip. "The fellow

said he only came to discuss a matter of business with Ravenswood."

Jasper only just stopped himself from swearing out loud at the revelation. "Who was this man?"

"I don't know his name," Sophie whispered. "Blue coat, silver cravat pin. Tall."

"Northcote." Jasper ground his teeth, exasperated by his friends' duplicity. He'd hid his motives for attending Jasper's party very well. Northcote was ambitious. He rubbed his jaw. "It would be a feather in his cap, a boost to his political aspirations, to be known to consort with the Duke of Ravenswood."

But thanks to Sophie, Northcote would not receive further invitations from Jasper or a second chance. No one ever used him twice.

Sophie's hand twitched toward him but she let it drop. "I am sorry to be the bearer of bad news, my lord. I just thought you should know what he said."

Jasper studied Sophie again. She'd wanted to comfort him. He ought to thank her for the warning about Northcote and did. "Was that all you wanted to speak with me about?"

"No, my lord. About the drunkenness."

"Yes, yes. I know." He waved the matter away. "Seymour will water the wine for the remainder of the party. I will ensure the misadventure to the upper floors does not happen again, too."

"Watering the wine will not be enough."

He'd noticed a few of the men indulging a little too freely from the wine cellar *and* the women before he'd been called away to the stables. If he wanted to continue his enterprise in the future, he would need to make changes...and perhaps some new friends, too. However, the last person he'd ever expected to point that out was a supposedly prim governess.

"I suppose you think I should send them all home?"

"Then you assume wrong, my lord. I think you need my help."

He couldn't help it. He laughed. Mrs. Radcliffe could have no knowledge of how to maintain order at a scandalous house party. All she could do is glare at a man. "I think I can manage the party without your interference."

"I don't mean to interfere but to help you and ensure those women remain safe."

"I beg your pardon?"

"I have an acquaintance in London who might be interested in your future amusements," she said, and then cocked her head to one side, watching for his reaction.

"Who?"

"I can write to her tomorrow and arrange a

meeting," Sophie promised, wetting her lips. "Madam Clover understands the trade intimately and is the soul of discretion."

Jasper gaped. "How the devil do you know Madam Clover? She runs the most scandalous pleasure house in all of London."

Her gaze lowered slightly. "No one begins their life as a governess, my lord. It's not important how I met her, only that I can help you."

He drew back, baffled and in shock. Madam Clover's Violet Gardens Pleasure House was the preserve of the richest gentlemen and was expensive. Jasper had never had the pleasure, but he'd heard stories of what went on there.

And Sophie Radcliffe claimed to know the madam well enough to arrange an introduction.

He'd never known her to lie. A proper woman would never have mentioned such a connection unless she was forced. Why would Sophie tell him this now? What did she want from him?

He decided to play along, find out if she could be making a jest of the connection and see what she had to say. That did not mean he would believe her. He would make up his own mind, as ever. "What do you believe my party lacks that Madam Clover could offer?"

"Control."

Her gaze shifted to look over his shoulder,

and then Sophie moved around him, peering down the shadowed hall as if searching for someone.

Jasper turned her back to face him. "Continue."

She shook her head, and then pointedly looked down at his hand where it rested on her arm.

Jasper let his fingers caress her flesh instead of releasing her. Her breath caught and her eyelashes fluttered. Jasper leaned close, intrigued by her reaction. "Tell me, was there ever a Mr. Radcliffe?"

"No." She frowned at him. "Mrs. is an honorific title all governesses assume in their employment."

So, no husband in her past. He met her gaze and realized he yearned to kiss her. It was quite a shock to discover she could affect him twice. He was never usually drawn to proper women. And yet this one claimed to know a madam. "Tell me, are you an innocent?"

She took a long time to answer that question, but when it came, a slight shake of her head, Jasper's breath rushed from his lungs. Relief and anticipation coursed through him. For the whole of their acquaintance, he'd treated Sophie a certain way. He'd thought her dull, timid, and uninteresting. Forbidden. Proper. A stickler for the proprieties. He'd avoided her to spare himself the difficulty of speaking to a woman of supposedly high morals. "Well now. That changes things indeed."

She raised her chin. "I am no whore."

Despite her words, he grinned. Not prim, but not utterly fallen, either. That made him like her more. Could that be the reason he needled her so often? Why her pert responses tormented him? This feeling stirring between them was lust and frustration on his part. She was more of a kindred spirit than his opposite. Somehow he'd sensed that from the first time they'd met.

He bent his head down to whisper, "If I had kissed you yesterday, what would you have done?"

"You didn't." Her fingertip landed on his chest, flexing slightly against the wool of his waistcoat. Jasper captured her finger in the same fashion she'd held him yesterday, and she did not shove him away, just as he hadn't been able to do. Her eyes lifted to his. "You don't like me."

The blood pumping through his veins right now, loud and urgent, claimed otherwise. This was a woman he wanted. "Apparently, that doesn't appear to be the case anymore." He smiled as he touched her hair where it hung forward and then moved it back over her shoulder. Touching Sophie seemed a luxury he never knew he wanted. "However, it is not up to me if we kiss or not. I'm sure you would rather my brother put—"

Her lips were suddenly on his, and a whimper broke from her throat as she jerked him close.

At last.

Sophie's arms wound tight around his neck, and her lips parted to admit his questing tongue. She was warm and lovely, and Jasper's surprise died quickly as he got lost in the taste and feel of her slender body pressed against his. With next to nothing between his hands and her skin, he eagerly learned the delights of her curves.

He drew back, panting, and then kissed her again, wrapping her in his arms tightly, pressing her against the wall. He could get lost in her kisses...and discovered he'd always wanted an excuse to shut her up with his mouth.

But before he could decide what might next happen between them, she pushed him back with a hard shove and turned her face away. "Wait!"

Jasper looked at Radcliffe and heard only the rush of desire coursing through his veins, turning his world upside down. "It's natural to feel unsettled by a good kiss," he whispered.

"Oh, I know exactly what a wicked kiss makes me feel." Her head swung around to the nursery door, then she turned to glance down the hall again. "Is that crying?"

Radcliffe fled down the hall, leaving him standing in front of the nursery, alone and aroused.

Jasper stormed after her, shaking his fist. "Don't walk away when we are finally kissing each other! You liked it, I know you did."

"I did not say I didn't," Radcliffe threw out and then rushed down the stairs a few steps more. She stopped; head cocked to one side. "I'm sure I heard..."

"Woman, how do you expect me to hear or even think about anything besides getting you into my arms again after that kiss," he complained.

But her steps away from his arms continued, at least until she rushed into the family wing, where his own room was located. He brightened. Well, it seemed she was eager for more than just kisses.

He pursued her, grinning, but Sophie paused every few feet and put her ear to every door. When she stopped at his door, she finally turned to look at him. There was confusion in her expression as she caught his gaze. Her shoulders slumped. "You should deal with that."

He shook his head. "Deal with what? The fact that you're an impossible flirt?"

"Don't you hear the crying?"

"Crying? What crying?" He stormed toward her and then stopped dead, his gaze moving beyond her to his door. "There should be no crying coming from my chambers."

"And yet there is," she said. And then without so much as a by your leave, she threw open the doors of his bedchamber and slipped inside.

He heard the wailing, clear as day then. A vastly unhappy sound was coming from his rooms when none should have been heard. Jasper pursued the governess—and then froze to see a tiny figure flailing about on his enormous bed. "What the hell is this?"

The governess looked at him. "Where's the mother? Downstairs at your party?"

"No friend of mine should have brought her child to my party."

"For a moment there, I thought you were different."

Jasper put his hands on his hips. "What is that supposed to mean?"

"Rakes never want reminders of their scandalous ways once their fun is over, do they? I should have remembered that."

"That is not my child," he declared, pointing at the ball of misery on his bed.

Sophie sighed. "You should treasure something so precious."

"Me? How is this my responsibility?"

"She's on your bed so clearly she must be yours."

"The only thing clear to me is my bed is occupied by a loud-mouthed brat that interrupted an exceptionally good kiss between us. That does not make her mine. I do not even have a lover at present. I haven't for a while." The wailing intensified, and Jasper put his fingers in his ears. Sophie went to the bed to look down at the small being who refused to be comforted by their mere arrival. "Radcliffe, will you do something about the noise?"

Sophie grimaced. "What makes you think I know what it needs?"

"You're a governess, aren't you? Mother it the way you do the other pair. They never cry when you are around."

Sophie drew back from the child, fingers twisting together at her waist. "Your nephews were told to like me."

"Well, I can do that for you, too. Child, this is Sophie. Do as she says," he demanded. "There now, it's easy. You can pick her up and all will be well."

"And how should I do that?" Sophie asked, eyes overly wide.

"Oh, for heaven's sake! Here, let me show you how it is done." On occasion, Jasper had cause to pick up his two nephews when they were young, even younger than this child seemed to be. They were weak and wriggly, especially when they were crying. He made sure to get a firm grip before he hoisted the child into the air. The child turned into his chest of its own accord, and Jasper held her against him, relieved that the noise subsided to mere hiccups.

"It seems she knows her papa," Sophie said, stepping away from him.

He scowled at the woman. The governess had tricked him into holding the child—and was about to abandon him. He couldn't have that. They had a kiss to discuss.

"Children sense competence, not ownership," Jasper insisted, following Sophie. "Bounce them around a bit and they'll coo and gurgle next. See? It's a simple problem to solve."

"I wouldn't do that if I were you," Sophie warned.

"Nonsense. I used to do this with my nephews all the time." He brought the child closer to his chest. "It's perfectly all right."

The child burped, and Jasper felt a sudden splash of warmth hit his chest. He jerked the child away from him and stared at her. The child had stopped crying, but a bit of drool dangled from her lower lip in a revolting way. He glanced down at his shirt and cursed roundly to see it soiled. The child had cast up its accounts over his cravat and the shirt beneath, too. The excess rolled downward toward his favorite waistcoat even as he watched.

Jasper shoved the child at Sophie blindly, desperate to strip away the soiled garments and the smell. Thankfully, Sophie grabbed the infant as he fled into his dressing closet to change.

When he emerged minutes later, refreshed, the child had been placed back in the center of his bed. "What are you doing? Don't leave it there."

Sophie turned her gaze on him. "What do you expect me to do?"

"I don't know." He set his hands on his hips. "Take her."

"I'm sorry, my lord, but I am charged with caring for two children, not three. This child is obviously your responsibility."

"Why do you keep saying it's my child?"

"Because she is." The governess held out a scrap of paper toward him. "This was tucked into the shawl she was wrapped in. Isabelle is addressed to you," Sophie said, glancing down at the bed with a sad smile on her face now.

Jasper snatched up the paper. The front bore his first name, the inside said *take care of our Is-*

abelle. "It's not signed," he protested immediately, unable to believe his eyes.

"That hardly signifies," Sophie whispered.

"She can't be left with me," Jasper complained. "None of my lovers have conceived that I'm aware of."

"Now you're aware," Sophie said, fingering the child's clothing and frowning. "This is an expensive garment. The child comes from a wealthy household."

Jasper drew closer to the child for a better look. Isabelle had plain brown hair and was dressed from head to toe in thickly embroidered white muslin garments. But it was her feet that drew his eye. She wore embroidered silk slippers bearing the family crest.

"This is a mistake." Jasper reached for Sophie's hand as his stomach lurched. "How did she even get in here?"

"Many of the doors stood open for your guests tonight when I was downstairs."

"Yes, I heard you *were* roaming the halls earlier, dressed like that. What did you want with me? To show me this?"

"I want nothing now." Sophie turned away, headed for the door.

Jasper rushed after her. "You can't leave her with me!"

"I've no reason to stay," she warned. "This child is not my responsibility."

"Think of the child," Jasper warned, casting his eyes about the room in a panic. "Where should I put her to sleep? In the closet with my boots?"

That made the governess pause, but then she smiled. "Perhaps you should carry her with you everywhere you go tonight, while you get used to the idea that you are a responsible parent now. I'm sure your guests will understand."

Jasper blanched at the idea of anyone downstairs seeing him with an infant. They'd want to know where she came from. Jasper had not the slightest idea. His last lover was too new to have a child of this age. The one before that, a longer-term mistress, had not fallen pregnant to him. She was married now, and had every chance to tell him about a pregnancy long before that event.

So, this could not be his child...but it might bring disgrace to him and the family. He had to hide Isabelle until he knew the truth about her parentage. "I can't take her downstairs with me. I'll be made a laughingstock."

"You might have thought of that before you trifled with...well, whoever you've trifled with and can't now remember. There are always consequences for our actions, my lord."

"For the last time, this child is *not* mine. I would own up to my responsibilities if I had any."

"So you say," Sophie muttered, and with that she left the room, slamming the door behind her.

Jasper blinked as the child started crying again. "Damn her. She ought to believe me." He looked down at the infant as it continued its whimpering. "Why won't Sophie believe me?"

The child's cries increased, her face scrunching up to prepare for an even louder outburst. Jasper rushed to pick up the child, turning her face away from his chest in case she cast up her accounts a second time, and tried to think of what to do.

He jiggled her gently as he walked about the room, until he eventually passed close to a tall mirror and saw that Isabelle had closed her eyes, falling fast asleep in his arms while he panicked.

"Damn," he muttered. He went to put her back down, but she stirred immediately, uttered a little squawk, and grumbled. Jasper wanted to leave her there, but the longer she wasn't in his arms, the more restless she became. Before another bout of loud crying could erupt, he scooped her back up, and she settled once more. He circled back to the mirror in time to see her fall asleep in his arms a second time.

"Devil take it," he muttered softly, glancing down at the annoying infant. He had to get back downstairs to oversee proceedings before some other calamity befell the palace. He couldn't neglect his duties as host. What he needed was another pair of hands, willing ones, and more experienced than his own, too.

He turned on his heel and stalked to the door. He peeked out into the hall, but Sophie was long gone. "How am I supposed to get anything done with you...and without Sophie to help me?"

CHAPTER EIGHT

THE CHILD WAS SILENT AGAIN, as had happened on and off since Sophie had first laid eyes on the poor little thing, kicking and screaming in the center of Lord Jasper Sweet's enormous bed.

It had taken all her strength to leave the girl in Lord Jasper's unprepared hands. To leave him after a kiss that never should have happened felt even worse.

She could still feel Jasper's hands on her body, his tongue teasing hers, and the devastating heat of his body pressed against her full length. Although she should never have allowed a moment like that to sweep away her good sense, she'd uncovered a truth about herself. She was not immune to a rake's kiss, after all.

Not since the last rake, a man who'd broken her heart, had kissed her had she experienced such excitement. Thank heavens for the child's interruption. The little girl's arrival had put Sophie's position in the household firmly in her mind again.

The child was Lord Jasper's offspring, although he denied the responsibility most strenuously. There was no doubt in her mind that Isabelle and Lord Jasper were family. Isabelle had been named after the man's late mother, Isabelle Sweet, Duchess of Ravenswood, and there was a strong family resemblance between them. He ought to care for her for at least one night.

Isabelle had a family; a father, and a mother somewhere. She had asked around discreetly that morning, but no one else had seen a stranger and child wandering the palace. Isabelle was lucky to have Jasper, unwilling or not.

Seeing the child abandoned on Jasper's bed had brought back painful memories of Sophie's time in the orphanage and a loneliness that she had believed long buried. Sophie had been left in a wooden box on the poorhouse's front step at a similar age, wrapped in rags, not heavily embroidered muslin robes, and without a note accompanying her. Sophie didn't even know the name her own mother might have given her once. She'd been named by the woman who'd run the orphanage and then handed off to an indifferent servant's care. The painful reminder of Sophie's abandonment had nearly robbed her of speech in front of Lord Jasper. Almost, but not entirely.

Isabelle was fortunate to be here. Lord Jasper could be made to make provisions for her by his brothers. Lord Nash and the duke would ensure it, no doubt.

She glanced at the nursery door, curious about Isabelle's prolonged bout of silence now. Perhaps the mother had returned, or Lord Jasper was getting the hang of his child at last. It had taken all of her powers of persuasion to keep Thomas and Liam from running off down the hall to see the infant for themselves once they'd recognized the sound for what it was. The children had excellent hearing, far better than their uncles, and they were painfully curious about the intruder in their midst.

Sophie judged the girl around a year old by the look of her. She might have told Lord Jasper that last night, but she'd been too embarrassed to discover Jasper could turn her head. Lord Jasper's half-voiced insinuation that she preferred Lord Nash had taken her by surprise and made her do something reckless to prove it wasn't true. She was not attracted to Lord Nash at all, and she did not like the feeling thinking of Lord Jasper stirred in her today. She would prefer to avoid Lord Jasper, but she probably ought to check on the girl's welfare. If only for a moment, to appease her own conscience. Make sure the child was being fed and kept clean.

Sophie glanced at her charges. The boys were occupied enough that they might not miss her if she slipped away alone for a few minutes. She should leave them behind when she made her trip to Lord Jasper's bedchamber again, anyway. Lord Nash would not like his children to become aware of their uncle's wickedness at such a young age.

Sophie edged toward the door.

"Where are you going?" Thomas asked, standing to face her.

"I'll be right back," she promised them, hoping that would be enough to appease them.

"We want to see the baby," Thomas announced, hurrying to her with Liam following suit.

She'd hoped they might have forgotten the child with the prolonged silence but clearly they had excellent memories, too. "I'm only going to fetch another shawl from my room," she lied.

Thomas, however, clearly did not believe her. He frowned. "We'll be quiet."

Sophie sighed softly. "Thomas, she's terribly young and could be asleep."

"I know how to tiptoe," Liam promised. "Thomas taught me."

Thomas puffed up his chest then and addressed her with such a stern tone, Sophie was taken aback. At times Thomas seemed too much like his father. "Radcliffe, we will see the child. Now."

"I think—"

"You are not employed to think," Thomas continued, parroting the old duke when he delivered a set down to other servants. "But to obey."

Sophie was stung by that. She wet her lips, pained by the realization that as much as she cared about Thomas, he likely saw her as nothing more than another servant to be ordered about. And his younger brother would likely follow in his footsteps soon after.

"As you wish," she answered. "But Lord Jasper might not want you there."

Thomas ignored her warning and strode to the door. Liam grasped her hand and dragged her out the door with them. Thomas took the lead toward their uncle's bedchamber, marching down the hall and down the main staircase. Liam, however, tiptoed by her side but kept glancing up at her.

At the door, Thomas paused and turned to her, a look of uncertainty on his face at last. "Should I announce myself?"

"It would be polite," she murmured, hoping his sudden burst of arrogance might only be fleeting.

He scratched at the door and then ran behind Sophie, putting her at the front of their little group.

The child inside was hiccupping, working itself up to another wail by the time the door was flung open.

Lord Jasper looked a mess. Sophie ran her gaze over his bloodshot eyes and whiskered jaw. Given the rumpled state of his clothes, and lack of coat, it was obvious he'd not slept a wink since she'd seen him last.

He caught Sophie's gaze. "Help."

Such a plaintive wail from a grown man-made Sophie's resolve crumble, and she ventured inside cautiously, the boys following. "I take it her mother did not return?"

"Obviously not, and I still don't know who she could be, but I'm going to have a few choice words to say to her when I find out her identity," he grumbled, following close on her heels.

Before Isabelle could launch into another bout of wailing, Sophie picked up the child to look into her eyes. "Now, now, Isabelle. What has your poor papa done to deserve so much un-happy wailing?" She took the child into her arms, running her hand from shoulder to rear, and then detected an unmistakable odor about the child. "Ah, I see."

Jasper was at her side in an instant. "See what?"

"Calm yourself, my lord, but someone needs changing into something clean and dry."

Lord Jasper turned in circles, looking about the room, appearing frantic. "What do I do?"

Sophie deposited Isabelle on the bed and glanced at her charges. She was loath to involve them in Lord Jasper's problems, but supplies were easily at hand if one knew where to look. The children did. The question, though, was if Thomas would be a help or not. "There is some clothing for an infant in the nursery cupboard. They were once Liam's, I believe."

"I don't want those anymore," Liam said, climbing up onto the bed nearer to the girl's head. "I'm too big."

"Indeed you are, my dear. Perhaps someone could fetch them for me," she said, without looking at anyone in particular.

"I'll go," Thomas said as he paused a moment beside the bed. He looked up at Sophie, nose wrinkling. "She smells."

"She does indeed, but in a little while, she'll be clean and you can be introduced properly. *If* your uncle approves."

Thomas raced off, and Liam put his face right close to Isabelle's and her hand slapped onto his cheek. Liam laughed and Isabelle chortled, delighted to see a friendly face so close at hand.

Sophie smiled at the pair. "Children never hesitate to satisfy their curiosity, do they? Perhaps, while we wait for Thomas, you might open the windows to draw in some fresh air, my lord."

Jasper rushed to the windows and threw them open, causing a cool draft to swirl around her skirts. Sophie removed her shawl from her shoulders, placed it aside on the bed, and then rolled up her sleeves. "I'll need a bowl of water, soap, and a washcloth."

Lord Jasper was quick to do her bidding, silent and apparently content for her to make decisions for once.

He'd brought the washbasin to her, including the stand it usually rested upon, by the time Thomas returned with his arms overflowing. The boy had brought everything. "This is all I could carry!"

"Thank you. Perhaps we might have a little privacy now," she requested, and Jasper kindly pulled the bed curtains closed around one side of the bed and ushered his nephews to the far side of the room with him.

Sophie glanced down at the child and smiled at her unhappy expression. "I think you will be glad to have this taken care of, won't you?"

"What was that?" Lord Jasper called.

"I was not speaking to you, my lord," Sophie replied, and then cleaned up the little girl. A task of a moment for someone well accustomed to the chore. At the orphanage, she'd tended to her share of helpless little children. Given the delay in changing her, Sophie elected to dress her entirely in fresh clothing, too. Nothing so grand as what she had arrived in, but appropriate for the day. "I'm surprised there's nothing for you to wear. Was your mama in such a hurry that she forgot?"

The child said nothing to that question, of course, but she kicked her legs about happily. Such a pretty child. She had Lord Jasper's eyes. Sophie spent a moment in contemplation of the mother's identity, but then shrugged the problem away. It was none of her business. The child was clean and healthy and happier now.

Sophie emerged from behind the curtains with the soiled clothing rolled into a ball in one hand and Isabelle balanced on her hip. She asked Lord Jasper to clean the clothes. He looked so befuddled that she had to explain what she meant. "They should go to the washerwoman. I assume she remained behind?"

"I think she did." He shook his head. "I suppose I cannot keep this a secret from the servants."

"No. Have your guests noticed your distraction?"

"Not yet, I think. Thank God." He gnawed on his bottom lip.

"You will have to do something about them," she murmured, thinking it expedient to end the house party. A bastard child would be widely gossiped about.

"You were right, I did not think well enough about hosting the party here with so few servants remaining."

She nodded and held out the happier child to him. "Here you go."

"Ah..." Jasper said, pulling a face and swiftly putting his hands behind his back.

Sophie made him take the child back by forcing Isabelle against his chest. She wasn't about to be saddled with his offspring so easily. Isabelle was his responsibility.

She stepped back to allow the children to crowd their uncle and meet the infant. "Be gentle with her," she warned them, worried about their enthusiasm for tickles. The boys could be a little rough with each other at times.

Isabelle seemed quite taken with more faces around her, and when Jasper laid the child inside a makeshift crib—a drawer pulled from furniture in the room—the children started talking to her.

Lord Jasper backed toward Sophie slowly. "Thank you."

Sophie wrinkled her nose. "I would say it was my pleasure, but I'm sure you understand it was not."

"I do understand. Again, thank you from the bottom of my heart," he said, and Sophie scoffed.

"Yes, I do have one," he assured her, grimacing. "I'll have you know if I wasn't so taken by surprise, and knew who her mother might be, I would have accepted the blame as my due."

"At least that is something in your favor," she conceded. "Many so-called gentlemen do not."

"Now, while I have you here with me and she's quiet, I wanted to return to our discussion of last night. You had more to say on the subject of my parties, I suspect and I want to hear it now."

Sophie didn't feel equal to offering her advice anymore. For a foolish moment, she had forgotten her place in the grand scheme of things. He wouldn't want her advice on how to run a proper pleasure house. He was merely dabbling in the trade. "It's not important now."

"No, it must have been. Otherwise, you would not have summoned me like a recalcitrant child in your care," he said, throwing a teasing smile at her that made her skin heat with a blush.

"I should return the children to their lessons," she told him, instead. Eager to get away. It had been an idle fancy, borne of a moment of foolishness, and nothing more needed to be said. She was better off staying out of his business. He had more important things to worry about now.

When Isabelle began to fuss, the new father rushed to pick her up, and the girl quietened immediately.

Sophie gathered up the children and went to leave, but Lord Jasper followed her into the hall. "Walk slowly and tell me when my brother's children are beyond hearing you. Your concern for the prostitutes' welfare was unexpected...and truly kind, by the way."

She pursed her lips, and after a moment of debate, told him about the flaw in his plan as she saw it. "I suspect I know what this week is about."

"Do you?"

"Every servant at the palace is aware that money had become a scarce commodity."

Jasper pursed his own lips and nodded. "Go on."

"You're looking for an effortless way to replenish your funds. But to make money of the size you must need, you must understand what drives men like yourself to spend. Men like you want luxury in everything and expect to snap your fingers and have it delivered immediately."

"You hardly know me."

"I've known men *like* you. Rakes with means

and little care for what they take from others." She shrugged away her resentment of that attitude to focus on practical matters. "When it comes to running a profitable business, everything and everybody in it is a commodity with a short lifespan, unless it is managed well."

"What does that mean?"

"The women you hired were already exhausted, and it was only the first night. In a pleasure house, a madam of experience would have sent each of the ladies to rest and refresh themselves several times during the night. She would never expect them to entertain all those men, all night long."

"Well, of course not." Lord Jasper asked, stopping suddenly in the hall. "That is obvious, now I consider it further. But how do you know so much about the workings of a pleasure house?"

Sophie held his stare and chose not to answer that immediately. "You must think on a different scale. Hosting a party in a large and opulent home might have been a simple decision for you, but such a vast setting is problematic. It is too easy to lose control of proceedings. The pair on the stairs making love last night, for example."

"Seymour mentioned them," Jasper confirmed.

"The gentleman was drunk and held a lit candle?"

Jasper reeled back. "No!"

"You could lose everything through carelessness like that. They could have pitched down the stairs or over the railing and died or been severely injured. Every guest needs to be controlled."

"I did try, but I was called away to the stables," Jasper complained. "These fellows are used to having their own way."

"One man is not enough to control the dozen you have here, if they are allowed to roam. You cannot be everywhere at once, which is why you need the right sort of help."

Jasper wet his lips. "All right. Let's say I agree with your criticism that setting a party here was not my brightest idea. How do I fix that now?"

"You need a madam. A strong woman to keep an eye on all amorous proceedings, protect her ladies from misuse, and collect the funds to share from each tryst. That leaves you and your second —a dedicated servant would be best—free to mingle and encourage the gambling. Makes sure no one wanders away. At the end of the night, the combined profit should be greatly increased over last night."

"Seymour has been run off his feet helping me already. And what makes you think I can just snap my fingers and a madam will appear?"

Sophie turned away. "It's just a thought I had. A foolish one."

Jasper hauled her back. "You may as well tell me the rest now, or I will hound you until you do."

Sophie's breath caught. It was too late not to tell him it all. Most likely he would dismiss her idea out of hand. "You invited a dozen wealthy gentlemen, no credit extended? They would have arrived here with a limited amount of funds to spare in their pockets. But next time, lured by the promise of more experienced London companions, far more funds would change hands. Wealthy gentlemen will pay for good sex. Bad sex, they can get anywhere for free."

"That is an incredibly cynical observation, but unfortunately it rings true to me," he agreed. His lips brushed the child's head, as if in a single night he'd grown fond of the little girl as he pondered her words. "Very well. I agree with all you say. The next party must be better arranged. Now, if only you can point me toward a madam to help with *this* house party, I'd pay you a small fortune."

"You don't have a fortune to give away," Sophie reminded him. "In the meantime, those women need someone to look after them. You only have *me*. I know what to do. I could act as their madam for the rest of the week, if you wish."

Sophie took in the changed expression on Lord Jasper's face and knew she had said the one thing he'd never expected her to suggest. She laughed a little nervously as his silence continued. She might just have gotten the last word again. She could get used to that, too. But she had irrevocably changed how Lord Jasper saw her today, and perhaps forevermore. She hoped that would not set them further at odds.

CHAPTER NINE

"YOU CAN'T BE SERIOUS?" Jasper gasped out after the initial shock of her suggestion subsided enough for him to understand what he was being offered. He held Sophie's gaze, saw her amusement, and scowled until her cheeks turned a fiery red and she had to look down.

Sophie studied her fingertips. "It would only be pretend. But of course you would not consider me. Why would you trust I know anything about anything?"

"I didn't mean it that way," he protested. "I'm sure you're capable of many things, it's just that... it's not at all proper."

Sophie laughed. "What makes you think I'm proper?"

"Oh, you are," he insisted. "And I care about you and your good reputation continuing. I did not want you involved with my party for good reason. If Nash finds out..."

"He'd dismiss me. I know. Should one servant tell him, I'll lose his good opinion forever, and perhaps that is for the best." Her lips pursed, and she looked at him with a calculated gleam in her eye. "I assume the other servants have been promised a generous compensation to still their tongues about your party?"

"Yes, they're to be paid well," he admitted and then scowled as she smiled. Sophie wanted something from him. Just like every other woman he'd known. "The butler will compensate them fairly."

"I hope so," she said. "Then you only have to convince the butler that it's necessary for me to play a role, and he'll convince the others to hold their tongues. Look, there isn't another woman with the knowledge I possess around, unfortunately, so what do you have to lose?"

He shook his head. "Knowledge you may have, but you have the children to look after."

"And you have a daughter now, too," she reminded him.

"Your safety is important."

Sophie laughed, but it was a sad laugh. Bitter. "I know how to protect myself from scoundrels."

Jasper pursed his lips. "Tell me how you came by this knowledge you possess."

"I became acquainted with a madam in London, and through that friendship became familiar with the internal workings of a highly profitable pleasure house. I have been taught well by my friend and know how to manage an entertainment for the best possible outcome. Games of chance will make you some money, but it takes a concerted effort to earn a lot, and that is only possible with an experienced madam and courtesans in attendance who know how to entice and tease. I could provide you with an introduction."

Jasper adjusted the child in his arms and drew closer to Sophie. "If I was going to follow your suggestion for the next event, I must know more about this acquaintance of yours before I let anyone peddle her wares inside Ravenswood."

"Never inside Ravenswood," she warned him, then pointed to the windows. "If there's no better venue available, an outdoor event on the grounds would be a better choice, weather permitting. Less disturbance and wear and tear on the palace's opulent rooms and furnishings. I think the type of men you consort with would be satisfied with a more rustic location near this exquisite family home."

He set his free hand on his hip. "I can't do that. My guests require some luxuries."

"I'm not suggesting roughing it entirely." She rubbed her hands together, as if warming to the topic. "The long gallery and the palace attics are filled with everything we need to create an atmosphere of exotic excess, a bazaar, if you will. Brocade pillows and other luxurious fabrics are easily found. Old carpets no longer needed. Imagine a secluded grove dotted with lanterns hanging from the trees, champagne and beautiful women who dance, sway and sing, accompanied by unseen musicians. Violin or fiddle, you can decide upon which with the madam."

"How the hell could you imagine such a scenario?"

Sophie sighed. "Because I've seen it done. I helped dress a scene just as I described. That time, of course, it was an indoor event, a temporary stage for a birthday celebration, but the same principles apply for your endeavors. In the right setting, with the right variety of companions, you will exceed your own expectations. Believe me, men will pay handsomely for the thrill to continue all night long."

"You describe an orgy." Jasper hadn't imagined his shock could increase, and he drew Isabelle protectively against his chest. "Who are you and what have you done with that prim, disapproving woman my brother foisted upon us?"

Sophie shrugged, but a smile tugged on her lips. "First impressions are not always accurate, my lord. We all hold back something of ourselves in conversation and you have never sought my opinions before. I hold a mercenary view of the transactions that occur between men and women during intimacy, thanks to my experience of the world. I'm no giddy debutant who believes in love or good intentions. Something for something is fair. Everybody wins this way."

Jasper was baffled to discover Sophie was a woman he could actually understand. They even shared similar opinions. Yes, there was as much money to be made in peddling sex as in gambling. Everyone knew that, but few ever spoke of it so bluntly. Sophie was opening up to him, sharing her thoughts with someone she felt comfortable with at last. It was up to him to make use of her suggestions or not. But it was clear she hoped he'd consider some before his next party.

The problem of his current event, however, still required some discussion. Yes, he needed help. But what would it cost him in the end? And what of Sophie's reputation? If Nash ever learned of her involvement, Nash wouldn't want her then. She'd be dismissed without question— without a reference. Sophie was already on the outs with the duke. She just didn't realize it yet.

He gulped. The solution to his problem might imperil her future employment, and that would be all his fault and his responsibility to fix.

"I should go," she whispered, and turned toward the children's room, perhaps keen to forget his problems and his kisses. Jasper certainly wouldn't allow the latter for long. He stewed over the fundamental problem—how to control a roomful of rakes—and came to a swift and startling realization. He needed Sophie.

Jasper *could* do this alone, but he didn't *want* to.

"If I follow your advice, I will need your help and I will pay you well for it," Lord Jasper called out softly. "With Isabelle, as well. Something for something. Everyone wins. What do you say? Partners?"

Sophie glanced back at him and seemed confused by his suggestion. "Partners?"

"I could not offer you any less since you risk your position to help me," he said. She should be outrageously flattered by his offer. He was wicked, a rake, but not unfeeling or selfish.

Jasper hardly ever cared about other people's opinions or his own reputation. But he suddenly cared about Sophie's. If she lost her position for helping him, she would not be sent away empty-handed. She would have money from his own pocket to support herself and a letter of recommendation from him, if that at all helped her. He was a father now. He could say she'd been his daughter's governess and write her a glowing character reference.

He glanced down at the child and smiled. "If my brother were to dismiss you, Isabelle still requires a governess, don't forget."

Sophie returned to him. "I'm not sure I could work for you."

"I could promise a vastly more pleasurable situation with me if you ever wanted it. You can arrange things to suit your own rules rather than my brother's. That must be a chore. You know more about the raising of a child than I ever could, and I would defer to your opinion, I'm sure. And when you're done with the child, there'll always be me to spend your evenings with."

Her brows shot up. "Such a rake."

"Always a rake," he answered. "But I do have some other sterling qualities."

"Such as?" Sophie asked as she tickled Isabelle's cheek.

"Loyalty," he promised sincerely. "I would treat my partner, my governess, very well indeed."

She swallowed and looked away, seemingly not at all accustomed to flirtation or the thought of a future with him.

"We can discuss this in greater detail later if you like," he said.

"After the party," she whispered.

"Yes," he promised. The matter of them

kissing could wait. Sophie wasn't going anywhere until the party was over, anyway. "What do you need from me? I assume you mean to begin immediately."

Sophie wet her lips and then met his gaze. "I need to speak with the ladies you hired. Then you need to speak to Seymour and the footmen about why I'm there. They need to understand they must follow the madam's orders and not question me in front of the guests."

"I can do that," he promised. He looked her over. Sophie's attire was utterly suitable for the nursery, but not for a scandalous house party. She looked like no madam he'd ever met. Would any of his guests believe she was one? "What are you going to wear to my party?"

Her smile burst over her face. "Something entirely appropriate for presiding over wickedness, I promise you that. I will need a mask, though."

He nodded, wondering if one was possible to find. The only women's clothes he'd seen about belonged to the ones wearing them. "I can loan you my own mask. I doubt my sister-in-law left many articles of clothing behind when she left."

"Lady Win?"

"No, Lady Laura Sweet."

"Oh," she said, wincing. "I ought not to wear

something of hers. Yours will have to be good enough."

"Are you sure?"

"Yes."

"Very well then." He delayed a moment more. "Are you certain about this, Sophie?"

"You need me," she asserted. "Here, give Isabelle to me for the day. You need a shave and you've responsibilities with the guests and the estate. Ask Seymour to send the maid Kate to me at three o'clock and I can begin my preparations for the evening ahead."

He nodded, burning with curiosity about what those preparations would entail, but gladly handed Isabelle over to her, knowing she'd be treated so well she might never want him to take her back. But he *would* take the child back. Isabelle was his responsibility for now.

Jasper leaned toward Sophie and dropped a gentle kiss on her cheek. "Thank you."

Sophie glanced up at him a little shyly from under her lashes. "Just remember to come back for the child."

He'd be back for them both.

He waved and went on his way, down to the butler first to deliver Sophie's request.

"I will send someone along to the nursery at the appointed hour," Seymour promised, but he didn't look happy about involving Sophie in the coming evening. Certainly not pretending to be a madam, either. "Mr. Threadwell was looking for you earlier, my lord. Knowing where you might be, I suggested you were out in the stables instead."

"Good. Sophie has taken the child off my hands for the day, so I'm free to resume my responsibilities as host. I'll better go see what he wants first," Jasper decided and headed out of doors.

The gardens were deserted, but the stable yard was busy with grooms exercising the animals.

"Good morning, Threadwell," he called as he joined his friend as he admired the duke's horseflesh.

"Sweet," Gulliver Threadwell replied, eyes trained on the livestock in their stalls. "This is a fine-looking gelding you've got here. One of your father's best."

"My brother's now," Jasper corrected.

"Yes, of course. You know, I lost quite a few pounds betting against this beast last spring."

"You should have known better," Jasper chided, giving the horse a passing glance. He wasn't as interested in racing or horseflesh as his friend. Threadwell was obsessed.

Threadwell smiled. "I didn't want your father and cousin George proved right about his chances of winning at the time. Your father was always an insufferable prig when his horse won."

Jasper leaned against the railings. "That he was."

"It must be nice," Threadwell mused.

"Nice?"

"Being here without him. Neither one of us had an easy time with our family." Threadwell turned around, studying the palace through narrowed eyes. "If I had inherited all this, I'd have burned the palace to the ground. Wiped my awful father's crowning glory from the Earth and started over anew."

Jasper looked at his friend, startled. "Luckily for everyone concerned, neither you nor I will ever inherit our families' estates."

"Yes, it's a great pity," Threadwell agreed, turning back to study the racehorse again and then thumped his fist on the rail. "I want this horse."

"I beg your pardon," Jasper said,

"The horse. I want to race it, and I hear your brother has no plans for the track."

That wasn't common knowledge. Only family members should have known about that so far. "Where did you hear that?"

"Your cousin George, of course." Threadwell complained. "He was befouling my family estate the last time I was home. Without his wife. You do know she left him?"

Jasper shrugged. "I had heard something to that effect, but not where he'd slunk off to."

Threadwell pursed his lips. "Put a good word in with Ravenswood for me. I'm not my brother. Tell him I'll pay double for the beast," he murmured. "I want to see the looks on my brother's and George's faces when they learn the animal is mine."

"Why would your brother care about you owning the duke's horse?"

"My brother had been using George to whisper in the duke's ear for years," Threadwell warned. "And George is not above spreading ill news about your brother back to him to cause trouble. Keep him at arm's length."

"We always do." Jasper pulled a face. "I'd gladly convey your interest to my brother if you were ever known to be here. My party would not please him."

"Tell him I stopped for an hour, on my way back from where my mistress was spending her confinement." Threadwell grinned. "She's delivered me a son, by the way."

Jasper drew in a breath. "I wasn't aware she was with child."

"Our third. But you know it is the damnedest thing. After a few days with this new one, I swear

I can still hear him crying at all hours, even from this distance."

Jasper gulped. Isabelle's cries carried farther than he'd ever imagined they might. At least Threadwell thought it merely a memory. Perhaps it would be best if the child slept in the nursery with the other two from now on. But that meant the governess would always watch over Isabelle, and Sophie might not agree to that. Yet, that is what a nursery was meant for—for children and the ones who looked after them. He supposed that meant himself now, too. Would Sophie mind if he spent his nights in that part of the house with her?

Probably not. He laughed and glanced at Threadwell again. "You have three children?"

"Yes," he said with a careless shrug. "Illegitimate, but I'm fond of them."

"Why did you never marry her?" Jasper had met Threadwell's mistress and liked her. She was elegant and witty and undemanding.

"I might still inherit," Threadwell suggested with a tight smile. "I'll need a wealthy bride then to unravel the damage my brother has done."

"Only if your brother dies," Jasper pointed out.

"Yes, and I think my chances of that improve every year." Threadwell straightened. "He's reckless, drinks to excess. His wife won't share his bed, so he'll never have a son or heir by her."

"There is still another brother ahead of you in the succession, don't forget," Jasper said.

"That bumbling idiot would ruin us entirely within a month," Threadwell complained. "I could never allow him to inherit. There are ways to ensure he never will."

Jasper drew back, startled. "I suggest you not say that out loud to anyone but me."

"I'm sure you've thought the same thing about your brothers, too." Threadwell removed a flask from his pocket and drank. "They've treated you as shoddily as I've been treated by mine."

"My father was far worse," Jasper said, refusing the flask when offered. "There's nothing my brothers have that I could ever want so badly as to commit murder to get it."

Threadwell smiled and took another long swig. "Then you're a better man than I, my friend."

Jasper made up an excuse to walk away from Threadwell before he heard any more that might incriminate the fellow later.

Jasper glanced up at Ravenswood. He did not want this estate the way Threadwell had suggested he might. Jasper wanted...something more than what he had now, though. Unfortunately, he did not know what that *more* could be yet.

But when he came clean about the child's existence to his brother's, things would have to change. The duke might not want him or Isabelle staying at Ravenswood, and she couldn't be kept a secret forever. He wanted her provided for, too.

Isabelle was yet another reason he needed money. He would need enough for her dowry, so that she could make a good match one day when she was old enough. She would need an education and love and...well, far more than he'd imagined ever thinking about. He'd have to ask Sophie what that entirety might be.

Later.

When he might find them alone again.

CHAPTER TEN

SOPHIE LEANED TOWARD THE MAID. "Do you have questions?"

The maid Kate shook her head. "No, Mrs. Radcliffe."

"Excellent."

Sophie slipped from the nursery and rushed toward her own chamber. In the last hours, she'd made several brief excursions through the upper floors and attic space of Ravenswood and uncovered a remarkable collection of mismatched items. She had a feathered headdress of what she thought was from swans. A woman's mask had not been found, but she had found a length of black mourning lace that she could drape across her face to wear as a veil that suited her better than Lord Jasper's mask ever could.

Sophie had everything she needed now. Last week, while confined to the upper floor, Sophie had stumbled upon a lovely gown that had been left behind by a previous guest. A red dress, so sheer it was almost indecent, hung forgotten on a peg inside an unused guest chamber. No one was likely to return to collect it anytime soon.

The gown had been soft as it ran through her fingers, with the silk ties teasing her skin. The last time Sophie had worn a gown of this exceptional quality was at the Violet Gardens Pleasure House Masquerade Ball. Madam Clover had insisted she dress the part of a lady of the establishment to blend in—if being seen by her guests could not be helped.

This was indeed such an occasion when a gown like that was needed, but there was no one but herself with the necessary qualifications to watch over those poor hired women. Sophie could not appear downstairs in her governess clothing or her nightclothes again.

She slipped into her room and locked the door behind her. She was excited and couldn't keep the smile from her face. She took the gown down from the hook behind her door where she'd hung the gown hours ago and headed for her small mirror. She held the dress before her and admired the color against her skin and what little she could see of herself. With her hair arranged properly, she could appear to belong. With a little cooperation and instruction, Sophie could also help those poor women manage their would-be lovers better, too.

There was no need for them to deal alone with an amorous fellow who wanted their favors too frequently. They should also not be wandering off where anything could happen to them in the dark. Falling over the staircase balustrade or being set on fire due to carelessness could indeed be prevented under her watchful gaze.

Sophie threw the gown across her narrow bed and then stripped down to her plain and sensible undergarments. Unfortunately, she would have to forgo most of them to carry this off. Sophie redressed herself, aware the festivities were soon to get underway. The gentlemen were at dinner presently. The ladies were not required to join them. They had not dined together last night, either. They were to wait for her arrival and her little talk. Sophie hoped that went well, given they'd no reason to go along with her suggestions, which were only for their protection.

Once buttoned into her gown, she released her hair from the pins that had held it back all day. She brushed the long lengths, twisted them together and allowed them to drape over one shoulder.

Then she went to her mirror. She had always kept cosmetics, a gift from her time with Madam Clover. Although the creams and powders were getting old now, it was the work of a moment to make them usable again. She dabbed at her face with a powder and then brushed most of it off again. She rouged her cheeks sparingly and applied dark kohl around her eyes, as well as a touch more to her eyebrows. And then stood back to consider her changed appearance.

She still looked like herself.

Sophie took up the length of black lace next and stitched it to a headpiece. She used pins and a comb to hold the lace across her face. Finally satisfied, she nodded to her reflection in the mirror.

Sophie had become someone who turned heads, was listened too, and maybe earn a little more approval from Lord Jasper. He thought she disapproved of anyone having fun, and that was hardly the case. Since becoming a governess, she had worked hard to present a respectable image. She enjoyed caring for children very much and had wished to keep her position with Lord Nash. But she also was a woman with an understanding of the scandalous world.

Lord Jasper was about to get the second shock of his life where she was concerned.

The first had been, of course, the moment she'd somehow aroused him. That had shocked her, too, but not enough to end the encounter before she'd won a small victory over him. He'd almost tried to keep her there with him, she suspected. Sophie would not have allowed that. She knew how to defend herself from the persistence of rakes' unwanted advances, if necessary, now.

Governess she might be, but every woman wanted proof that no matter their age, they could still turn a man's head even if they never thought they'd want to again. Sophie wanted a chance to change Lord Jasper's low opinion of her. She wasn't just a dowdy governess. Sophie could be just as captivating as any other lady he might know.

She just would never do anything about those unwanted thoughts or feelings. They always got her into trouble.

Sophie picked up a fashionable beaded reticule she'd also found—a size perfect for carrying money—and hurried out of her room.

At the top of the stairs, she paused to look down, her stomach clenching with tension. But she was committed, and Jasper expected her. Needed her in a way no one else ever had for a long time. She couldn't disappoint him now or abandon those girls.

She started down. Hardly any of the guests could have laid eyes on her before tonight. She'd have to be careful about that in the future, too. She was being paid to pretend to be a madam, though no amount had been specified. Lord Jasper didn't need to pay her for this, but it obviously soothed his conscience to offer compensation. If she was dismissed over this, he might feel bad about it later. She had to think of her future, too. Hers was not to be a governess forever.

She too often thought of returning to London, to her scandalous friends and a less restricted lifestyle. She missed her old life, the one she'd taken up after her ruin. Meeting Madam Clover had opened her eyes to a wealth of possibilities and exciting new experiences. Moving to the countryside, even a grand estate such as this, had been vastly disappointing. It was not at all the idyllic life that had been described to her by Lord Nash.

There was also the worry that Lord Nash had developed feelings for her that she did not and could not ever share.

The extra money Jasper offered could go a long way in her hands if she was ever without this position. And there was always Isabelle. Sophie would not mind helping Jasper care for the little girl for a while, either, though she would not let him know about that just yet. He was too used to getting his own way. Isabelle was a sweet little thing, all told. Hardly more trouble than her current charges had ever been.

All things considered, what could it hurt to

help this particular rake? At least Lord Jasper was honest about his nature, his interests, where another had not been so forthcoming. He did not pretend to be something other than what he was unlike some she could name.

She would simply have to ignore that little voice in her head that suggested he was entirely too handsome and kissable.

Sophie moved downstairs, passing no one, and turned away from the dining room where she could hear the voices of Lord Jasper's guests. They were not her concern just yet though.

The ladies had been sequestered in the morning room nearby, and she let herself in without knocking. Six mouths ceased speaking immediately, and six pairs of eyes looked her up and down with deep suspicion.

Only one woman rose and came forward. The woman from the staircase last night. The one she'd helped with getting her gentleman back down safely. She approached Sophie, bold as brass, clearly the leader of their little group. "Are you the madam?"

"Yes."

The woman laughed. "We told him we don't need a madam to take our money while we do all the hard work, do we, ladies?"

Sophie winked. "I'm not here for your money. I'm here for *you*. To protect you."

The woman frowned at her, taking her seat, and the other ladies looked just as confused. She noticed one of them sported a bruised cheek and went to look at the injury. "One of the guests did that to you last night."

The woman pulled away. "It's nothing."

"It's not nothing." Sophie gently captured the woman's face again to see if she was bruised on the other side as well. She was relieved to see her other cheek was clear of any injury. "A bit of cosmetic will hide that blemish, but remember—what you allow is what will continue." She addressed the room. "Did any of the men give you trouble last night?"

"Of course they did," the first woman informed her.

Sophie turned her gaze on her. "Might I know your name?"

"It's Giselle," she told Sophie smugly.

"Is that your real name?"

"Course it is," she boasted.

"Never use your real name with any of your dance partners," Sophie warned. "Always change it."

"It isn't a dance we're doing with them," another mumbled, and ribald laughter followed her words.

"I am not only speaking of the act of lovemaking, but the beginning of the encounter, and the aftermath, too." She pointed to the door and grimaced. "These men are rich, powerful, but they want something from you. That means you have power over them."

Giselle narrowed her eyes. "What's your name?"

"Regina, of the Violet Gardens Pleasure House."

Giselle was suddenly on her feet. "'Ere, I've heard about that place in London. Classy. But what are you doing here with us?"

"Madam Clover has friends everywhere. She sent me to meet you. If you want to make more money off these so-called gentlemen, I suggest you listen to what I have to say and keep an open mind. You can do better if we work together." She pointed to the injured woman. "I want no more *nothing* bruises on anyone else's features tomorrow morning."

"What do you want us to do?"

Sophie smiled. "Gather round and I'll explain."

For the next half hour, she explained how things worked at Madam Clover's pleasure house. How the ladies moved constantly from man to man, limiting the opportunities for being pawed at. How it drove the men to compete for their favors. How it drove their asking price up, too.

Giselle caught on quickly, and the others eagerly followed her example.

"Now, to the manner of your presentation tonight."

Giselle's hands flew to her face. "What's wrong with how we look?"

"I'm not referring to your appearance, though less rouge would be preferred on all your cheeks." She counted the number of ladies in the room again and glanced at the clock. It was almost time to join the gentlemen. "There is no need for you all to troop out together like pigs to a slaughter. A pair of you will remain behind."

"Then the others will get all the money," an older woman complained.

"The money comes to me to disperse to you all here at the end of the evening," she promised.

"I knew she was after our money," Giselle warned.

"An equal split." Sophie lifted her wrist. "It all goes in here. You will have your hands full with the gentlemen. We don't want them stealing back their money when you're distracted, do we?"

There was enthusiastic agreement to that.

"That fat fellow did that to me last night," one girl complained bitterly. "Pinched a penny and wouldn't give it back unless I kissed him again."

"Another reason to make use of me," Sophie said with a shake of her head. "And that brings me to another point—no one takes a penny from any man that they did not earn. It all comes through me to be shared," she warned. "So, we have a man who used his fists, another who short-changes for services rendered. Are there any other problematic gentlemen the others should know about?"

No one volunteered anything further, and Sophie nodded.

"If you encounter an unpleasant situation and need help, signal to me or each other."

"How are we to do that? Shout out that he's pinching my bottom too hard?"

Sophie laughed along with them all. "Nothing so obvious. Simply do this." She stretched up one arm high, then brought her hand down onto the back of her neck slowly.

"Lud, that's hardly a signal of distress," Giselle, said and then mimicked her movement. "Twill make him hungry for our titties."

Sophie laughed again. "A distraction for him, and a signal to any of us to come to your rescue. Madam Clover's ladies use it all the time. Distract, withdraw, and return to tease again."

Giselle was nodding enthusiastically now. "That we will. What do you say, ladies? Shall we try it her way tonight?"

There was a chorus of agreement around the room at last.

Sophie breathed a sigh of relief. "Now one last thing, no more than three men each tonight."

"Only three?"

"Or less. The gentlemen got a generous taste of you last night. This evening, they pay dearly for their pleasures," Sophie swore. "I promise if you let me do all the talking about your fee, the combined income will be split evenly between you all by morning, and you may be on your way less exhausted than you were last night."

"What if they don't want to pay more?" Giselle asked, worrying her lip again.

"Refer them to me, and if you genuinely want them, the gentleman will have to convince me to accept a lower payment. Believe me, I'm not easily swayed by a man crying poor."

"Lud, Madam Regina," Giselle exclaimed. "You've a hard heart and that's needed in our line of work. I'd be happy to go to London and be a whore in Madam Clover's pleasure house if you were there, too."

Sophie nodded. Giselle certainly had the ambition, and mind, to have a future with Madam Clover if she wanted to make something more of herself. "Please decide between yourself who'll remain behind at first. We'll switch everyone over each hour."

"Are you going to be entertaining the gentlemen, too," a young girl asked, coming up to her side. "I bet Lord Jasper's got his eye on you."

"She's probably had him already," the oldest woman complained. "They're devils, those Sweet gentlemen."

The women laughed and looked at her for a response. Sophie drew in a breath and instead of answering that question, memorized the names to go with their faces. "I will circulate through the room and watch over you all night."

A tap sounded on the door. "Care to join us?" *Jasper.*

"Coming, my lord," she replied and faced the room again. "Ladies, it is time. Shall we join the gentlemen?"

"I say let them wait a few minutes more," Giselle decided. "It will increase their anticipation and I like having the upper hand for once."

The ladies agreed with her about that and fussed with their appearances before they formed pairs. At Giselle's signal, they swept out the door ahead of her.

The ladies left behind moved to surround Sophie before she could depart. "What will we do, madam?"

"Put your feet up, and get some sleep if you can," she told them. "It's going to be another long night for you all."

Sophie headed for the doorway and shut the door on the other ladies with a wink, which they laughed at.

Jasper was waiting. "Sophie?"

"Madam Regina tonight," she warned.

"Your middle name?"

She was surprised he knew it, but nodded. "Do I look different enough for my new role?"

He swallowed. "You look good enough to undress and I have never thought that before about you."

"I'll take that as a compliment," she murmured, pleased with his reaction. She'd been dressing the part of a governess for so long that it was a relief to dress this way again.

"You should most definitely do that," he said, tugging at his cravat to loosen it. "Threadwell, do go away. She's not for you."

Sophie turned and faced a wall of male chest and looked up slowly into a rake's knowing eyes.

"But I'm here to take this ravishing creature off your hands," Threadwell said, extending his hand to her. "You don't mind, do you?"

"I mind," Jasper warned, his tone low and deep. Possessive. Sophie shivered. She glanced at Threadwell's hand, and then at Jasper. "Would you introduce us?"

"Sophie, may I present Mr. Threadwell? An old friend. Very old, indeed."

The man ignored Jasper's teasing about his advanced age, though he didn't look much older than Jasper was, and kissed the back of her hand when she offered it out to him. "My dear, might I offer you a glass of Ravenswood's finest sherry?"

"Another time, perhaps," she murmured. "It is imperative I continue to speak with Lord Jasper right now. I'm sure you understand."

"Until later, then," Threadwell said, kissing her hand again and letting his fingers draw slowly along her palm before he took himself off to where the other ladies were holding court.

She glanced back at Jasper and laughed. "Do you have any friends who are *not* rakes?"

"Probably not," he warned in a low tone, gaze dipping to her breasts briefly. "Perhaps this was a bad idea."

Sophie linked her arm through his. "Nonsense. I am alert to all the tricks a rake uses to charm a lady into his bed. They are obvious, after all."

"What tricks?"

"The fingertips tickling my palm," she said, but Jasper looked baffled. "Oh, do you not use that one? Here, let me show you."

She reached for his hand the way Threadwell had done and slowly drew her fingers across his palm.

Jasper's spine straightened, and he turned to

glare at Threadwell's retreating form. "Devil take it! He was attempting to seduce you right before my eyes and he already has a mistress."

"He's a rake. Seduction is all you all think about."

"True, but tomorrow, you and I are going to discuss what other *tricks* rakes have used on you," Jasper warned, turning for a moment into her protector and would-be champion.

"Why?"

"So I never try them on you myself," he said with a soft chuckle. "You won't fall for any of them, so I may as well not bother."

Sophie laughed, caught up in the night's excitement already. "I like you more now, you know."

"And I like you, too, and the dress as well," he said, eyes dipping to her breasts again. "I'd like nothing more than to peel you out of it with my teeth right now but we have guests to entertain."

"Indeed we do," Sophie murmured, fighting a blush as Jasper led her deeper into the drawing room with one hand firmly settled at the small of her back. She looked about the chamber, noticing the changes. "The chair's gone."

"What chair?"

"The chair we squabbled over last time we were in this room together. Your favorite chair."

"It was damaged last night," he said sourly.

She sighed. "I will miss that chair."

"When it is repaired, you can sit on *my* lap rather than me on yours," he offered, and then began the lengthy process of introducing her as the madam to everyone.

They parted ways not long after and for the next several hours, Sophie collected payments, chaperoned the couples to and from rooms for lovemaking, and made sure the women, if not satisfied, were well afterward.

The largest guest haggled heatedly for the privilege of bedding the youngest whore, but it was clear she was not in favor of the match. Knowing he would be more trouble than she could handle alone, Sophie stretched up and rubbed the back of her neck.

The man was staring at Sophie's breasts as Giselle smoothly stepped up to his other side and kissed his cheek. Sophie sent the younger woman away to rest with a discreet flick of her hand without the fellow noticing she'd even done so. Giselle stretched up as he stared at her breasts, too, and Sophie could slip away from the pair, knowing she'd be replaced by another lady soon. The fellow was in expert hands. Giselle knew how to conduct her business well.

Sophie headed to the gambling table to see how Lord Jasper was faring. He looked to have won more often than not. In fact, his game seemed to be near its conclusion.

She leaned over his shoulder boldly and picked up a coin from the center of the table to admire, even though some protested. Then, just as carelessly, let it slip from her fingers back to its spot on the table's surface.

However, in leaning over the table the way she had, she'd offered Jasper's opponents a glimpse of her breasts too. Those men now tracked her movement round the table, and she let her fingers drag over their shoulders as she went round. Madam Clover had done that often when a distraction was needed during heated games of chance. It was a way to cool tempers. She paused behind Jasper, briefly resting her hand on his shoulder, and then turned away, swaying her hips more than she ordinarily might as she left the table behind.

It was just like being back in London, and yet she'd never been brave enough to do all she'd done tonight at the pleasure house. But she'd done it for Jasper. A rake who made her forget the last one. She did not understand how that could be good for her heart. For now, she had a role to play in making his evening the success it should be.

Someone grabbed her hand, and when she looked, it was Jasper by her side again. He scowled at her suddenly. "Lean over my shoulder like that again and you'll start a riot."

"But did you win?"

He nodded. "Yes, but I'd rather have had the view the others enjoyed. I've never seen my friends so instantly smitten. What are you wearing under there?"

She looked at him and fluttered her lashes. "Nothing at all, my lord."

His arm slipped around her waist immediately, and he held her tightly to his side. "You should not have told me that, madam. I can't possibly let you wander around alone now. We're sticking together tonight, partner, till dawn."

She couldn't escape the rush of pleasure that swept over her at his promise. She'd like to spend the evening doing nothing else but being with him, too.

CHAPTER ELEVEN

JASPER GAZED out over the beauty of the Ravenswood Palace estate, a sense of pride filling him. Father might have run up debts everywhere but had never stinted on the estate or livestock. Of course, there were dozens of improvements he could easily see that could be made still though. He made a mental note to write them down later, something he'd been planning to do for days, but of course the party and the arrival of the child had thrown his life into utter chaos, and so had Sophie, too, in a way.

The child was more problematic, of course. For the life of him, he could still not imagine a lady of his intimate acquaintance keeping such an important event from him. They should have told him, hinted at making a marriage between them or, at the very least, applied to him for financial support.

The latter, he would not have stinted on. He wasn't heartless. He owned up to his mistakes, and he liked his brother's children well enough to want some of his own. But marriage would have been an entirely different kettle of fish.

Jasper had many flaws as a man; he was a third brother and, as Sophie had been quick to point out, a proud rake. He wasn't the first bachelor any respectable lady thought about for a husband.

He patted his horse's neck as it stamped its feet, keen to move on with his tour of the property. Jasper was impatient, too. But he was concerned by the flavor of his own thoughts since last night to want some time alone. The possessiveness in him when he was around Sophie was unexpected and troubling. He wanted more. He always had, but the *what* had escaped him...until now.

He turned his horse about and started back toward the distant palace, to a child who might be his and the governess he now seemed to crave more conversation with. The governess had reinvented herself in the space of one day and there was no turning back now. He liked Sophie very much—far more than he'd ever expected to.

He did not know what to do about Sophie.

She was like him in so many ways, but better at hiding her jaded experience of the world.

A flash of movement among the trees caught his eye. He wheeled his horse around and reached toward the pistol he carried strapped to his leg in case it was needed. There ought not to be anyone lurking about in the trees. Poachers were not unheard of on the estate, and he would deal with any trespassers if he must. This far from the main road, from the palace gardens, signified a stealthy incursion might just be underway.

To his surprise, a rider in an inky black cloak emerged from the trees, followed by a man on horseback. Jasper squinted at the pair, recognized the former was a woman riding sidesaddle. There was nothing furtive about their approach, though, and Jasper kicked his horse into a gallop to reach them. "This is private land."

The woman raised her chin, revealing her entire face to him. "I am well aware of that, Jasper. Do you intend to shoot me for trespassing?"

"Of course not," he hurried to promise, knowing full well how stupid he must seem for not immediately recognizing her. "Sister?"

Lady Laura Sweet inclined her head. "My lord."

Jasper urged his horse alongside hers and reached out, hoping to touch her fingers to confirm Laura had come home at last. She did not oblige to lift her hand from the reins though, and he dropped his own after a moment. "I can hardly believe my eyes, but it is you."

"It would oblige me to know where my husband is?"

Jasper frowned at the question, and the frost in her voice. "It's good to see you again, and looking so well."

"No thanks to your family," she said bitterly. "Tell me where he is."

Jasper and Laura had gotten along passably well before her departure from the family fold. Clearly, she was no longer fond of him. He'd done what little he could to protect her, but of course, Father had despised Laura's presence by the end and wanted her sent away almost as soon as Nash's second son had been born. She'd stayed only long enough to nurse young Liam past his first months of life and then slipped away early one morning, leaving no trace.

"He's away with Algernon. Do you know Father died?"

"Of course," she said, gesturing to her dark clothing. But her eyes darted about the clearing still. "When will Nash return?"

"Oh, any day now," he lied, and Laura's grip on the reins tightened slightly. There was definitely a furtiveness to Laura's visit to the estate that Jasper did not care for. He felt it in the way she sat in her saddle. Poised to take flight. "So, you have come home?"

"No."

"Your husband misses you."

"Nash has my money, my children, and that's all he has ever wanted from me." A sour smile turned up the corners of her mouth. "He has found other comforts, anyway."

Jasper drew back in surprise. How could she know what Nash was up to? Had she spied on her husband? "You have been misled," Jasper promised. "He has been faithful to you."

"No, he has not."

Jasper blinked. "Why would you think that?"

"Believe me, I know all about his secret London affair."

Nash and Laura had married young and, until recently, Jasper had never doubted Nash's fidelity to Laura. The flirtation with Sophie, if that was even true, would be forgotten now Laura was back. "Then confront him about the matter. Don't let him get away with it."

She glanced his way. "I thought you would have been on his side in this."

Jasper shook his head. "My brother's behavior has always mystified me at the best of times. But when it comes to you, I cannot fathom how he let you slip through his fingers."

"I did not *slip* anywhere, Jasper. I ran." She

adjusted her grip on the reins. "I wish to see my children."

"Of course, I'll not bar your way into the palace."

"I want you to bring them to me here."

"I cannot do that, but please come inside." And then he remembered he had guests who would see Laura and gossip about her return. He'd have to risk it. "Take tea with us in comfort. Ravenswood is your home still."

"It never was. Bring them here and without the governess," Laura demanded.

Jasper gaped. "She'll never agree. Sophie is devoted to those children, and they are hardly ever out of her sight for long."

"The nursemaid I left behind was devoted to them as well," Laura bit out. "Delphine was more than capable of looking after the children in my absence. But as soon as I was out of the way, your father discarded a loyal woman and Nash replaced her with his tawdry bit o'muslin."

Jasper was taken aback by her accusation against Sophie. "Delphine could no longer manage the stairs, or keep up with them. She was pensioned off with a generous amount of coin to go live with her sister. Sophie is a competent re-placement."

"How naïve do you think I am? Do you think

I don't know Nash met the current governess at a brothel?"

Jasper's horse sensed his unease at hearing that information about Sophie's past repeated and it pranced under him. He settled the horse quickly, but he was puzzled by his sister-in-law. Her accusations Nash meeting Sophie at a brothel, but how could she know that when he'd only just learned of it? "Sophie Radcliffe is the furthest thing from a light skirt."

"So, he still keeps secrets from you?" Laura murmured. "Poor Jasper. Always the last to know what is going on in the family. The forgotten brother. Never told anything important until the last minute. I had hoped things might have changed for you with the passing of your father."

Jasper blew out an exasperated breath. Laura had been his friend and neighbor before her marriage to Nash. He'd confided in her things he'd rather she'd forgotten all about. Being born third meant he'd felt slighted as a boy. Algernon and Nash had always been close and had been given the best of everything. Nash had taken Laura from him, in a way, not that they had been in any way romantic with each other. They had been friends once, but it seemed those days were a distant memory now. "I won't be drawn into an argument with you, Laura. Stop this nonsense and come and meet Sophie yourself. You'll see the only thing she cares about is the children's welfare."

"Are you in love with her?"

"Are you daft?"

"Oh, you are!" Laura laughed in his face. "No wonder you defend her so well."

"I'll not listen to your slander, either. Come to the palace and you'll see your fears are for naught about Sophie."

"In some respects, you are very much like your brother. Demanding all women to forget their principals to keep your favor." Laura smiled tightly and leaned forward in her saddle. "Be your most persuasive with the governess. Women have been falling all over themselves to do you and your brothers bidding since you came of age. One woman should present no difficulty if, as you say, she's not Nash's creature. Bring me my children here in an hour."

Laura wheeled her horse about and dashed back the way she'd come into the woods, headed in the opposite direction to her family estate. The other man nodded to him and turned to follow her more slowly. Jasper attempted to follow, but lost sight of them almost immediately when he entered the trees. They clearly knew where they were going, while he did not.

He cursed and turned about, and headed back to the open field to think. He wanted to reunite Laura with her children, but he was worried. The eldest rarely mentioned his mother. The youngest might not remember her at all. And there was also something sinister about Laura wishing him to bring them to the edge of the woods. Why not come to the palace? Nash was not even there. No one would prevent her from leaving if that was her heart's desire.

He replayed their meeting in his head on the ride back to the stables and by the time he'd handed his horse off to the groom had decided not to tell Sophie about the encounter with Laura yet—or to give in to his sister-in-law's request. The main reason being her accusations against Sophie. Sophie might find that upsetting.

Nash might have made Sophie's acquaintance through a London madam, but he could not imagine Sophie entertaining countless strangers in her bed. After last night, the idea was ludicrous. Sophie might not be the woman she had first seemed, but she had held herself aloof from proceedings and not for one moment portrayed interest in any of the gentlemen who had circled her. She had only blushed for him and he'd been charmed by that.

No. Sophie was a proper lady. Nash would never have employed a whore to be a governess to his children, anyway.

Jasper hurried into the palace and immediately went looking for the children and Sophie and found them sitting in the nursery together. Isabelle was in the center of them all, on the floor, kicking her little legs into the air and gurgling about some nonsense only children could understand.

Sophie glanced up and smiled so warmly at him, he nearly tripped over his own feet. "Careful. How fares the estate today, Lord Jasper?"

"Nothing beyond the expected," he promised, blushing at his clumsiness as he perched himself on the open window ledge across the room. He gripped the window ledge and smiled at her. She had changed from last night into the sensible, governess uniform she had always favored. Yet he could still remember how she had looked last night and the pleasures he'd found in her whispered confessions. He shook his head, feeling foolish and almost besotted by this other side of her. The friendlier side. "Sheep grazing in fields, birds taking flight from the long grasses. The estate does very well, I'm pleased to say."

The boys left Isabelle and proceeded to pepper him with questions for so long that it quite naturally led to an offer to take them with him for a ride to see the distant fields. "Both of you could fit upon my horse together, but it is up to your governess to decide if you might enjoy such a boon."

"We can go," Thomas informed his uncle.

Jasper knew better than to assume Sophie didn't have some concerns, and yet she remained silent. But her fingers were busy, twisting the ends of her shawl into neat folds.

Something had changed in the nursery lately, besides the distraction of Isabelle.

Jasper caught Thomas' gaze and saw a flicker of rebellion in his eyes. Thomas was going to be a handful soon for the governess, unless it was stopped by someone with more authority than a servant. Thomas was too young yet to start lording his position over the palace staff, especially Sophie, who was currently acting as mother to him.

And Laura was out there. Her return, if she ever did, might create more difficulties for Sophie, too. He could not have his nephew getting too big for his britches yet. "The decision is Mrs. Radcliffe's."

"But she's just a servant!" Thomas argued hotly. "If you say we can go, we will. My father—"

"Your father made a point of mentioning that Radcliffe is in charge of you both before he left the estate, and I'll not go against his wishes, young man. You would do well to remember you answer to him as much as her," Jasper warned.

Thomas looked down, jaw clenched, as he sulked over the fact that he was going to be treated as just a child still. Jasper had been gentler with the boy than anyone had been with him in such a situation. The first time he'd tried to assert his authority over a servant, he'd earned a hard slap across his face for the impertinence.

Jasper turned his eyes on Sophie and saw her discomfort, and his heart went out to her. There was little he could do to soothe her feelings and offer reassurances while the children stood between them.

She had value to him, and to the family. She made sure these children were better cared for than their absent parents ever had. "The polite thing to do would be to ask for Radcliffe's permission to go. She might have made other plans for tomorrow."

Liam ran to her and asked, begged, to go with Jasper. Thomas followed reluctantly and grudgingly asked for permission as well. "I've no concern other than to ask you not to take them out in the rain to become soaked, my lord."

He smiled. "That is my hope, too."

"Please, Radcliffe. Please! Let us go," Liam begged. "I'll make sure my brother and Uncle Jasper are on their best behavior."

"Oh, will you now?" Her soft laugh lit up the room, and even Thomas joined in, eventually. The idea that Jasper needed a keeper seemed to amuse them all.

"You could come with us," he offered. Jasper held his breath in the seconds it took for Sophie to decline to join them.

"Isabelle and I shall be content and read together while you are gone."

"Sounds very pleasant."

He dropped his gaze to Isabelle, who was lying on the rug in front of Radcliffe and still happily kicking her legs about. She seemed highly amused and reaching for any toy Sophie held over her head. He felt himself smiling at the warmth of the scene. Sophie really was good with children. Even his own. There was a glow about her face now when she smiled at them that had been forever absent around others in the family, and especially him until recently.

He'd never seen her cross with the children, only disappointed in Thomas' behavior just now. Jasper's own mother had hardly spared him a glance or even a pat upon his head. Of course, his memories of himself at this age were almost nonexistent. From what he could remember, Mama had been interested in everything but her sons. Any affection he'd received had been from servants like Sophie and an occasional pat on the head from his elder brother, Algernon.

It was the way of the aristocracy, of course. Children were seen and not heard until they were caught doing something wrong. Parents lived their own lives, separate from their children. The lower classes lived a different life, he knew, from observation over the years. Yet Sophie cuddled her brother's children as if they were her own, and that made him wonder about her. "Where are you from, Sophie?"

She glanced his way, clearly startled by the question. "London."

"I didn't mean it quite that way," he drawled. "Your parents and family? They must miss you very much."

She frowned and did not look up. "I'm certain they could not."

It was his turn to frown now. "Why would they not miss you?"

"I grew up in an orphanage, my lord," she said. "I've no memory of any family."

Sophie rose, and he rushed to help her stand, catching her by the elbow and pulling her close when she was on her feet. Holding her seemed the most natural thing to do. He glanced down at her face, but she wouldn't meet his gaze and pulled her hand away.

Was she embarrassed to admit she was an orphan? He had to admit, he couldn't imagine what her life in an orphanage might have been like, but assumed it had not been warm or loving.

"I'm sorry for that. I suppose that is where you gained your great affection for other people's children," he teased.

She shrugged. "It was expected in the orphanage that I must help the young ones," she said, bending to pick up Isabelle. She settled the girl on her hip. "I am content for now," she promised, and then turned away. "To your beds, children."

Ah, the afternoon nap. Every day on Nash's schedule, the children were to be sent to their beds, tired or not. On the far side of the room was a cradle he'd only just noticed, though. Sophie put Isabelle down in her bed and gave it a little rock. He watched the child settled for sleep and the boys lay themselves down without a word of complaint.

Jasper perched more comfortably on the floor, leaning against the wall beneath the window and allowing the breeze to stir his hair as he watched the governess tend to everyone. He'd not spent much time in the nursery in recent years, but it was a place he'd always felt safe as a boy.

Sophie straightened and turned about. She was startled to see him still there, but she passed him by to tuck his nephews into their beds, smooth their hair back and kiss their brows.

He smiled as she stopped to regard him and he grinned up at her. "You're a very gentle woman, Sophie Radcliffe. Exactly the sort of woman who should have the care of my nephews, and Isabelle too."

Jasper then tilted his head up and pursed his lips, teasing Sophie that he, too, was ready for his bedtime kiss.

But she shook her head and seated herself opposite him in a chair. "You can leave Isabelle with me for a few more hours if you like."

He stretched out his legs. "I've nothing pressing that needs my attention this afternoon."

She shifted. "Still, there are more comfortable places for you to be."

"I am content here with you," he told her honestly, amused that she was trying to get rid of him. "Besides, I wondered if we might talk about your splendid idea again."

She glanced across at the children pointedly. Most likely they were too young to understand if they spoke of a scandalous topic in a whisper.

He scooted across the room until he could sit leaning against Sophie's armchair. "How much time would we need to set your idea in motion if we had Madam Clover involved?"

"A few days at least. Four at the most."

"There's only a few days left until my guests depart." He winced and had to wonder if Algernon and Nash would be gone long enough for him to host a second party at Ravenswood. He was very keen. "And this madam of yours? You really think she would really be interested?"

"Indeed, yes. She's always looking for new opportunities to make money off wealthy men."

"Tell me how you met her."

Sophie rubbed her palms on her skirts. "I was very ill, and she took me in until I recovered."

"A good Samaritan," he noted.

"A good woman. She was kind to me at a time when I desperately needed a friend, and since I possessed an education she lacked, when I was well enough, she let me repay her kindness with honest work. To read and write her correspondence and tally her profits each night. Your brother was aware of my employment there before he hired me, if you ever wonder about that."

Jasper pursed his lips, seeing easily how Laura might believe Sophie had earned her way on her back at such a place. There were not many women who left a brothel with their virtue intact. But if the woman was well educated and could figure and write, any madam who possessed none of those accomplishments herself would use Sophie's talents for their benefit.

"Your friend. Write to her and send it off in

my carriage with an invitation to visit Ravenswood to discuss the matter in private with us. I think it is better if any negotiations occurred face to face."

"Agreed," Sophie said, and then swallowed. "But I don't know if she'll answer promptly. She has not replied to any of my letters for months and months. But I took the liberty of writing a letter to her this morning again and mentioned your idea in it. Madam Clover will want to meet you before agreeing to any business dealings."

"Thank you. I'll need you there with me when we speak," he said, reaching up over his shoulder for her hand. "This is your idea, too, and you are my partner."

Sophie slipped her hand into his after a moment. "As long as the children do not need me, I'm yours."

"You have to let go of them sometimes," he said, toying with her fingertips and smiling. He'd never had anyone ever claim to be his before. It brought an unexpected warmth to his chest. And then, since he was a rake, he stroked her palm with his fingertips, just as Threadwell had done last night. "You know, one day they'll be gone off to their studies."

"Yes, next year Thomas will go to Cambridge," she said, her voice sounding a little breathless as he continued to seduce her palm.

Jasper let her hand go and turned to face her. She wore a becoming blush now. A blush he'd like to see more of. "So soon?"

"Yes. Lord Nash had everything planned out for their education and for the next ten years," she whispered, casting an anxious glance toward the boys. "Nothing has been left to chance. Liam is to go live with a tutor near Cambridge. An old friend of Lord Nash's, from what I understand."

"And Isabelle will remain behind alone."

"Yes, I suppose so, unless her mother returns for her."

"Let us hope for that," Jasper said and turned around again. Isabelle would be left with him and perhaps Sophie to care for. He could imagine many afternoons like this up here in the nursery. The thought of being a father to Isabelle held a great appeal right now. Because of the child, he knew Sophie far better than he ever might have.

Sophie squeezed his shoulder. "She'll come back."

"What if she doesn't?" Jasper asked, grasping her hand again.

"Then it is up to you to do the best you can. You're all she has. Believe me, she could do worse."

Jasper pulled her hand forward and kissed the back of it. "That is kind of you to say so, but we both know how ill-suited I am to such matters."

The woman's breath caught as he dropped a kiss to her wrist. "Nonsense, all you need is practice."

Jasper turned to face Sophie again, and when her hand wrapped around his head, he pulled her forward in the chair. Sophie did not resist him, and Jasper pulled her down to kiss her lips.

Their kiss was prolonged and quiet, so the children wouldn't hear what they did together. Sophie had him panting for more, though. Jasper wanted this woman. But he would have to be careful in his seduction. He did not want to make the mistake of falling in love with her, or her with him, either.

Everything he'd ever cared about always went to someone else when he put his heart on the line.

CHAPTER TWELVE

SOPHIE SPRINTED out to the front drive as a familiar old carriage came to a stop before Ravenswood Palace. She danced on the balls of her feet as the slow-moving grooms jumped down, groaning. The carriage steps were finally dropped, and the most elegant woman Sophie had ever known descended to the gravel drive. Regal. Proud. Clearly exasperated with Sophie's behavior, too. The woman wagged a finger and laughed. "Sophie Regina Radcliffe. Did you really run out to meet my carriage?"

"Yes, Madam Clover," Sophie confessed, laughing in return. There was just one woman who she'd ignore the rules of proper decorum for, and that was Madam Clover. The woman who had saved her life just by showing her a little kindness and compassion. "What are you doing here so soon?"

"Soon?" The woman frowned and glanced around. "I'm here to see what has befallen you."

"Befallen me?"

"I see now my fears were for naught. Come here, child." Madam spread her arms wide, and Sophie rushed forward to receive her warm embrace. "I have missed you so much, my dear," she said

"And I have missed you, too," Sophie promised. "You never answered my letters."

The madam cupped the back of Sophie's head the way a mother might her own child and held her close as she whispered, "We received no letters from you. Not for months now."

Sophie drew back, shocked. "But I wrote to you every first of the month?"

"Never mind that now." Madam Clover brushed a lock of fallen hair behind Sophie's ear and sighed. "I am relieved to know we were not forgotten." She gestured behind her. "I brought some friends of yours with me. I hope you don't mind. They were as concerned as I was about your silence."

Three equally elegant ladies descended from the carriage. Eleanor, Persephone, and Ruby. The most sought-after courtesans of the Violet Gardens Pleasure House squealed to see her and rushed over.

Sophie hugged each and found herself near

to tears. "I never thought you might come all this way for me. What will the gentlemen in London do without you?"

"Pine away to nothing most likely and flatter us with jewels upon our return," Eleanor murmured. "Or at least they had better."

"Goodness Soph, look at you," Ruby exclaimed. "Do they really force you to dress the dowdy just to be considered a proper governess? If we'd known, we'd never have permitted you to leave us."

"No, indeed. She should have stayed with us forever," Persephone said, glancing up at the facade of Ravenswood Palace and suddenly smiling. "Now, what deliciousness do we have here?"

Sophie glanced over her shoulder to see Lord Jasper watching them from the top of the staircase. She whispered his name to them. But heat warmed her cheeks as he strolled down the stairs —swaggered, really—and extended his hand and a charming smile to Madam Clover. "My dear lady. Welcome to Ravenswood."

"Ah, you must be the Lord Jasper our Sophie has told us so much about in her letters."

His smile faltered as he glanced toward Sophie, but he inclined his head, eventually. "Guilty. It is a pleasure to make your acquaintance, Madam Clover. Sophie speaks so highly of you. Ladies, you must be tired after your journey.

Would you care to follow me inside for re-freshments?"

"That would be very agreeable after our long journey, my lord," Madam Clover said as she smiled up at him. "It has long been a dream of mine to be reunited with our dear Sophie. She is quite the treasure, isn't she?"

Lord Jasper glanced at Sophie and smiled wider. "Agreed."

Sophie could feel her cheeks turning red. She had never been comfortable receiving compliments in front of other ladies. "You're too kind."

"No. No. You know me. I'm not given to false praise of anyone." He extended his arm to the older woman. "If you will allow me, madam?"

"I certainly will, my lord. I have dreamed of a good rest and long talk for hours," Madam Clover said. "Carriage travel rarely agrees with me."

"I understand completely and for that reason alone, you must stay with us a few days to recover from the ordeal," Jasper suggested as the pair dis-appeared through the doorway ahead of Sophie. What response he might have received from Madam Clover could not be heard because Perse-phone caught Sophie's arm and held her back.

"We could all agree to a lie down with the handsome bachelor like that, too," she whispered to Sophie. "Lud, Sophie, I thought you said he was horrible?"

She had not described Jasper's looks in her letters, but the way he'd acted toward her. From the very start had been horrible.

Ruby giggled. "I think he's perfect for any of our beds."

Sophie winced inwardly but managed a smile as they hurried inside, past the butler, and headed straight toward Jasper. It became clear immediately that he was flattered by their attention and remarkable beauty. Sophie had quite forgotten how forward her friends could be sometimes when there was an unattached man anywhere in their vicinity. She felt the stab of exclusion as flirting began in earnest between them all. Lord Jasper lapped it all up as his due, and of course he could. But would Sophie be minding the children alone tonight while Jasper was *entertained* by her bolder friends?

She took a seat close beside the madam, and took up her hand, still unable to believe the madam come all this way to check on her. "I'm so happy to see you, madam."

Madam Clover cupped her cheek gently. "You're too good a woman to simply forget, and as I was telling Lord Jasper just now, I was worried about not having received any correspondence from this part of the world."

It was odd that her most recent letters had

not been delivered, and she looked across at Jasper, who frowned, too.

"Lord Jasper has assured me all is well here, but that Lord Nash is away for the summer," madam continued.

"Yes, that is true. He is traveling with the duke," she said.

Madam Clover pursed her lips. "A pity, for I had hoped to have a long conversation with him."

Sophie grasped her hands together in her lap. Madam Clover and Lord Nash had been acquainted long before Sophie had ever met him. He had, occasionally, tended the ill and injured at the pleasure house—before, during, and after her time there. "Is everyone well at the garden?"

"Yes, yes indeed. We ladies are in the best of health."

"It's so odd you're here when I have just sent a letter to you about a matter of business." Telling Madam Clover now, in person, would speed up the discussion. Sophie glanced at Jasper, and he offered her a subtle nod.

"Business?" Madam glanced at Jasper, who merely smiled. "We'll, I'm doubly glad I'm here now. You've a head for business, my dear, and it has always been to my benefit to hear you out."

"Thank you," Sophie murmured.

"Would you excuse me a moment," Jasper asked. Sophie watched Lord Jasper step away to confer with the butler at the door. She had expected him to be involved in all the discussions, but perhaps his absence was for the best.

Sophie told Madam Clover her idea, and Lord Jasper's intentions for the future, and by the end she could tell Madam was clearly intrigued.

"Tea shall be delivered shortly," Jasper said as he returned to sit nearby. "Now, Mrs. Radcliffe, perhaps now the initial pleasure of your friend's arrival has subsided, you'd do me the honor of performing the proper introductions to these remarkably pretty acquaintances of yours."

Sophie managed the introduction but cringed inside as the flattery between Lord Jasper and the ladies escalated. She adjusted the collar of her plain gown a little self-consciously and turned to Madam Clover, "How have you really been?"

"I am very well enough, and the business thrives. Mr. Peters sends his warmest regards," she said. "He's asked more than once if you're happy buried in the countryside and longs for your return to our society."

Lord Jasper, done with his flirting for now, took a seat close to Sophie and the madam. "Who is this Peters character?"

"A neighbor in London. Quite handsome in his own way, rich and still terribly alone, especially without our Sophie to smile at each evening." Madam grinned at Sophie's discomfort.

"I think he might have called on you here if I'd told him where you'd gone."

Lord Jasper sat forward a little more. "Why wouldn't you tell him? There's no shame in Sophie being a governess to my brother's children."

Sophie brushed her skirts smooth while watching Lord Jasper from under her lashes as the madam answered.

"I did not tell him more because Sophie did not favor him," Madam Clover murmured, patting her hand.

"Soph is too particular," Ruby exclaimed. "He would have married her!"

Madam Clover shushed Ruby. "Enough. Sophie decided against him, and that's all there is to it."

Ruby shot out of her chair, muttering to herself as she went to look out the nearest window. "He could have asked *me* to be his wife. I would have said yes to him."

Sophie winced. Ruby desperately wanted to be married and had been jealous that Sophie had attracted the interest of one of her gentleman friends.

Persephone begged Lord Jasper to open up the pianoforte for her, and he got up to assist her to the instrument, casting Sophie a questioning look as he went away.

Sophie caught the older woman's eye. "You

should not talk about suitors in front of Lord Jasper. He could hardly care."

"Why not? Every young man needs a little push to see what's right in front of them," Madam teased. "It would ease my heart to know you were admired."

"Not by him."

"And why not him? Is he the heartless rake you described in your letters or the man you're starting to feel something for? The tone of your last letter to reach me was a great deal cooler toward him than the heated looks exchanged between you today suggest. You are nervous around him."

Sophie swallowed a lump in her throat at the very distressing idea that the madam might be right. But she should feel nothing for a rake or her employer's brother. Lord Jasper had until recently despised her. But if anything more should happen between them, it would only lead to disappointment and shame. She was courting enough scandal as it was simply by offering her aid.

When the tea came, they talked of the roads the ladies had traveled, the sights they'd seen, and then the madam requested to be shown to her room so she might rest before dinner. Lord Jasper offered his arm and led her away to the stairs. The other ladies elected to remain behind with

Sophie and when it was clear he wasn't returning, the ladies crowded around her.

"She tires easily nowadays," Ruby whispered. "Lord Nash warned that prolonged travel was ill advised. We couldn't bear to let her journey all this way alone."

"She mentioned no illness to me," Sophie said, worrying her lip. "Lord Nash hasn't mentioned it either."

"She probably told him not to tell you," Persephone grumbled. "There are some requests that ought to have been ignored. Madam hides it well, but she's a little worse every day."

Sophie put her hand to her throat in shock. Madam Clover was the closest thing to a mother she'd ever known. It pained her to realize she might lose her. And because her letters had not been delivered, she'd come to find out if Sophie was all right, and that might have been the worst thing for her health. "I appreciate you all coming with her," Sophie said. "If I had known, I might have already returned to London."

"Your silence has worried her no end, but we're glad you're all right," Eleanor promised. "She just decided to come and nothing could stop her."

"The sight of you so well and the prospect of making money cheered her right up today though. We haven't enjoyed an orgy since you left us. If madam agrees to it, the others will be so jealous that they're not sent for."

Sophie laughed. "I'm sure there will be others."

Ruby pulled Sophie to her feet and hooked arms with her. "Will you be joining in the fun this time?"

Eleanor took up Sophie's other arm. "She'll need the loan of a better dress first."

"No one will care what a governess wears," she explained to them both as she was pulled from the drawing room and up the main staircase.

"We do. And your hair! Something must be done about that monstrosity at the back of your head," Eleanor chided. "Do you not even have a maid's help?"

"No."

"Well, you'll dress properly for dinner tonight," Persephone insisted. "We must show Lord Jasper the jewel hiding right under his nose. We can tell you like him more than you want him to realize. Your blushes said it all."

"Persephone don't say such things. I'm just the governess," she reminded them, stopping on the landing. "I have children to look after."

"And who looks after you?" The ladies all smiled. "That handsome gentleman hardly noticed us. Couldn't keep his eyes off *you*, though."

Sophie blushed fiercely and shook her head in denial.

"Don't pretend you don't see it and probably have all along," Eleanor said, taking up her hand. "You're a lovely young woman with needs not being met. I knew it was a mistake to allow that starch-shirted physician to take you away from us for a respectable position."

"And now we've met his brother, we know exactly why you don't complain loudly enough anymore. You were made for more than this. We shall ensure Lord Jasper understands what a treasure you really are before the day is through."

Ruby stopped talking abruptly, and her smile grew wider. "My dear, Lord Jasper. Just the man we were talking about."

"Oh?" he replied, approaching the women.

"Sophie must come to dinner with us. Tell her she can be excused from her dull duties as governess for the evening for a night of fun and frivolity."

He inclined his head. "A fine idea. Mrs. Radcliffe is welcome to join us, but tell me truthfully, have you ever managed to change her mind once it's fixed a certain way?"

"I'm sure you could be very persuasive if you wanted to be," Ruby teased, fluttering her lashes at him.

Sophie discreetly poked her friend in the ribs, and Ruby pouted.

Lord Jasper only laughed though. "Ladies, there are servants waiting to show you to your guest room. Until the dinner hour."

Ruby, Persephone, and Eleanor hurried away, giggling, and whispering and smirking over their shoulders as they glanced back at Sophie.

Sophie waited until they were gone before she met Lord Jasper's gaze. "I hope you do not mind my friends arriving unannounced."

"Not at all. A remarkably friendly trio, and Madam Clover is a delight. It is also nice to see you looking so happy. Actually, I was just seeking you out."

"You were?"

"Indeed, I was, *partner*." He jerked his thumb over his shoulder. "You cannot leave me alone with those women. I know they are your good friends, but I honestly fear for my virtue around them," he warned, and then a shy smile broke over his face. "I like them...but not the way they might hope for."

An odd sort of relief flooded her to hear it. "They are good women."

"Together, they're more than I could ever endure," he teased.

She laughed at his statement. "Perhaps just the one, then?"

"No. I shall leave that privilege to those who attend our orgy." He grinned. "Madam has already decided in our favor, by the way. Seems she's eager to do anything you suggest."

"If only I had the same influence over young Thomas," Sophie muttered darkly.

"If he gives you trouble, I'll deal with him. We're in this together now," he promised.

Sophie worried her lip. "If I'm to join you all for dinner, who will look after the children tonight?"

"The matter has been taken entirely out of my hands and Seymour will not budge on his decision to watch over the children himself. I think he's become smitten with Isabelle."

"And what of her reluctant father?"

"If I am her father, it is a safe bet to say I might feel an even greater attachment to her one day soon."

"Might Madam Clover be allowed to know of Isabelle's existence?" she asked carefully. "I don't keep secrets from her, and she has always sensed when I'm hiding something."

He smiled. "Then tell her everything, including how you took charge of a delicate situation by flinging the child at me."

"I did not fling her at you," she chided.

"Indeed, you did," he protested. He drew closer and lowered his voice to continue, "You're very bossy, and I don't seem to mind that about you anymore. Now, I need to know what you think—it has been an age, and I wonder if you've given any thought to being kissed again?"

Sophie's heart pounded in her chest as she regarded him. "It's only been a few days."

He glanced at his pocket watch. "So many hours. I did not want to assume you liked it, but when I heard your friend mention you had needs not being met, I decided I've neglected discussing the matter long enough. I'm here and willing, madam."

She looked away from him. Confused by her own excitement at the prospect of being sought after. The courtesans in Madam Clover's employ were surely much more to his taste. But Jasper's fingers curled under her chin and gently drew her back to face him.

"Sophie," he murmured. "Yes or no."

Oh, she might just murder her friends for putting ideas about her needs in her head, and in his, too. This was going to end badly. She knew it. He was a rake and surely had no designs on making an honest woman of anyone. But she could not deny she enjoyed the thrill of being pursued by him. Of being tempted by a worldly and handsome gentleman. He was not offering her forever, and she did not expect it either. And he was waiting for an answer so patiently.

"Yes, my lord. Please."

His hands landed on her hips. Warm, firm, and her breath caught as she was overtaken by memories and sensations she'd thought never to feel again.

"Never beg for my attention, Sophie," Jasper whispered. "You deserve it and more."

He steered her out of the hall and into his bedchamber—his gaze locked on hers. She could not look away from him and what she'd started.

She was about to be made love to. Again. This time, though, she was under no delusions that love had anything to do with intimacy.

But she ought to make sure there were no consequences from what they did together. There were ways to avoid conception, and she mentioned their use to him.

He nodded slowly. "One child is more than enough for me to think about right now. Trust me to take care of you. I won't take things that far," he whispered as he kicked the door shut behind them. His lips descended on her neck next, and Sophie twined her arms about his shoulders, holding him close against her skin as they started their affair.

Lord Jasper was stronger than he looked. His scent was delicious, too. Sandalwood and some sort of spicy berry in the mix. She held him close as his lips worked their magic on her senses, scattering them to the wind. His kisses aroused her, and he probably knew that.

She felt herself pushed gently against a wall and opened her eyes.

Jasper lifted his head from her neck as he framed her face with his hands. "You are lovely. How did I not see that from the start?"

"You were busy looking at the other women invited for dinner that night," she noted. "Probably wondering which ones breasts would spill from their gown before the dessert course could be cleared away. I had no interest in you then, either."

"We must have been mad," he said as he peppered soft, darting kisses on her lips with a smile tugging up the corners of his.

"You were *always* mad at me," Sophie whispered. "No matter how small or innocuous I tried to make myself, you always frowned at me."

"I apologize." He drew back, frowning. "You know, it's not the done thing to pay too much attention to servants. I can only apologize for my behavior and beg your forgiveness now. I should not pursue you."

Sophie stared at him in surprise.

The man she'd been ruined by had not apologized and he had done far worse. Sophie might have expected Lord Jasper to have avoided the same. He was rather obviously in an aroused condition, but he had more control over his desires, and she acknowledged that he had more honor, too.

Sophie reached out a shaky hand and touched his face to lift his gaze back to hers. He looked flushed and flustered. Uncertain of his welcome. Sophie had told him what she wanted, and now he hesitated.

She teased her fingers boldly along his jaw, feeling it flex under her light touch. She drew closer to him and smiled. "I do not work for you or Ravenswood. I choose you of my own free will. Expecting nothing but the kindness, the warmth, of your passionate embrace."

He gulped. "Sophie. Do you even know what you're saying?"

"Yes, Jasper." It was time to tell him everything. "I was ruined by a man who I thought loved me above all others once. By a rake much as I assumed you to be until now. He did not care for my objections. He took advantage of my vulnerability to ensure his own satisfaction was reached. I have not voiced any doubts to you, have I? Do not imagine I wouldn't say no to you. I would if I did not feel as I do."

"How do you feel?"

She wasn't sure how to answer that question and not sound as vulgar as Ruby could be. But she felt *something*. A tingling excitement to be nearer to him. "Kiss me, my lord, and find out."

He pulled her close and whispered her first name. "Sophie."

She was back against the wall in an instant, Jasper's kisses urgent and hard. Sophie returned them, hungry for the passion his kisses aroused in her. He brought her arms above her head and held them there with one hand. His other hand slithered down her body to rest upon her rear. Jasper slowly molded them together. The evidence of his arousal pressed against her sex. Those gentle movements ignited Sophie's passions, made her long for the moment he might slide inside her and make her forget even her own name.

Despite what had come after her ruin, the moments leading to it had been exciting once. Passions stirred for the first time in years as she buried her face in his neckcloth and dared to nibble on his ear. Jasper moaned, and his thrusts against her sex became quicker and harder, and then he lifted her up in the air.

Sophie expected them to move to the bed, for her skirts to be lifted and her body taken possession of. Instead, Jasper merely widened her legs where they stood and renewed his thrusts against her sex. Only now it felt so much more intense with her legs wrapped about his hips. He kept hitting that hidden pearl between her thighs. The place she'd touched herself and exploded from. Jasper made her feel that same way. She could not get enough of the sensation, or this man.

She was lost to passion again. Desperate for more.

Jasper turned his face to hers and sealed their lips together. They kissed and ground against each other, caught up in their unexpected hunger. Sophie tightened her legs about his hips and the next thrust against her sex exploded her world and she cried out, over and over, overwhelmed and frantic to hold on to Jasper while she could.

When her spasms subsided, Jasper moved them finally to his bed and lay her down.

CHAPTER THIRTEEN

JASPER DRAGGED his fingers slowly over Sophie's gown, moving from her knee to her hip and up to her breasts, and knew he'd never had a more intoxicating woman in his bed. He was as yet unsatisfied, but he was vastly content. He was also profoundly humbled that a woman ruined by another rake might entrust her pleasure to him. Even if she said they were different, he was still a rake, and he was not offering the woman forever.

But for now, Sophie Radcliffe had become his.

He leaned close to nuzzle her ear as he playfully teased her nipples. "Are you all right?"

"Yes," she whispered, catching his fingers where they circled and holding them still.

"That was quite the moment, wasn't it," he whispered, and then chuckled softly.

"It was, but just a moment and it is over for

me." She sat up abruptly, pushing down her skirts over her calves. "What of you?"

"Me?"

"Did you...?" She waved her hand over his lower anatomy, where he was slightly less stiff than when she'd come against his thrusting.

"No."

"Oh." Her brow furrowed and her expression changed to one of confusion.

"Don't worry about me," he whispered.

But that statement seemed to worry her even more. "But don't you want to climax, too?"

Jasper sat up beside her. "Men do not need to achieve release every single time they become stiff. In fact, a repetition of excitement and softening over the hours of a day can make a later release more intense. At least that is my experience, and if you doubt me, just ask your friends down the hall what other men say."

"Oh," she said slowly and glanced down at his lap.

Jasper grinned and leaned close to drop a kiss at the corner of her mouth. "You've much to learn yet about the many ways of passion, my dear."

"I see that." Her gaze flew to his. "Can you teach me soon?"

Jasper gaped. Who was this remarkable creature? So confident one moment and yet so uninformed. "I could," he said slowly. "But why the urgency?"

She shrugged. "It's probable I shall never marry. I would like to know what other women, like my friends, sell their bodies to enjoy."

"Not all intimacy is enjoyable, especially not for whores," he warned sternly.

"Oh, I know that. That is why I should like to enjoy this time with you while I can," she told him, nodding to herself.

He pulled away from her. "Are you going somewhere?"

"No. But you will, and I will move on to another situation one day, too."

Jasper got to his feet. The matter-of-fact way she spoke of leaving and a next situation far from Ravenswood diminished his enjoyment of what they'd done together somewhat. He'd pursued and seduced a governess, and she was already thinking about the end of their affair—but he wasn't. He didn't want pleasures to be over so soon between them. "There will always be more children in this family to keep you busy and employed."

"Yes, your young brother has married, and your cousin, Mrs. Crawford, seems pleased with my work for Lord Nash. But I cannot assume they'd want me for their children."

"Why not?"

"You, of all people, should see why." She jumped off the bed and started smoothing down her gown, and the bed too. "My skirts are a little wrinkled," she said, and then laugh softly, "but luckily I am almost always a little that way after playing with the children, so none of the other servants will wonder about it. Liam likes to climb into my lap for hugs many times a day."

She spoke naturally, as if she were accustomed to confiding in him. He liked that change between them very much. "What of Thomas?"

"He's almost too grown up to need my comfort."

Jasper crept behind her and wrapped his arms about her waist, pulling her close and pressing a long kiss against her cheek. "He's a fool."

Sophie laughed softly again. "He's young and thinks differently to a full-sized gentleman with amorous inclinations."

He marched Sophie to the mirror, holding her from behind so he could see her face clearly. There was a pretty blush to her cheeks still from their lovemaking. "Amorous indeed, but not indifferent to your needs. See? Not a hair out of place."

Sophie twisted her head from side to side. "I think you might be right. Well done, my lord. I doubt my friends will guess what we've been doing, as long as I can keep a blush off my face."

"Jasper," he whispered, correcting her. He did not enjoy women *my lording* him once they'd shared his bed. "A blush suits you."

Sophie caught his eye in the mirror and she smiled shyly. "Jasper I never knew you could be so sweet."

The softness of his name tumbling from her lips made his heart melt just a little. "The smile suits you, too."

Jasper normally would ruthlessly quash any sentiment attached to lovemaking. Sophie had come to him for pleasure. And now it was over, she'd go on her way, as all others had. Resuming the duties of a governess and proper woman, at least on the surface.

But Jasper had her measure now. Perhaps that was why he'd been compelled to argue with her all these many months. He'd been seeking ways, poorly, perhaps, to draw her out of her shell. She had never been true to herself around him and he'd sensed that somehow. The only people she'd ever been genuine with were her friends from the brothel and those under four feet tall.

She was exceptionally good for Nash's children, too. She cared enough about them to be herself at all times. He remembered his promise to his nephews though and sighed heavily. "In light of our unexpected guests' arrival, I will have to postpone the ride I promised Thomas and Liam."

"I'll tell them."

"No, I will tell them myself and now. I will not have you make excuses for me like you do for my brother. That is not fair."

"Thank you," she whispered to him, nodding.

Jasper set his fingers lightly at the base of her throat. Sophie had such soft skin, and he would like to see more of it too. "Will you come to me tonight?"

Her eyes widened, not in shock, but with a renewed glimpse of desire. Sophie's needs would never again become neglected while she was his. She swallowed. "The children?"

"Yes, the children and our guests require entertaining." Isabelle was in the care of Seymour still and he ought to check on her welfare soon. "Some other night, perhaps."

He released Sophie, determined not to reveal his disappointment that it must be so.

Sophie turned to look at him though. Her gaze dipped to his groin, and a smile tugged on her lips. "Some other time, certainly. Soon."

Jasper put an arm about her shoulders, ready but reluctant to part with her now. "I really do like you better now, Sophie Regina Radcliffe."

He walked her to the door and peeked out first. There was no one about in the hall, so he gently propelled her from his bedchamber. He waited a few moments and then followed, heading directly to the nursery on the upper floor. Sophie was already there and surrounded by the boys. Jasper explained he could not take them out riding. They were disappointed, but Sophie promised them treats from the kitchen. They were satisfied with a compromise. Boys always thought with their stomachs.

Jasper dismissed the butler and took up his position beside Isabelle.

As Sophie passed him, she lightly tapped his backside, giggling as she tripped out the door following the children.

Jasper shook his head and grinned. Yes, he quite liked Sophie Radcliffe after all. She knew how to have fun and he would look forward to the day, the hour, when he got her alone again.

He scooped up Isabelle, despite her still being asleep. She grumbled, but immediately went back to sleep in his arms. The child was adorable indeed, and his heart swelled with happiness to have her in his life. To think he'd tried to deny any responsibility for the child. He couldn't imagine not having her around after just a few days.

He went to the window and peered out in

time to see the children sprint away to the kitchen garden. Sophie followed at a more sedate pace.

"Ah, I see I am too late," Madam Clover said, entering the room and catching him by surprise.

He pointed to the open window with one finger. "Only just."

The older woman drew close. "Perhaps it is for the best as it is really you I wished to speak to, anyway."

"Oh, is there a problem?"

"Indeed, there could be." She inhaled. "When your brother, Lord Nash, first posed the offer of employment to Sophie, I assumed—we all assumed—she would not be hidden away here the way she has been."

"What do you mean, hidden?"

"I had expected to see her in Town again, and yet she mentions no plans to return from the countryside. And now I discover that Lord Nash has gone off for the entire summer, abandoning her here alone with his children. That was not the conditions I imagined her living under."

"'Tis the life of a governess, madam," Jasper reminded her.

"Your brother hinted Sophie would become more than a governess to him."

Jasper gaped. "What more did you assume

she could be? I'm sure you know full well my brother is married."

The older woman snorted and then she smiled. "Lord Nash could divorce and make Sophie his wife instead."

Jasper stilled as the potential for a divorce became all too clear. Laura didn't want anything to do with her husband. And Ravenswood had feared something was going on between Nash and Sophie before they left for the summer. If the madam suspected a divorce was in the wind, Nash must have been considering it for quite a while and let something slip.

But Sophie was with Jasper now. "Nash would never do that. Divorce."

"Why not? Is our Sophie not worthy of his adoration? She respects your brother, and adores his children, well enough to make a comfortable companion in a marriage of convenience, so the problem is not with her," Madam Clover complained.

Jasper hugged Isabelle a little closer to his heart. "Is that what she told you she wants?"

"Not in so many words, but it is clear she greatly esteems your family and her life here."

Jasper ground his teeth together. That possessiveness rose and lashed out in impotent fury. "What is it you would have *me* do about it?"

"Support the match. Your brother is dragging

his feet unnecessarily. If you think it will help, make him jealous by showering her with attention so he sees what he is missing out on. Our Sophie is meant for more than a governesses life and anything closer to my profession is an insult to her intelligence. She has the wit and charm to do anything but is forever plagued by self-doubt and her humble upbringing. When I took her in, it was with the intention to see her make a great match one day."

"I see," he mumbled. Numb. The idea of Sophie married, and to Nash, made his stomach turn. She was *his* lover...or had that just been a mistake borne of loneliness and disappointment on her part? It wouldn't be the first time a lover had chosen him when they'd really wanted his older brothers' favor instead. And to find out Sophie's friends expected her to marry Nash one day made him feel ill. "If my brother had any plan to divorce and to marry anyone, I am not privy to it. My brother is ambitious, so why would he choose Sophie? A penniless orphan?"

"Because she is my heir, young man. When a woman gets to my age, she begins to think and plan for the future. I was never blessed with children, but when I met Sophie, I found the daughter I'd always longed for. Sophie can be counted on to look after my ladies and my business interests when I'm gone. After all, she was responsible for most of our recent success. Your brother knows this."

Jasper turned away, troubled. Nash's priority would always be to the duke and to Ravenswood. If he divorced Laura, and remarried anyone, any new money from the union would flow directly into the family coffers. "So he knows Sophie will inherit a fortune?"

"Not in so many words, but he will ensure my wishes are carried out I'm sure."

Jasper turned back to the woman, dread in his heart. She expected Nash to marry Sophie. But Jasper was almost certain her faith had been misplaced in his brother. Nash wouldn't care about Madam Clover's employees once she was gone, and he already did not listen to Sophie's opinions, or so she recently had told him. Marriage would only take Sophie's inheritance and control of it out of her hands entirely. He did not like what he'd heard today.

"I will broach this matter upon his return to Ravenswood."

"Good." She smiled at him. "You know, it is a shame. I should think you would have made a much better match for my Sophie had you ever been in the market for a wife."

"I am not, madam," he blurted.

"Every rake says the same until it is too late," the older woman said, and then drew close to him, her eyes on the sleeping child. "So much like her father."

Jasper couldn't help but smile at the compliment.

"And her mother too," the woman said, turning away. "A pity she could not bear to live with the man."

"Wait," Jasper called out to her. "Who is her mother?"

The woman frowned and met his gaze. "Why Laura Sweet, of course?"

"What!" He recoiled. "No. I would never bed my sister-in-law."

"Oh, dear...so it is as Sophie claims." She came closer. "You really believe the child is yours, then."

"Isn't she?"

The madam shook her head slowly and there was compassion in her eyes.

Jasper felt the news like a punch in the gut. From the beginning, he'd believed the child was not his, but Sophie had insisted and he'd reluctantly conceded he might just be a father. He'd fallen under the little girl's spell too and had begun to think about what sort of future she might have. What he might have to do to raise her and protect her when she was grown up. But if she was Laura's child, born within a legal marriage, Isabelle was Nash's responsibility whether he liked it or not.

He looked down at the infant and squeezed his jaw tightly together as regret hit him squarely in the heart. And yet, he only had Madam Clover's word for it. Gossip. He glanced at the older lady and wondered what else she would say about his brother. "Madam, how did you come by the information about this child?"

"I have made it my business to keep a close eye on Lord Nash for Sophie's benefit. Any arrangements he made with other women keenly interested me."

He raised a brow. "Other women?"

The old lady smiled. "Thankfully, there was only his wife."

"How do you know Laura?"

"I do not, but your brother attended a rather scandalous masquerade and engaged in a tryst with a woman who later fit the description I had been given of his estranged wife. Imagine my surprise at that discovery when all of society knows they cannot stand each other. He skulked away at dawn from the masquerade and she went her own way. I had her followed." The older woman quirked her brow. "Should you like the date of conception and the delivery too?"

Jasper blanched but nodded and filed the information away to consider later. Nash had said not so long ago that he'd not seen his wife since she'd left him. But did Nash realize he'd lain with his own wife at that masquerade?

And what of that letter that had been left on his bed? It had been addressed to him.

If Laura had indulged in a tryst with Nash and hidden her pregnancy from him later, that would be yet another scandal to rock the marriage and the family.

Jasper wet his lips and then met the madam's gaze. "If Sophie doesn't know about the events that led to the fathering of this child, I don't want you to tell her yet," Jasper said slowly. "I will get the truth from Laura myself and then deal with Nash immediately upon his return."

"But Sophie believes you the father of this child now," the woman murmured. "You are innocent of any wrongdoing. She ought to know the good about you before it is too late."

"She will know it all, when I have all the facts."

The older woman's smile grew wider. "I can clearly see now who the better brother is. Be gentle with our Sophie's heart, Lord Jasper. It is easily broken by insincere men."

"I'll do my best," Jasper promised and left the nursery, carrying Isabelle, his niece, but wishing that was not the case. For a few days, he'd been a man with responsibilities and they had settled easily on his shoulders. A man who Sophie had begun to admire, despite their bad start. A lover, a friend, and a partner. Could Isabelle really not be his child?

Jasper ground his teeth. If he wasn't, Laura should have told him instead of muddying the waters with a damn unsigned note left on his bed with Isabelle.

And when Nash returned, Jasper *would* force Nash to acknowledge the child as his too and attempt to get him to make up with his wife. Even if she was difficult. Even if Laura ran away again. There had been times during the marriage when Nash and Laura had gotten along. Clearly they had no problems in the bedchamber.

In the mean-time, Jasper would continue playing the role of Isabelle's papa and hide his regret that it might not be for long enough.

CHAPTER FOURTEEN

SOPHIE TURNED as a twig snapped behind her and saw Jasper emerging out of the darkness around the grove. "Is there a problem?"

"No," he promised, coming to a stop by her side. "Were you expecting one?"

"Not from my side of the arrangement. The ladies know what they are doing."

Jasper's orgy had taken only a day and a night to set in motion, and all seemed to be going well so far. Tonight was the culmination of his party. His friends had not been able to believe their good fortune when Madam Clover and her ladies had suddenly appeared in their midst. They had been so enthusiastic about the prospect a night of unrestrained passion beneath the stars that Jasper had been hailed almost a hero in their eyes.

They would all be gone by morning, though. Even Madam Clover.

Sophie was keeping her distance from the festivities, but Madam Clover was reclining on a chaise lounge in the shadows, keeping a watchful eye over the event and her ladies. Madam had met and instantly brought the local whores into her troupe and treated them as if they were her very own, too. Sophie now had little to do with the event taking place.

But she was not forgotten. Jasper had shadowed Sophie closely all night so that none of his friends could approach her, mistaking her for the entertainment on offer. She was surprised with his hovering so protectively, but glad for his company. "Are you pleased?"

"How can I be anything but? I've made more money from this one night than I did in the whole of last year. And I owe it all to you and Madam Clover."

"She is a marvel," Sophie told him.

"You are, too. I am still curious how you became such good friends with prostitutes though. I would not have thought to see such a close bond existing between you all after so long apart."

She turned her head to the side, considering how to answer that question. She owed the ladies her life, a debt she could never repay, but that was not a subject open for discussion tonight. However, it was a question that deserved acknowledgement. "I met them in London before your brother hired me."

"Yes, you told me that."

She smiled slightly, vaguely remembering being carried into the pleasure house by those kind women, in pain and with no hope left in her heart. If not for them, she dreaded to think what might have happened to her. "We became friends almost at once."

"Well, that tells me nothing at all." Lord Jasper pursed his lips. "Very well, Sophie. I won't pester you for the truth. Keep your secrets."

"I shall," she promised, and although he let out a frustrated breath, he said no more to drag any particulars from her lips. She was relieved he would let the matter go so easily. She valued the women of the brothel, but her past, and what had brought her to their door, was deeply personal. "Don't let me keep you."

"From what?"

She pointed to the lighted grove some distance away. "From enjoying yourself with them."

"Who says I'm not enjoying myself now?" he murmured.

She raised a brow at his remark but kept her eyes on the distant glow of light, where a dozen rakes were being entertained by equally enthusiastic women under the stars. Sophie wished she did not understand what drove her friends to seek pleasure with unsuitable men, besides the money, of course. Lord Jasper's acquaintances were much like him. Seeking short-term passion with no thought for any consequences. "They mentioned a hope you might join the fun."

"Which one?"

"All of them at one point or another," she replied, although there was no telling if they might still have the energy for another man at this late hour. It was an orgy taking place over there, after all.

"Not to my taste," Jasper announced.

"Oh," she said, frowning. Lord Jasper had been so keen on the idea of an orgy, at least once he'd gotten over the shock of Sophie suggesting it. She'd expected, assumed, he would change his mind and become a participant during the night. "There were others left behind in London who might interest you more next time."

"Not interested in those either," he said.

Sophie turned to look at him, utterly confused. "But I thought a rake..."

In the dark, the white of his teeth appeared as he smiled at her. "I know what you thought, and you were wrong about me."

"But you've gone to so much trouble to..."

"For the money," he assured her. "Not in search of pleasure for myself, madam."

"I see."

"I'm not sure that you do." He drew closer and his hand settled low on her back. "I'm glad I could surprise you. I wouldn't want to be like all the other rakes you've known. You and I are not done. Not by a long way."

Although that shouldn't please her, Sophie had trouble keeping the smile off her face. "I'm...glad."

"Only glad?" he teased. "I had hoped for more enthusiasm for my company than that by now. But then you really don't know the first thing about me or what I want, either."

But she was starting to get an idea of him now. Lord Jasper was not quite the heartless rake she'd first assumed he'd be. He was wicked and ambitious, yes, but there was a reason for that. He wanted to increase his fortune, and this was the only way he thought he was qualified. Hosting parties for a fee. Courting scandal.

Yet, he knew the land, the demands of the estate, she'd noticed. He wasn't quite the useless younger brother everyone had made him out to be.

But he was impatient, hence his enthusiasm to make money through scandalous evenings such as this. She'd also detected his appreciation for the ladies from London, too. They were beautiful and graceful, skilled at bringing a man pleasure. Accomplished in ways Sophie would never have a chance to be. "What do you want in a woman, Jasper?"

He shook his head. "I don't know yet. But for now, you'll do."

She sputtered at his offhand compliment. "Well, thank you so very much."

"See, I knew that last bit would get a rise out of you." He laughed and his arm curled around her back to pull her closer. Sophie was compelled to laugh along with him. She rather enjoyed their banter. He was more at ease around her now and much, much friendlier outside of the bedchamber, as well.

The man who had dismissed her at first as just another insignificant servant, then with growing suspicion and outright scorn, had been looking at her the last few days as if she was interesting to him. Such consideration had gone to her head. Making her wish things could stay this way between them forever.

But it was not a good idea to think too far ahead. Not for her. Not again. She wouldn't mistake the excitement of a new lover with the beginnings of a true friendship or even something deeper. Lasting. She'd made that mistake before. And when Lord Nash returned? She'd have to become proper again to keep her position.

If she still wanted that now. She was worried enough about Madam Clover's health to consider returning to London, too. But that would mean leaving the children, and Jasper. A man she might have grown too fond of already.

Sophie shifted her weight to one foot, subtly preparing to step away from him. She would not impose her impossible longing upon him, nor mistake his kind words for more than they really were. Sophie was not like the women she had brought to the estate for the pleasure of his friends, who could pass from man to man with ease.

Jasper released her and rubbed his hands together briskly. "Yes, indeed. The funds from tonight have more than exceeded my expectations for our partnership. I thought you were mad to suggest such a scandalous event. Your friends' attendance, beauty, and warm welcome to my friends, has ensured a night those men will never forget. They'll be clamoring for the next scandalous evening we arrange."

Sophie wet her lips. "When might that be?"

"Madam Clover and I are yet to have that discussion on the subject, but she was clearly interested in a second event. It would have to be somewhere else, though. Somewhere I can guarantee His Grace could be far away from for the planning but close enough that you can be involved."

"I don't have to be involved at all." She

shrugged. "It would be wise to move the event from place to place, anyway. Intrigue and secrecy add to the excitement. They might even pay more, too."

Jasper's arm snuck back around her waist, and he pulled her close again. "You and I are of the same mind, then. Exclusivity makes a difference. You must be involved in all the planning and execution. I insist."

She blushed in his embrace, wondering if such displays of affection between them were wise. He called them partners, but if she was a man, and this truly a business arrangement, he'd never behave in such a manner.

They stood there in companionable silence for a few moments more, listening to the indistinct sounds of the distant revelers. Judging from the occasional burst of raucous laughter, the evening was going very well. "Do you intend to stay out here all night?"

"Yes, to be sure they all leave before dawn without incident," he replied, releasing her again.

Jasper stepped back and made so much noise that Sophie eventually turned to see what he was doing behind her back. He was leaning against a tree now, one foot propped on the trunk. The pose was as carefree as she'd ever seen him in the whole of their acquaintance.

He glanced her way. "What will you do now?"

"I don't know. I had thought of going back in case the children need me."

He gave her a look. "They are amply supervised."

"Yes, but Kate is new and Isabelle has the butler but..."

"The palace servants can manage without you for one night, and perhaps the morning, too."

Sophie turned to the distant source of light again and worried her lip. This was the longest she'd ever been away from the children. They were the only reason she was at Ravenswood.

Yet she would like to stay near the orgy, for exactly the same reason as Jasper—but to know the ladies were treated well. Men could be beastly. Sometimes there was no warning when a change would come over their temper. Even though the ladies were no doubt more accustomed to dealing with such situations, they were not in London, where a dozen footmen could be easily summoned to protect them.

She squared her shoulders, prepared to stand here all night simply for her own peace of mind. "I will stay, too."

"I thought you might. Come over here and sit yourself down. There's an hour or more yet before the dawn."

Sophie turned, looking for a suitable place, and spied a log—and before it on the ground, a large wool blanket spread out and pillows. Another blanket was folded neatly on top. She was taken aback by the sight of such comforts sitting there out in the open. She'd not brought them. Jasper must have done so. "You were expecting me to stay?"

"I was expecting a chilly, uncomfortable night. Go sit down and keep warm," he said, jamming his hands under his arms.

"Thank you," she said and moved toward the log, keeping one eye on Jasper as she sat down alone. He seemed content to lean against the tree and made no move to join her, but he, too, would feel the chill soon. She shivered as a sudden breeze stirred the air around her face, sending a fallen tendril to tickle her nose, and thought about inviting him to sit with her.

Jasper moved then and picked up the other blanket. He unfolded it, shook it out, and moved toward her slowly. He gently wrapped the heavy blanket snugly up to her shoulders and down over her legs, making her blush. "There you go."

When he drew back, he seemed a little embarrassed by his act of kindness and went back to his tree and his earlier pose. Sophie watched him, his handsome features softened by the flickering light of the distant torches, and dreamed an impossibility.

If she were any other woman, she might want this man to look only at her forever. But she was Sophie, a woman far, far beneath even him. An orphan and a governess. What family would ever want her to join their ranks? Certainly not a family in need of funds. Jasper would only marry a woman with money, if he ever did.

Jasper could have and do anything he wanted though. He was sought by other women, not just those seeking to meet his elder brother's as well. He was also a man determined to distinguish himself any way he could, too. She understood what drove him. He wanted to prove he was good enough as he was.

Sophie wanted the same.

But Sophie sometimes dreamed of living another kind of life. One where she had a home, a husband, and children; where she could be with her friends, too, and be loved no matter what she did. None of that seemed likely here, where she was only a servant. Perhaps it was time to return to London and rejoin her friends. At least there she could be herself, like this, always and never have to change to fit in.

Jasper turned to her suddenly. "You know, you're very interesting, Sophie."

She was taken aback by the sudden remark. "Interesting?"

"If I'd said pretty, which you are, you might have hated me for saying it," he teased.

"I would have." Sophie drew her knees up to her chin and wrapped her arms around them, laughing softly. "There are far prettier women than me. They are over there, entertaining your friends."

"Not to me right now, and that surprises me more than I ever thought it could," he confessed. He walked away a few steps, hands under his arms. "I'm going to take a stroll around, make sure everything is in order."

"But it's so dark?"

"I know this place very well. I'll be back soon," he promised, and he strode away without waiting for a further response from her, his long legs carrying him into the darkness until she couldn't hear him anymore.

Sophie hoped he wouldn't be long and blushed, remembering how he'd held her tonight. She was only human. Compliments and kindness had always gone to her head for their rarity. Especially consideration from handsome rakes. That had been her mistake before. She'd believed the compliments a sign of a true romance and not what they really were; a remedy for boredom by an entitled and wealthy gentleman who'd decided she'd be grateful for his fleeting attentions.

She'd learned the error of her ways in the end. Men did not look at her and think of honor or matrimony. Jasper was no different, but he was honest about that. He was nice to her because she'd helped him, and he was with no other female companion that appealed to his sensibilities. He was lonely.

Sophie knew that feeling all too well, too. She huddled into her blanket to watch the distant lights alone and waited impatiently for Jasper's return.

CHAPTER FIFTEEN

"THAT'S IT. Done. The last man on their way home," Jasper crowed as Threadwell's carriage disappeared down the little-used laneway out of the estate. He turned to his companions and grinned. Madam Clover offered him a wry, tired smile. He walked to her and took up her hand to kiss the back of it. "I cannot thank you enough for coming to our rescue."

"We should all thank Sophie for her inspired ideas," the woman demurred, eyes turning to the blushing governess. Sophie had grown quiet since the first carriage carrying his guests had rolled away.

"She ought to be dancing a jig," Jasper teased, hoping to earn a smile from her.

"I'm much too tired for that," Sophie warned, sounding for all the world like she needed to go to bed. He wished it could be his own.

"Perhaps tomorrow we will celebrate our success," he murmured and turned back to the London madam. "This is your share, less the amount we agreed upon."

Madam Clover counted the money right in front of him and then added it to the pockets hidden under her cloak. "Thank you, Lord Jasper, for a most exciting stay. I look forward to the next time we meet. Perhaps then it will also be a day of celebration, and our Sophie *will* dance."

He inclined his head. But he was hoping she was not thinking it might be Sophie's wedding day to Nash. That would be over his dead body. Nash could not divorce Laura if they'd made another child together.

He offered his arm to the weary older woman and led her across the uneven ground to where her companions waited. Madam Clover and the ladies had been enthusiastic about the night just past, and the next orgy was highly anticipated, too. When he found the right venue, he was assured of success with their eager participation.

But he owed his success entirely to Sophie. A woman with a remarkable mind and unexpected boldness. To think he'd scoffed at the very idea that a plain governess could be of use to him. Except she did not seem plain anymore. There was a subtleness to her beauty that he'd come to appreciate.

Since the women had already said their goodbyes, Jasper helped the madam enter her carriage, and handed her companions in one by one next. It was a tight fit with the local girls included, but Madam insisted on delivering them back to the village herself. Some of them had decided to make the journey to London though and had possessions to collect.

When he looked around, Sophie had hung back and there were tears in her eyes. He closed the carriage door and stepped back a little. The women crowded the windows, blowing kisses to Sophie, who seemed to be getting more upset by the minute.

When the ladies were finally ready and shouted out to go, the coach rolled away and slowly disappeared from sight. He strolled back to Sophie.

"Thank you," he said, holding out his hand and the money Madam Clover insisted upon paying her. An advance on her inheritance, in case she ever needed the funds to return to London, where she would be welcomed again.

"What is that for?"

"For being the woman you are."

She took the money, counted it, and stared at him. "I can't accept this much from you."

"Well, if you don't accept it, I'll have to run to the stables, saddle a horse, and give chase after that carriage. It's not from me, but Madam Clover herself."

"I never truly expected anything." Sophie worried her lip. "You could keep it. Use it for this place instead."

"That would be stealing," he said, and then he jabbed his thumb into his chest. "Rake, not thief."

"Not so wicked either, or you would have joined the orgy," she accused.

"I've never been one for public nudity," he told her. At least not since he was twelve or eleven and swimming at night with his brothers. He moved closer to her and noted she seemed less inclined to cry now, thanks to their banter. He was glad he could pull her out of her mopes so easily. "I prefer a private and leisurely passion. Besides, it was damn cold last night. That can diminish a man's proportions, let me tell you."

Sophie sputtered a laugh and glanced around the clearing. He wondered if she might be regretting not taking part in the event. She'd been dressed for it under her cloak. Wearing the little red dress she'd found forgotten somewhere in the palace. Silk and satin had transformed her body into that of a siren.

A siren who had made no sign she'd welcome a renewal of his seductions so far.

Not wishing for them to become awkward with each other now, he looked around. The only evidence of the night just past was the trampled grass. The fire pit was filled in, torches extinguished, and chaise lounges used for beds carried back to the palace for a good beating and then a return to their rightful places. The only evidence left of the night just past was himself and Sophie, out on the estate grounds when they never normally would be found together at this early hour.

Yet he smiled. Staying up all night with Sophie wasn't a bad way to spend any evening. He'd enjoyed her company and their little talks. "I don't know about you, but my bed is calling me."

"Mine too."

He offered his arm. "Shall we?"

Her arm wound through his, and her cheeks dimpled with a smile. "Yes, indeed. The children will be waking soon."

"Not too soon, I hope," he murmured. "You do need some rest."

As soon as the children were up and running around, he would also lose any chance of talking to Sophie again that day. He'd always known their time together would be short because of the children, but it did irritate him now and then.

Because the grass was longish and damp with

dew on the journey back, Sophie had to let him go to hike up her skirts to keep the bottom dry for a few yards. Jasper couldn't help but steal a peek at her legs as they strolled along back to the manor at a leisurely pace.

He wanted to know Sophie better, see more of her than anyone else had. Without his brothers around, or the children taking precedence. He could not be himself, teasing or tempting Sophie in front of witnesses. But he did not want her to feel ashamed by their affair, such as it was, or pretend it had never happened. His own conscience was blessedly silent on the subject of getting too close and personal with his brother's employee. She'd made it clear that she understood his intentions.

"Where do you come from?" he asked again, reaching for her hand when he could. "I know Nash employed you while in Mayfair, but is that where you are from?"

"No," she said and looked away. "I was born far from there."

He smiled at her answer. "Again, no specifics, Sophie Regina Radcliffe?"

Her lips were turned up in an impish smile when she faced him again and curled her arm through his. "I knew the lack of detail would annoy you."

He grinned and patted her hand where it

rested on his arm. "Are we not beyond annoying each other now, Sophie dear?"

She turned narrowed eyes on him, but she was fighting a smile. "I don't know. Are we?"

"I swear I mean you no ill. In fact, my mind is awhirl with ideas that ensures my brother keeps you on long after the boys need mothering."

"Why would you do that? I've always known I would have to seek a new position when they were gone."

"But I still need you. We are partners, are we not?"

"Not really. Madam likes you, and enjoyed making money with you. She will not stop the arrangement simply because I go to another position or return to London."

"London?"

She shrugged. "I really missed my friends. If I stay here, I might never see them again. Madam Clover is getting older. I don't want to be trapped here when she might need me most."

Trapped? He frowned and walked on beside Sophie in silence. Mulling over her words. He did not want Sophie to go away and for *him* never to see her again. The orgy, and his introduction to Madam Clover, would never have happened without her. His success, and the money in his pockets tonight, was entirely because of her insights and valuable connections. And he wanted to continue to be as successful as this in all his ventures. "I want you here, too. Stay and I'll keep you busy and make you rich. I'll make sure you see your friends as well. I would never keep you trapped here?"

"Lord Nash promised that, too." Her hand slipped from his arm, and she stopped and faced him. "Helping you was never about making money for myself."

He turned to look at her, utterly surprised. "But you said—"

"I know what I said. It seemed the only way you would let me be involved."

"Why would you go to such lengths for no benefit?"

"Sentiment. Your family has been kind to me, and you needed the money," she told him. "More important than that, I wanted you to succeed, to prove I was not against you. Your pride might not have allowed my help when there seemed no reason for it."

Jasper felt a rush of gratitude sweep over him. He didn't know what to say for a moment—but then he pulled Sophie into his arms and held her head tight against his chest. "Thank you."

Sophie allowed his embrace a moment, then pushed him back. "You're welcome, Jasper."

Jasper caught her face in his hand and tilted it up to his. Sophie Radcliffe was a remarkable woman indeed, and she had become dear to him. "Clever and generous to one who surely did not deserve your help. What can I do to repay you? Name it and it's yours."

"I don't need or want anything from you, Jasper. I never have."

He brushed his thumb across her cheek, rediscovering her skin's soft and intriguing warmth. Those petty irritations that had kept them sniping at each other for months were long gone now, and in their place was a warm friendship that he never wanted to end.

It could be more if he let it happen.

However, that decision would not be his to make. He was not the marrying kind, and she knew that about him. "I think there is much more to discover about someone as lovely as you," he whispered, continuing to stroke her cheek with his thumb.

Her eyes had grown huge as she looked up at him and she shifted a little closer. "I'm dull and boring."

"That's a lie."

"I'm rule bound."

"Only when it suits you," he answered softly. "You know which rules you can risk breaking. You are wise beyond your years."

"An old hag," she muttered, lashes fluttering. "Older than you."

"Old enough not to be silly about certain things. Wise enough to spar with me and survive. A woman without equal. An incomparable in her own right."

Her breath caught as Jasper moved his hand behind her head, sliding over her extravagantly pinned hair. Sophie had been all frost on the outside, but a thaw had been coming over her slowly as the summer continued. It made his heart glad to know he might have been responsible for making her feel comfortable with him at last.

She sagged a little toward him, her chest rising and falling rapidly. Her eyes were luminescent in the early morning light. She was touched by desire, and so was he. The only question was if she would act upon it, or let the fire die of its own accord.

He hoped not. He wanted a chance to show her all the passion she'd asked about on the day Madam Clover had arrived.

Jasper slid his hand from her hair to her upper back, then stroked lightly down her spine and back up again. Just that much contact nearly brought him to his knees. He had not partaken of the pleasures of the orgy because none of those fallen women had made him feel even an inkling of this much yearning. Jasper wanted to do unspeakable things with Sophie, with her body, and be lashed by her tart tongue, too, during the day.

He wanted her in the worst way, and she had likely seen it in his eyes all along. Even before he had known it.

That was why she'd never dared encourage him. He was a danger to a woman trying to be proper.

Sophie was the forbidden pleasure. A temptation he'd tried so hard to ignore, too. To be with a proper woman who knew him, his ambitions and restraints, and accepted the way things would be with him had seemed impossible once.

Sophie shifted a little closer and bit her lower lip. When she met his gaze, there was sadness in her eyes. She knew what might happen between them and how it would end. She didn't want to want him because of that.

Jasper allowed his hand to fall away from her body, disappointed. He was wanted...but wanting him was the last thing she could do.

They would not make love today, or perhaps ever. But he was determined to keep her friendship and her trust no matter what. He took a step back from her. "We should go back."

Sophie gulped and nodded. "Yes."

Jasper gestured toward the palace. "Shall we, Mrs. Radcliff?"

A sad little smile crossed her face. "Yes, Lord Jasper."

They returned to the palace in silence, side

by side, Jasper painfully aware that he had lost an opportunity to be with her. He watched her discreetly, regretting his restraint, but knowing it was for the best. And it was too late now, anyway. He had an estate to run, the truth to discover about Isabelle, and Sophie had his brother's children to care for. They would not grow any closer when everyone else returned, either, and he regretted that very much.

And then one day she would be gone off to another place of employment, or return to Madam Clover in London, and he might never see her again.

He grimaced at the very idea of her leaving Ravenswood. Once, he had relished the idea of seeing the back of her. But now, Ravenswood would not be the same without her. He would miss doing all he could just to annoy her.

They parted ways with a polite nod before the house and he watched her slip away, through a different doorway.

Jasper cursed under his breath, and he stalked toward his private study where work awaited him. He put his money away and went through the motions of sitting down at his desk, taking out the lengthy list Nash had left for him to attend to, and crossed off the last tasks. He pulled out another set of papers from a desk drawer; one he'd made. His own list of improvements for the Ravenswood estate to show to the duke upon his return.

Yet all he could think of was Sophie: the softness of her skin, the scent of her body, and the rapid rise and fall of her chest when she met his gaze. Her laughter. Her conversation.

Her lips pressed against his.

They wanted each other.

He'd sell his soul for a taste of her one more time. But could a rake change enough for a woman like Sophie to trust completely? She had expected him to join the orgy. He wouldn't have done that without her beside him, too. But he wouldn't have let anyone else have her. He'd have kept her protected and for himself.

Jasper burst out of his chair in frustration. He could not conform. Jasper would not bend his knee just to have a woman kiss him back with as much need coursing through her veins as his. He would not become proper and marry Sophie even for all the money she would inherit one day, either. Marrying for wealth hadn't made his brother Nash's life any happier, but clearly, he had a chance to do it again, with Sophie none the wiser for his motives.

Sophie deserved to be married only because she was loved by her future husband.

Jasper paced the chamber, struggling to rid himself of his agitation at the very idea of Sophie as someone's bride. He'd never wanted to protect a woman as much as he did Sophie Regina Radcliffe.

He thought he'd almost mastered himself when a light step outside his door caught his attention. He spun toward the sound, yanked the door open to bark at whoever it was for the disturbance.

But it was Sophie.

He gasped as her body brushed his when she slipped into the room.

He shut the door. "What are you doing here?"

"I had to come."

"Why?"

She faced him. "I had to come—and so do you."

He blinked. Confused. Surely, she could not mean that the way it had come out of her mouth. He prowled toward her. She'd chosen not to encourage his seduction just ten minutes ago. "What did you say?"

"Everything," she whispered. "I want everything you offer and to hell with the consequences. I want my rake."

He was being propositioned. *His* Sophie wanted him. To...

He caught her head in his hand and hauled her close enough to kiss. He stared into her eyes and saw passion there again. "I promise you'll get all the education you asked for with me."

"Prove it."

He took her mouth in a brutal kiss. Hard and unrelenting, as Sophie wound herself into his embrace, her legs twining around his. He backed her up to his desk, deposited her on the edge and pushed her cloak back, then lifted her red silken skirts above her knees. She hadn't changed since they'd returned to the palace and he was glad there was so little between them. The skin of her thighs was so soft and distracting, but her mouth...oh, there was another world awaiting him in her kisses. He feasted upon her lips and delved his tongue into her mouth to tangle with hers.

He became aware of her tug on his clothing and opened his eyes to see what she was doing.

Sophie had her bottom lip between her teeth as she unbuttoned his waistcoat to slip her fingers across his chest, and damn if that didn't excite him unbearably. He shoved her skirts higher as she loosened his breeches and started to push them down his legs with impatient hands.

Jasper eased her backward, purely to see her sex better. A thatch of dark curls protected a place he very much wanted to devour with his mouth. He parted her with his fingers, catching the scent of her arousal in the air. She was glistening wet, and he met her gaze with a knowing smile. "What have we here, my dear?"

"What you need, I hope."

"Yes," he promised. "I want this and more." Jasper let his fingers explore, stroke, and penetrate her body. Sophie whimpered her excitement to be touched, and he fingered her with all the skill he could muster, though he could barely contain his excitement. He turned his hand a little, so his thumb rested over her clitoris. As he stroked her with his fingers, he pressed gently down, working to heighten her pleasure.

Sophie fell back fully across his desk, back arching, legs spread as she bore down on his hand. She was glorious in her passion, and Jasper couldn't get enough.

He bent down to kiss her sex to heighten her pleasure.

Sophie stiffened at the first brush of his lips and tongue, but her whimpers soon turned to urgent moans of "yes" and "oh, God" and "please, please come into me."

Jasper obeyed and was at her entrance in a moment. He slowly worked himself into her body, leaving his fingers dancing on her clit. She took him easily, bucked, urging him to take his pleasure in her. He was more than happy to oblige her request, but a woman's pleasure must always come before his own.

He caught her by her thighs, repositioned her, and threw her feet high in the air over his shoulders. Then he drove into her again and again, brushing over her clit from time to time. He bit his tongue to silence himself when he realized he was grunting with each and every stroke. Matching Sophie moan for moan in a way he'd never noticed he'd done with other lovers.

And then she bucked and cried out as she found her release unexpectedly soon.

He gritted his teeth as her sex tightened unbearably around him and held still until she softened, and he could move freely again.

Eventually, she lifted her head, gaze locking on his. There was a dazed look in her eyes, gratitude and relief as their stares met and held. Jasper lowered her feet to the edge of the desk and touched her clit again, expecting her to be sensitive, but another tremor rushed over her as she cried out a second time, shocking him completely.

He had yet to come, and wanted to, so he made the desk beneath them rock and bounce to every thrust as he sought his own pleasure. He broke free of her embrace to spill his seed into his hand. Sophie lay there on his desk, panting, legs open, undone and smiling up at him.

She reached up to touch his face with a tenderness that made his breath catch. Making love was different with Sophie. It meant something to her.

Sophie was special. Sophie was *his*.

He'd never let anything, or anyone, come between them. Especially not his own brother.

Jasper wiped his hand on his handkerchief, flipped Sophie over onto her stomach, and slid back into her, ready for round two. Their partnership had to continue.

CHAPTER SIXTEEN

SOPHIE LOOKED under the children's beds and then in a closet, balancing Isabelle on her hip as she moved through the room. "Thomas? Liam? Where are you?"

There was no answer. No response to any of her calls. At this time of day, almost noon, the children should be hard at work on the lessons she'd left behind and awaiting the delivery of their luncheon. The boys were not in the nursery, but they must be hiding somewhere close by.

The boys had never disappeared from the nursery like this before. But then again, Sophie had always been here with them at this time of day. They must have gone looking for her...and that made her angry with herself.

She had momentarily forgotten her sole reason for being at Ravenswood. Sophie was not a guest who could come and go as she pleased or ignore her responsibilities. She was a governess first.

Giving in to her desires with a rake was always a mistake.

Sophie thrust the child at the confused maid, who had been fast asleep when she'd come in after changing back into her normal clothing. "Take Isabelle to Lord Jasper."

"Yes, madam. Again, I'm so sorry," Kate whispered. "I did not know I'd nodded off."

"The children must have tiptoed out," she answered, and the maid hurried to scurry away with Isabelle.

Sophie watched her go with a heavy heart. It had been a mistake to entrust anyone here with Lord Nash's sons. She was sure no harm could come to them on their unchaperoned tour of the large house. But she liked to know where they were at all times.

She retraced her steps to her own chamber, then checked all the rooms until she reached the main staircase. If Thomas and Liam had gone in search of Sophie together, expecting to see her in her own room and not found her there, they must have gone farther afield after that. Perhaps downstairs.

The boys were not on the third floor. There was no reason for them to go up to the attics. Perhaps they'd gone to visit their uncle to ask where she might be.

She rushed down the stairs to the family wing. Kate was just leaving Lord Jasper's room, her arms empty of the child. Sophie went to his room and knocked at the door, hoping she might find the boys with him.

"Come in," Jasper called.

She opened his door and poked her head in. Jasper was in the middle of the room, Isabelle held aloft over his head and laughing down at her father. It was a charming scene, to see father and daughter at play, and at any other time she might have stayed to watch them together. But as she took in the rest of the chamber, her hopes of finding her charges were dashed. "Have you seen Thomas and Liam this morning?"

"No. Should I have?"

"I don't suppose so. Excuse me. I will have to check all the rooms in the family wing. Perhaps they have gone to Lord Nash's chambers."

"Sophie!" he called out, but she was already hurrying away and couldn't stop to explain.

Sophie had never had any reason or desire to enter the remaining bedchambers in the family wing before. This area was private, only for the duke, his brothers, and their immediate servants.

She opened Lord Nash's door, poked only her head inside and called out the boys' names.

They didn't answer, but she darted inside anyway to check under the gigantic bed in case they were hiding there. But they were not, and she got back up, frustrated. It was not like them to hide from her or go where they were not permitted. Their father's chamber was off-limits to them, as were all others nearby.

She put her hands to her head and then rushed for the door. Thomas had made the decision to assert himself and ignore the rules because his governess had deserted her duties for one night and morning. She backtracked and checked all the rooms in the family wing, even the duke's grand chambers, which she couldn't imagine they had cause to enter. They would be in such trouble if they had meddled with anything there.

She met Lord Jasper holding Isabelle on her return to the staircase. "Are you playing a game with the children? We could join you if you like."

She shook her head. "I'm uncertain if it's a game."

"What's that supposed to mean," he asked, eyes widening as she ran past him. "Sophie, wait!"

"I can't find them." A pit of worry was growing inside her belly. This was not a game, but a danger she'd not expected. In London, children disappeared all the time and were never seen again.

She flew downstairs, ignoring Jasper's repeated calls to talk to him, checking the library, drawing room, ballroom, cigar room, Jasper's study, and even the duke's too. No sign of the children anywhere in the house. From any servant she passed, she received a denial that they'd ever been there. The boys were not in the servants' hall, where they ought not to go alone, anyway. Certainly not begging treats from the kitchen staff.

On her return to the front hall, she felt a breath of air stir across her cheek and turned about, looking for the source. A breeze seemed to come from the morning room. The only room she had forgotten to check.

Sophie rushed in, calling out the boys' names again, and found a door to the rear lawn standing open.

Liam was outside the palace, and he was alone.

She rushed out and turned him to face her. "Liam! What are you doing? Where is your brother?"

"He went out."

"Out?"

Liam nodded solemnly and pointed to the estate grounds. "I told him to wait for your permission. Where were you?"

"I was in my room, dearest," she lied,

smoothing his hair mostly to calm herself because she was truly frightened now.

"I couldn't find you and Thomas wouldn't wait." Liam sobbed suddenly, and he turned into her skirts. Although he was a big boy, Sophie picked him up and held him tight in her arms, but her stomach sank with dread. She'd been with Jasper when the boys must have come looking for her. But how long ago had that been?

"I'm here now. Hold tight to me."

Sophie glanced desperately around the gardens, looking for signs of Thomas, and then set out, carrying Liam. But after a few yards, she realized there was no way to know which way the other boy had gone. The dew was long gone from the grass, leaving no sign of anyone's passage. There seemed no gardeners about either, who might have seen a solitary child pass them by. She glanced over her shoulder as she heard someone come up behind her.

Jasper had followed, and he held Isabelle. "I'm having the palace searched again, but I see you've found one of them."

"Yes. Liam wanted to wait for me, but Thomas has gone out there somewhere. He wouldn't wait. Oh, Jasper. I'm so worried!"

Jasper's arm snuck around her back. "I know. He shouldn't be out there alone."

Sophie stepped out of his embrace. "It's all my fault."

Jasper drew closer again.

"I have to find him." She put Liam back on his feet. "Can you take Liam back to the nursery maid, my lord?"

Liam wrapped his arms about her skirts tightly and held fast to her, even as Lord Jasper caught her arm to prevent her from going off alone. "No, Sophie. You take Liam and Isabelle back to the nursery, and I will find Thomas and bring him back to you. I will have a few words to say to him about his behavior first, though."

Sophie worried her lip, but she could see Jasper was annoyed by his nephew's behavior. "Are you sure I shouldn't go with you? He is my responsibility."

"We're in this together—partners, remember? This morning is as much my fault as yours," Jasper whispered grimly, and then he brushed his fingers across her cheek. A sweet, affectionate gesture that touched her deeply. He nodded. "I think I have an idea of where he's gone."

"Where? He's never done this before to me and he has no special place on the estate that I know of."

Jasper winked. "'Tis a secret between us men in the family. Never fear, I will have him back to you shortly."

And with that, he passed Isabelle into her arms, kissed her brow, patted Liam on the head and ran off, coat flapping as he sprinted through the garden and disappeared out of sight.

Sophie considered swooning and then soundly rebuked herself for reading too much into his kiss goodbye. If she hadn't given in and gone to Jasper this morning, the boys would never have left the nursery without her.

She would be relieved when Thomas was recovered and everything could return to the way it used to be. While she was here at Ravenswood, she belonged in the nursery. With the children every single moment. That meant not sharing kisses or pleasures with the rake in residence. Helping him with his schemes, while fulfilling, had to stop, as well. She would have to spurn Jasper, although that thought brought her no happiness.

She had become complacent. Relied upon others in a way she'd not experienced since her time with Madam Clover.

Sophie stood there a moment longer. Torn. She wanted to find Thomas herself, but Jasper was much quicker on his feet. And he did say he had an idea of where to find the boy while she had none at all.

She soothed Isabelle as the child seemed to realize her papa had gone off without her. Sophie caught up Liam's hand and led him back to the palace. She turned before entering, to look out over the gardens one last time. If anything happened to Thomas, she'd never forgive herself.

Reluctantly, she went inside and shut the terrace door to keep the chilly breeze out. She glanced down at Liam, who was wearing a frown still. "We had better get back upstairs."

"Is Thomas in trouble?"

"A little," she admitted. "I was so frightened when I couldn't find you. I looked everywhere."

"I wanted to take you with us," Liam complained, glancing up at her.

"I appreciate that."

He shrugged. "I don't want to make another friend like Thomas does. I just want you."

Sophie leaned down to hug the child, overcome with emotion at his remark, but a little sad over what he said about Thomas. She had tried so hard to win him over, but she wasn't enough, apparently. She ushered Liam back to the nursery.

Once he was settled and Isabelle was playing with some toys, she turned to the window to look outside again. The view had not changed, and that worried her. How far could the boy have gone? She'd no real idea when the boys had left the nursery, but he could be anywhere. Liam did not seem to know when she asked him about that. She watched over Liam, but it was clear his older brother's disappearance was seemingly forgotten already. Sophie took a deep breath, striving for calm and then settled at the windows to watch for the return of her charge.

Thankfully, she spotted Jasper and Thomas returning within a few minutes. She put her hand on the glass, peering down at the pair, utterly relieved to see the boy obviously whole and sound still.

Lord Jasper stopped, leaning down to speak with Thomas, and then the boy looked up at the nursery window. Even from this distance, she could detect a sullen mood lay over the child. He was likely angry with her for telling his uncle about his disappearance.

Lord Jasper might have shouted at him or possibly even punished him.

Either way, it was up to her to smooth his way back into their normal routine as soon as possible. She hurried to the door, standing there waiting for Thomas' return. It seemed to take much longer than it should have, and her relief and welcome were in proportion to the fright she had suffered that morning.

Thomas, however, was not as pleased to see her. He rudely brushed by her, went directly to his bed, and threw himself face down on it. She was a little hurt that he didn't seem to care about her feelings or that she'd been anxious about his whereabouts.

Lord Jasper appeared and smiled ruefully. "Let him sulk if he wants to."

"What did you do to him?"

Jasper shrugged. "Nothing, but I said enough so that he will never do that to you again."

Sophie bit her lip and then nodded. "Was he where you thought he'd be?"

"Indeed, he was, more's the pity." He drew closer and lowered his voice. "I don't mean to tell you what to do with him. I know I'm not your employer or the child's father, but I think I might have said enough for both of us this morning. Let the matter of him running off be forgotten. He knows what will happen if he does it again."

"What will happen?"

"He'll be sent off to school early, separated from everyone. That was the punishment my father used with us. Thomas did not like the sound of that at all."

Sophie impulsively put her hand on Jasper's arm. "That is a cruel thing to do to a child."

"So was what he put you through this morning," Jasper whispered, brushing a strand of hair behind her ear. "He doesn't need to know it might not happen. But the threat is a good one. It always worked on me. I'll be keeping a closer eye on him from now on, too."

He turned away, but Sophie rushed after him. "Jasper."

He stopped and turned back. "Yes?"

"It would be best if I concerned myself only with the children from now on." She hoped that would be enough to explain why she'd never be alone with him again.

Jasper frowned and drew closer. "You've never not put them first."

"I failed them this morning. That cannot happen again, my lord. I hope you understand. I'm only here for them. Not myself or even you."

Jasper seemed to reel back from her words.

"I'm sorry," she whispered. "I don't have the luxury of breaking all the rules the way you can."

"I broke my own for you...but so be it," he said in a tone so curt, she realized he was upset by her decision to end their affair. Disappointed and maybe even a little hurt.

"I'm just a governess."

"No, Sophie, you're much more than that to me," he promised. "But have it your way. I'll not bother you again."

He spun about and started down the hall, shoulders hunched.

"Jasper!" she called but he did not come back to her.

CHAPTER SEVENTEEN

"SEYMOUR," Jasper shouted as he stormed through the lower floor of the house on his way to his study and then spewed out every curse he knew. He was bloody angry now. "Damn woman. The damn nerve of her! She's no right to come sneaking onto the grounds when she could walk bold as brass right up to the bloody front door and be welcomed inside," he muttered, not caring that anyone might hear him.

Seymour came rushing in. "Is there a problem?"

"Yes." Jasper faced the butler and strove for control of his temper. "Lady Laura Sweet just tried to abduct her son."

And because of that, Sophie had called a halt to their affair, too.

The butler's eyes widened impossibly. "Lady Laura? She's here?"

"No. She *was* out there, but I think I scared her off. For now, at least. I only glimpsed her galloping away."

Seymour moved farther into the room. "I don't understand."

"That would be two of us," he bit out, and then explained what he knew about the morning and the previous conversation he'd had with his sister-in-law.

He also shared the news that Thomas had told him a strange woman had beckoned him outside that morning. When he hadn't found Sophie to ask who she might be, he'd gone down to see for himself, taking Liam. Liam had not wanted to go without the governess, but he had and the woman had lured Thomas farther away until he's seen sense and stopped following her.

Thomas was confused and angry, and rightfully so. He'd been led on a merry dance by his own mother, not that he'd recognized her from a distance.

Seymour slumped into a chair. "Why would she try to take them away?"

"How should I know? I'm not privy to every facet of her estrangement from my brother. I knew they didn't get along, but I never thought there was so much hostility on her part." He paced the room, unable to settle himself.

The boy had known he was in the wrong as soon as their eyes had met. Jasper had shouted, Jasper had threatened, and Jasper demanded he never do that to Sophie again.

Thomas had asked who had been drawing him away from the palace. Jasper hadn't known what to say about her but hoped that would end any more of Thomas' wanderings for now. But he was seriously worried. Was Laura even in her right mind? What did she think she would accomplish in stealing her children back? "I will need men posted on every path leading to the palace."

"There are more ways in than there are servants," Seymour warned.

"Damn it. Why now when we are so short of staff?"

"Perhaps this has occurred *because* there are so few on hand."

Jasper grunted, acknowledging the truth of that. "I wonder how long she has been spying on my brother, and the estate, waiting for a chance."

"And the gathering behind the palace, with the departures so soon after, made her brave enough to strike this morning. It is a good thing I personally make certain every single door and window is locked each and every night."

"At least she couldn't get inside last night."

But Jasper's stomach pitted as it occurred to him he hadn't locked the door behind him when he'd returned either. He would have to be more careful.

Laura might have retrieved Isabelle, too, if she'd discovered that oversight. He had been preoccupied with making love to Sophie. Over his desk, because he could not wait to reach his own bedchamber. He raked a hand through his hair in disgust with himself. He should have been more careful. Anyone could have walked in and found them like that, too. "Unfortunately, locked doors didn't stop her from calling the boys out to her."

"Does the governess know about Lady Laura's return?" Seymour asked.

"No, and I do not plan to tell her yet. Not until I have decided what to do about it." Sophie had told him she'd be sticking closer to the children and putting an end to their affair. That burned a little still, and yet, given the circumstances, it suited him very well to have her renew her dedication to his nephews and niece. Under Sophie's watchful gaze, they'd never have a chance to go anywhere without them knowing again. "We've had little to no trouble from Thomas before this."

"Once Lord Nash finds out..."

"Indeed. Thomas might not sit for a week,

should we tell him, and about his wife coming back too. You know how he is."

The butler grew pale. "Quite. What punishment will the governess mete out?"

"None, I hope," Jasper murmured. "I told her I had taken care of the matter of scolding the child and I think she believed me."

"I hope so." Seymour worried his lower lip. "It isn't right to punish the boy if he went to his own mother."

"My sentiments exactly," Jasper said, and straightened. "Alert the gardeners and the household staff. I cannot risk losing the children before my brother comes back."

"Agreed." The butler stood. "Perhaps it would be prudent to write to Lord Nash and beg his premature return from the house party."

"I'd already planned to once my temper cooled a bit. I'll write him and he can deal with his family himself."

Jasper would write to the duke as well. Ravenswood would be alarmed by any attempted abduction. He sat himself down at his desk and scratched out a note for his brother, and another for the duke, and gave them to the hovering butler. However, given the time it would take for the note to reach them, he could not expect any response for weeks.

And notes could go astray.

The missing correspondence between Sophie and Madam Clover was very much on his mind. Months of missing letters were unusual and smacked of interference. He would do a little more snooping about when he had the time to spare.

Now, though, he would have to keep a close eye on the children. Spend more time with Isabelle and make sure the governess never left them alone. That meant he could not lure her back to his bed. Not until his brother returned to take charge of his family. Jasper had to keep the situation contained for now. But he hated the idea of it, and of keeping Sophie at arm's length, too.

He stood and tugged down his waistcoat. Starting today, he was going to become the most constant uncle that had ever existed.

Jasper heard steps as he glanced at the clock on the mantel and smiled tightly. He knew the children's schedule by heart now. He knew exactly where they'd be every single day, and when.

He could always find Sophie. He would not be deprived of her company.

Jasper strolled out to meet them in the long gallery. Sophie appeared startled to see him and dipped a curtsy. "My lord."

He bowed in return. "Radcliffe. How do you do?"

She rose, a frown of confusion on her face. "Very well, thank you."

He turned aside, nodded to his nephews. They were on the floor around Isabelle and even from here, he could tell a bond existed between them. It surprised him that Sophie hadn't considered the possibility that the child might just belong to Nash instead of himself. But the note had suggested he was the father, and he had no way to prove otherwise yet. Jasper would carry on until Isabelle's parentage was confirmed by Laura or Nash.

He glanced out the window.

To have that conversation with his sister-in-law would require her to return. He wasn't sure where she was staying, but it couldn't be very far away. Most likely, she was at her family's old estate, or with old friends. Yet her family had moved away soon after the marriage. He should have gone round to see if she was there already, but he'd had guests that required his attention.

And so had Isabelle, too.

He glanced down at the babe. As far as children went, he'd not be upset to learn Isabelle was still his. But the question of her future would have to wait until his brothers' return to the estate. The sudden appearance of a surprise daughter would stir up gossip Ravenswood might not like. They might have to take her and Laura away from the estate for a while, away from Sophie, unless they took her with them.

He faced Sophie. "What games are afoot today?"

"We haven't decided." She crossed her arms over her chest, drawing a little away from him. But she whispered, "Thomas is very cross with me."

He shrugged. "That is to be expected of anyone when their will has been crossed."

She wet her lips. "What are you doing here?"

"Seeking Isabelle. I thought I might take her out on the lawn with me."

The governess frowned. "I cannot stop you."

"You could if you tried," he teased. He strolled down the hall and went to the cupboard. He knew few games that might appeal to a child so young. But he found a ball...a bowl that she could roll about with her hands. Something easy would be best. He scooped up Isabelle, threw a smile at Sophie and whispered, "Join us if you care to."

From the lawn, he could watch the grounds for signs of Laura lurking about. She might still be close. The children might lure her back.

It took all of ten minutes for Sophie to emerge from the long gallery, followed by two boys, one of which looked very uncertain about his welcome. Sophie, too, looked worried about joining him, so he gestured them to come closer. "What kept you?"

The trio stopped nearby, and the children fell to the ground near Isabelle again, attempting to teach her how to share the ball with them.

Thomas glanced his way. "We wanted to join you."

"Asking permission is the right way to go about it," Jasper said, nodding with approval. "But why don't you run back inside and fetch the bowls? We'll have a proper game, and if you don't know the rules, I'd be happy to teach you."

Sophie followed the boys a few steps, but turned back. "You don't have to play with them."

"It's my pleasure to prepare them for the future," he said. "Bowls are a favorite pastime in my family. When they are old enough, their father might just let them have a game with him."

"I would hope so," Sophie answered. "It might bring them closer, as a family, if Lord Nash could interact with them more."

"That would take a miracle," Jasper murmured under his breath. "My brother is highly competitive. The children's feelings could be easily bruised by that. Best they start with me. I instructed their mother."

"If I could ask, what was she like?" Sophie asked. "Mrs. Crawford told me you grew up as neighbors."

"Ha, I'm sure that's not all she said about me," Jasper replied, and then shrugged. "We were good friends, but she ended up married to my brother."

"What did you like about her?"

"She was smart and funny and strong-minded. A bit bossy with me, now I think about it. She played the harp beautifully."

"I wish I had met her. I have always hoped she might one day return for the children's sake," Sophie whispered as the boys reappeared. "Why did she really leave?"

"My father did not make her feel welcome and Nash could not be anything other than he appears now. The family was too cold to her, and she felt smothered in rules and left ignorant about many matters that concerned her and the children. I didn't know how desperate she was to get away from us. I would have helped her had I known and I think she would have taken them with her if she could."

"I see," Sophie said, and bit her lip. "I can't imagine Lord Nash would have been happy about that."

"I'm sure he would not be now either," Jasper muttered grimly. And then he forced a smile to his face. "I'll answer any question you put to me about Laura, Sophie, for I'm sure you have many, but let's not discuss her in front of the children,"

Jasper suggested, getting to his feet to help the boys prepare for a game.

Sophie remained behind with Isabelle while he instructed the children and when he returned, he helped her up and collected Isabelle. "Let's join the game."

"I'm not very good, my lord," she reminded him.

"You have strength, but perhaps not the focus you need to win. Perhaps this time, try not to think of me when you release the bowl," he teased.

Her eyes turned his way. "I was not thinking of you that night."

He frowned. "So it was the other rake you despise?"

"Yes," she admitted, and then walked around him.

Jasper followed. "That is a relief and a worry."

"I don't want to talk about him," she whispered.

Jasper wanted to know more about the man who'd come before him, but he could understand her reluctance. He was the one who'd taken her innocence and perhaps broken that tender heart Madam Clover was so worried about.

Despite being rebuffed, Jasper still wanted to be good friends with Sophie Regina Radcliffe.

The remarkable woman who had gotten under his skin well and truly. A woman he could bear to have on his arm and in his bed for many a year.

At the thought, Jasper tripped on a clump of lawn and cursed under his breath at his inattention.

Years? Could Sophie be his for that long and remain a governess? Probably not, yet he wanted Sophie in any shape or form.

He picked up a bowl, his cheeks burning.

He was *smitten* with Sophie. Putting himself directly in her path to make her notice him again and again.

He'd never known what he wanted in a woman, but he would like Sophie to be his. His friend, his companion, perhaps his...*wife.*

He stuck his finger under his collar as the realization hit him that he knew exactly what he craved most in the world. He wanted Sophie to be his in every way possible. She was too good to be a governess or mistress.

Jasper had fallen in love with her.

He found himself suddenly out of breath. In *love.* He steadied his breathing, and his hands, which had started to tremble. He was the third son. Overlooked as a husband by many, and women had climbed over him to reach Nash's or Ravenswood's notice. He'd known never to covet anything or anyone for himself because, in most cases, he would end up disappointed.

But as he watched Sophie step in front of him to bowl and then laugh as her shot went terribly wide, he knew there was no denying his feelings.

Love and other disasters had shown him what was missing in his life.

His first and last thought of every day for quite a while had been about Sophie and what she thought of him. There was good reason for his growing attachment to her. Jasper could be himself with her, and she didn't seem to expect anything better. He could misbehave with her, and also enjoy doing nothing much of importance at all, and still be content. He was not constantly aware of his shortcomings or disliked for his ambitions. Sophie had her own, too. To be good, to be with those she loved, to be his friend.

They had knocked heads simply because they'd sensed the other's needs perhaps, and feared them. But that earlier aggravation, the way they'd come together now, made him realize the sort of life they could have together. Open, honest, fun, and wicked, too.

Jasper had spent his life reluctantly bending to the will and needs of others. He would bend willingly if Sophie ever asked him to.

He prepared to bowl and placed his ball right

beside Sophie's instead of trying to always win. Wide of the mark, but sure of his target at last.

Jasper knew what he wanted, if he had the nerve to ask for Sophie's hand. But what would Sophie say when he did? Could she believe a rake loved her and might never change his mind about that?

CHAPTER EIGHTEEN

SOPHIE RUSHED the boys outside to take up their positions in a flurry of excitement to welcome the duke's carriage home to Ravenswood the very next day. Lord Jasper continued past her, hurrying down the stairs to the carriage door to greet his brothers still seated. There was no sign of Isabelle with him, of course. He must have left her behind somewhere in the palace. "Your grace, welcome back."

"It's good to be home, brother," Ravenswood called out, sounding weary to her ear.

"I didn't expect you for weeks yet?" Jasper replied, leaning inside the conveyance.

What the duke said in response, she couldn't quite catch.

"As you see," Jasper he said, stepping back and gesturing with his arm, "the estate is as safe and sound as the day you departed."

"Let's go inside," the duke said as he emerged, resplendent in black and frowning. "We need to talk."

When Jasper threw a glance her way, Sophie grew concerned that the duke had learned about his visitors and the orgy.

Lord Nash emerged a moment later, his brow deeply furrowed as he looked up the steps at everyone. Sophie flexed her fingers on the shoulders of her charges, willing Nash to look down at his children and show some sign he'd missed them. It had been many weeks since he'd been home.

She curtsied deeply to the duke as he passed her by with the barest glance. "Your Grace, welcome home," she murmured.

Ravenswood paused then, stared down at her and then at his nephews. "Thomas, Liam. I trust you've behaved while your father was gone."

"Yes, they have, Your Grace," she blurted out. The duke didn't need to know about Thomas running off alone yet.

The duke grunted and went on his way. Their father came next and stopped to ask how she fared.

"We are very well, my lord," she replied. "It is good to have you back at home."

For a moment, she thought he might offer the boys a gesture of affection, or at least acknowledge them in some meaningful way. Unfortunately, it wasn't to be that day. Lord Nash nodded to them. She flexed her fingers on the shoulders of her charges again, willing them not to move a muscle.

He nodded. "I should like to see you in the drawing room, Mrs. Radcliffe. Be prompt if you can."

"We'll be there directly."

"No, Mrs. Radcliffe. Just yourself."

"Of course," she answered but was pained that Lord Nash would exclude the children after being away for so terribly long. They would never know their father if he kept this up.

He moved away, and Jasper took his place, frowning at her too. He looked at Lord Nash's back and then at her. She could tell he wanted to ask her about the meeting, and what she might say about what had gone on while his brothers were away.

Nothing was her plan. Lord Nash did not need to know about the house party, their affair, or about Madam Clover's surprise visit. And no one would hear about the orgy from her lips. If Lord Nash ever suspected anything had gone on, she would pretend ignorance and leave Jasper to explain everything.

There was also Isabelle to worry about now, too. She wondered how the duke would react to the presence of Lord Jasper's bastard offspring being brought to the estate. Would they even notice the girl straight away? The duke surely might and have something to say about it. Sophie had grown very fond of the little girl and hoped she might continue taking care of her, too, along with Lord Nash's sons. She could easily care for three.

Yet that was for Jasper and Lord Nash to come to an understanding about. The manner of Isabelle's upbringing was entirely out of her control. For the moment, she assumed, the child was safely tucked away somewhere with a servant watching over.

She waited her turn to return indoors and then ushered the children upstairs and regretfully left them in the care of Kate. "I'll return shortly. Keep them here."

"Of course, Mrs. Radcliffe. We'll play a game until you come back."

"Thank you." Sophie stepped out into the hall and closed the door.

"Sophie?" Jasper stood not far away, a worried frown on his face. "What does Nash want with you?"

"I've no idea, but since he asked to see only me, and not the children, I assume it is about them." She went to move past Jasper but he called out her name softly.

She stopped. "Yes, my lord."

"I will miss the way things have been over the summer," he whispered, "and the time we spent alone together, too."

Sophie would miss him as well, yet she said nothing about her feelings, because he'd had plenty of time to move what they had to a more permanent footing already. She'd known he would not offer for her in the end.

Sophie trudged downstairs with her heart heavy but resigned to resume her role as a silent observer of the family she worked for. What she had with Jasper must be over, and it could never have been enough for him, anyway. She didn't want to imagine the looks, the outcry, should the family discover she'd been intimate with him.

She headed into the drawing room and found the chamber empty. Lord Nash was occupied still, no doubt with the duke, and settling back in after such a long absence. He was always attentive to his duties. Serious about and concerned for the estate, too. Was it any wonder his wife had felt slighted, made to feel second when his priorities lie elsewhere? There was little room left in Lord Nash's heart or head besides his brother's concerns. He'd none for his children. At least Jasper was better. It was clear he doted on the little girl.

"Mrs. Radcliffe," Lord Nash exclaimed, his voice booming through the empty room as he strode in, unchanged from his arrival. "Good of you to be so prompt."

Sophie turned and smiled at her employer. "You wanted to talk to me."

"Indeed," he said as he snapped closed the doors behind him.

Sophie moved toward him, and he met her halfway across the chamber. "What about?"

His lips pursed momentarily, and he looked around. "Please take a seat."

She did and folded her hands in her lap as she waited for him to continue.

"You are no doubt aware of the state of my marriage," he murmured, settling nearby.

Although surprised he would mention it now, she nodded quickly. "Yes, my lord." It was nonexistent. A subject he infrequently mentioned, but every staff member whispered about the scandal of his marriage. After her discussion with Jasper though, her sympathies might lay on Laura's side now.

"I'm sure you've learned from others that the estate is in something akin to disarray. The duke will marry a wealthy woman soon, but I have already done so once for the good of the family," he admitted.

She nodded again. "I am aware of that, too."

"Some say I am ill-suited to wedlock, but it

occurs to me that my children need a mother and always will."

Sophie's heart leaped. "Has your wife returned to you?"

"No. It may well be that she never shall." He burst to his feet. "It occurred to me some time ago that, given the duration my wife has been absent from our lives, it might well be time to sever the knot between us."

Sophie blinked rapidly, utterly shocked. "You're not considering divorce?"

"I have it on good authority that she lives and breathes. I thought perhaps she might return once she heard of my father's demise, but that has not been the case as far as I know."

"Oh." Sophie gulped. He should not be talking to her about his wife like this. She'd never met the woman and could offer him no advice.

He nodded. "So, I have come to a difficult decision to seek a divorce in the new year and marry again so my children can have a mother."

Although Sophie knew better than to believe ending a marriage could be so simple, or as swift as he made out, she nodded and forced a smile to her face. "Have you someone in mind to marry?"

"Indeed, yes." He met her gaze. "You."

Sophie blinked and shook her head. "I'm sorry. Could you repeat that?"

"Your hesitation is to your credit. I'm sure

you are aware I have never been a man given to wild declarations of passion. But the two of us rub together well enough, and my children are excessively fond of you. I can offer you a life of mutual respect and dignity here with me."

Sophie could not have kept the shock off her face. "You want to marry *me*?"

"Yes, I do. I expect a wedding could occur next season. You can make a note of that in the children's schedule. There'll be no need to fear you'll be forced into society after we wed, either. Mrs. Crawford will act as the duke's hostess in Town until he is married, as already planned. You can stay here year-round and manage the household until my elder brother finally brings home a bride."

Sophie sat in stunned silence. She'd never heard so unromantic a proposal as the one Lord Nash was offering to her. And he seemed entirely serious about marrying her, too, despite her unsuitability to join his family. He was the duke's heir. If anything happened to Ravenswood, Lord Nash became the duke. And she might become a duchess!

A response was required, but any appropriate words of thanks and refusal became stuck in her throat. Of course, she had to refuse him. She could not marry the brother of the man she'd...

The brother of the rake she'd so foolishly fallen for.

She *loved* Jasper, not Lord Nash.

She licked her lips, shocked and uncomfortable. "My lord, you do me a great honor, but you must know what my answer will be and why I am completely unsuitable."

He came to sit at her side. "We have never discussed the night we met, have we?"

"No."

"I understand your hesitation to think of marriage again. You were left in a bad way. But in the years of our acquaintance, I've come to admire your inner strength and resilience despite the ill-use you suffered. I hoped you had have forgotten him by now."

Sophie blushed. She had not thought of her heartless rake very much at all lately. Jasper had somehow driven him from her heart and mind over the summer. "I was young and a fool to trust it was love then."

"You need never be a fool again with me," Lord Nash promised. "It will be a marriage in name only between us. You will have the children to love and a home and the protection of my family. I won't bother you in the slightest. In fact, you might keep to your current chamber close to the nursery if you care to."

"I was not worried about being bothered by a

husband," Sophie whispered, paling a little at the sort of life and marriage he was proposing they could share. Married in name only. Never to experience passion again. Never leaving the estate. *Trapped.* "My answer must be no."

He drew back, seemingly surprised by her reticence to wed and denial of his suit. "Consider the benefits. Take your time before you give me your final word tonight." Lord Nash smiled at her. "Now, I'm needed by the duke for all of this afternoon until dinner, but we will speak again of this later, and I will do my best to ease your fears about matrimony. You'll soon see marriage to me is for the best." Lord Nash's dry hand suddenly covered hers, and he squeezed her fingers. "Until dinner."

He was back on his feet and gone the next moment.

Sophie stared at the door as it closed. Lord Nash never did listen to her. Or perhaps he expected to wear down her resistance until she complied.

Why would he want her? It made no sense at all.

She thought of how different to Jasper he was, and blanched.

She wanted to be married to Jasper—not his cold brother.

Sophie sat there a few minutes more, uncertain what to do or what she should have said to be more clear. Lord Nash was so cold, so utterly foreign to her idea of a man she had ever imagined being bound to. So completely different from Jasper, the only man she'd rush to say yes to.

She had always wanted and expected to have children of her own if she ever wed, even after the terrible loss she'd suffered at the hands of a scoundrel. A loss Nash knew about, but Jasper still did not. How could Nash believe she might never want to hold a child of her own if she had a chance to?

He had seen her anguish. Her grief.

Apparently, he'd never even tried to understand her loss.

But Jasper had, although he didn't know what she'd done.

When she refused Nash again tonight, she doubted she could remain at Ravenswood for very much longer. She would have to return to London and Madam Clover. Leave Jasper behind and hope he would succeed in his schemes without her small assistance.

She stood and walked to the door on legs made of clay and opened it again.

The first thing she saw was Jasper, standing in the library across the hall and talking with the duke. Their eyes locked momentarily over the top of Ravenswood's dark head, but she turned away, embarrassed. She hoped he never found out what her conversation with Nash entailed, but not out of a hope he might become jealous.

That Lord Nash intended to divorce his wife to offer her a marriage of convenience was an embarrassment to her. He would drag her into his mess, the scandal of his first marriage ending, and not care how she or the children might be hurt by it.

Lord Nash didn't care about her feelings or about Laura. He hadn't bothered to learn of her hopes and dreams, during the whole of their acquaintance. He only seemed to do what he wanted. No wonder Laura had left him.

Sophie wanted London, and the noise and chaos found there. She wanted to visit Madam Clover and her friends at the pleasure house as often as she could. Nash had kept her in the countryside for so long and clearly intended to keep her here forever.

No, Nash was not the one her heart wanted to be with or love.

Sophie hurried upstairs and went straight to the children, gathering up Isabelle and Liam on her lap and hugged them tight. These children might have been her family forever, if she had a heart to barter for the honor of making a proper marriage. Becoming a wife on any terms except having her love returned was too high a price for a woman like Sophie Regina Radcliffe. Sophie had rules for how she lived her life now. She also no longer had a broken heart. It was repaired completely but it had been claimed by an unavailable man again.

CHAPTER NINETEEN

"SO, YOU'RE BACK EARLY," Jasper said to the duke when he was urged to sit in the chair opposite him in the library. But although pleased to see his brothers, Jasper was going to end this conversation as quickly as possible today.

He wanted to follow after Sophie to learn what Nash had just said to her. He had never seen her look so pale. She could hardly look at him, either. It made him fear Ravenswood had somehow learned of his scandalous secret house party and convinced Nash to get rid of her because she'd played a part.

The duke had given away nothing though while Nash and Sophie had been talking behind closed doors across the hall. Ravenswood turned over the paper, a picture of calm unconcern, as he studied the next one without looking up to answer. "Yes."

Jasper shifted in his chair. Watching others read his handwriting was awkward, even worse when it was his own brothers. Jasper had written his thoughts on the management of the estate instead of simply regaling the duke with an impossibly long recital of changes he thought should be made, only to have them forgotten. In total, there were seven pages detailing improvements that could save the duke, if not quite a fortune, enough money to make a difference over the years.

He'd yet to find a moment to mention the arrival of Isabelle. He would rather Nash was there for that announcement to watch the expression on his face. Cavorting with one's own wife was no scandal but not knowing he'd done so might shock Nash a little.

"And the house party? How was that?"

"Quite enjoyable for the most part, though our brother might disagree with my sentiment," Ravenswood said, a tight smile on his lips. "He found the company dull and grew more irritable as the days passed."

That sounded about right for Nash in any setting. "And Lady Stephanie?"

Ravenswood lowered the paper slightly. "She remains available for marriage."

"Did you ask her?"

"No." The papers lowered even more to reveal a troubled expression on the duke's face. "The right moment did not present itself."

Jasper nodded. He could understand how Ravenswood might feel about marriage. How soon was too soon to know that a change in one's life was meant to be?

The duke cleared his throat. "Well, get on with it. Rail at me, too, for my inaction."

He frowned at his brother. "Why would I do that?"

"Nash has not let up for days. But perhaps he's said enough on the matter for the both of you," Ravenswood murmured.

"Most likely he would. It matters not to me when you propose. You've said you'll marry, and I believe you will," he answered.

"Thank you, Jasper," the duke said, exhaling as if he was comforted by his faith in him. "You've always been the easiest of brothers."

And then he went back to reading Jasper's notes without another word about marriage or Nash.

While Jasper waited for the duke's response to those notes, he rang the bell and requested coffee be served. He could not leave until he heard what the duke thought of his ideas. But he kept glancing at the windows and the doorway, hoping to see Sophie come downstairs again.

Her schedule with the children would have

been thrown out the window with his brother's sudden return, and he wondered what she was doing right now. No doubt something Nash had ordered her to do, and unpleasant, judging by the look on her face a moment ago.

Jasper needed to see her, and it had to be before the dinner hour.

"Nash, would you come in here and kindly sit down with us," Ravenswood called out loudly.

Nash emerged from the ducal study next door and took a seat nearby. But he jiggled his knee, looking for all the world like there was somewhere else he'd rather be. When the coffee arrived, he refused a cup, too. It was unlike Nash to appear so impatient or so distracted, but then, he'd never had any interest in Jasper's ideas before.

The duke cast a sour look Nash's way. "Take a look at this."

"Why?" Nash bit out as he looked toward the door again.

Ravenswood handed him the sheets of suggestions with a heavy sigh and sat back. "Our brother has been busy, and I think his suggestions are worthy of consideration."

"Let's see them," Nash said, snatching up the papers.

Ravenswood glanced Jasper's way with a

proud smile. "Well done, little brother. I'm impressed."

Jasper felt his face grow warm at the praise. He hadn't really imagined the duke would be impressed. After all, what could a third son know about running an estate of this size? No one in his family. "I'm sure you already considered many."

"A handful only," the duke admitted. "I knew leaving you in charge would prove beneficial."

Jasper squirmed a bit as he waited for the duke to dismiss him. The duke and Nash would discuss his ideas thoroughly when he was gone. He didn't need to stay for that. Most decisions were usually made while he was elsewhere anyway.

He sat his coffee cup down, deciding it was time to leave the room and seek Sophie.

"Oh, would you just let it go!" the duke barked.

Jasper looked up, startled by the heat of the demand from his brother.

But the duke was addressing Nash, rather than him.

Nash mumbled something under his breath that Jasper didn't quite catch. The duke must have, though, because he scowled darkly and then glanced at Jasper. "Our brother has been in a foul mood since we left the house party, and I've grown weary of it. I didn't ask her. There's nothing to be done about that now. So what else is there to fret about?"

Nash glared at the duke. "I'm proceeding with the divorce."

Jasper blinked, shocked to the core. "What?"

"Our brother has a foolish notion stuck in his head for weeks, one that will not solve anything in the end," Ravenswood warned, sitting back in his chair. "Divorce is almost unheard of in our circle and would cause a scandal the likes of which we would not escape for years."

Jasper leaned toward Nash. "Why now?"

But Jasper suddenly knew why—Sophie. Why else would she look so pale? Had she heard of his plans, too? Had Nash come home and the first thing he'd done was press his suit with Sophie! What had she said in answer?

Nash cleared his throat repeatedly. "It is clear to me that my wife has forfeited any claim on a place in the family. Our marriage was arranged and there was never love between us. I would rather live as a bachelor again than as an abandoned husband forever."

"She is not the only one who abandoned the marriage bed," Jasper threw out, appalled by Nash's plan. "You hardly noticed the absence that first week."

"Jasper," the duke warned. "You know nothing of the matter."

Until now, Jasper had kept his thoughts about Nash and Laura strictly to himself, but no more. Not when there was Isabelle to worry about. "I know enough to see my brother is trying to absolve himself of any responsibility for the failings of his marriage. He was absent when she needed him most," Jasper complained, getting to his feet. "He left Laura alone with Father to be a victim of his whims."

Nash sucked in a sharp breath. "You were here, too. You were her friend," he snarled. "Her best friend."

"Yes, I was then, but I was not her husband. I held no sway over Father's decisions concerning her, and why should I have had any say at all? But I saw what was going on, and I wrote to you, suggesting you return more than once. You chose not to listen to me. You obeyed Father and did his bidding instead. Father separated you from Laura, and then separated Laura from the children. If you divorce her, you take away any chance those boys might have to see her again."

"She could have come back to me any time she chose," Nash replied so coolly, Jasper almost shivered.

He grew angry at the calm way Nash continued to speak of ending his marriage. There was no passion in him, save for his own ambitions for the family. Jasper could not fathom that they were even related by blood. "Did you tell her that? Apologize for what father was like with her."

Nash's jaw twitched. "It goes without saying that the mother of my children is welcome here."

"Not while Father lived, she wasn't," Jasper reminded him. "Father did all he could to make her feel an outsider. She had to make appointments to visit her own children on their last birthdays!"

"Jasper, that is enough," the duke warned again, standing up as well. He put a restraining hand on Jasper shoulder. "Leave him to make his own mistakes."

"No, I will not! Not this time." He turned on the duke, too. "I've said nothing for years and let him do as he pleases. But why divorce her now? It is not as if he'd want to be with anyone else at this point. He's too set in his ways to bother with romance."

Nash cleared his throat. "I will marry again. A bride has already been selected."

Jasper shook his head, but the duke appeared surprised. "You're making a jest."

"No," Nash promised. "It has been discussed, and I expect to marry as soon as the divorce is final."

"That could take years. What woman would agree to wait so long?"

Nash shrugged. "Mrs. Radcliffe understands the situation."

"Radcliffe? No!" the duke gasped. "I'll not consent to this."

Jasper shook his head again. "She can't marry you."

If Sophie married anyone, he hoped it was himself.

"I see no real impediment," Nash continued. "After I have secured a divorce, I'll promote a maid to take her place as a governess until the boys go off to school."

"What of Laura?"

Nash shrugged again. "What of her?"

"You'll humiliate her."

"Has she not done the same to me? Embarrassing me in front of my family because I did not defy Father while he lived."

"Yes, but now Father is gone, there's no reason not to reunite and make peace with her," Ravenswood argued.

"She's had enough time to come to her senses," Nash announced and slowly got to his feet. "No. A fresh start is what I require."

"A fresh start," Jasper said slowly. "So, you're courting Mrs. Radcliffe now?"

"No, no. None of that nonsense is needed with her. I know all there is to know about Mrs. Radcliffe already, to see she is the perfect choice for me. She will not require the romance you believe necessary to make a second marriage work."

Jasper gaped. "Why the hell would you think that?"

"Because it is to be a marriage in name only. I told her so. She will have the children to care for and our protection. She will remain here in the country where she can be comfortable."

Jasper narrowed his eyes on his brother. "Did she tell you that's what she wants for her life?"

"Not in so many words, but she could hardly want to return to London and the unhappy memories to be found there."

Sophie's friends were in London. Madam Clover, Ruby and all the rest. Jasper's senses came alert. What did Nash know that he didn't yet? "What unhappy memories are in London for her?"

Nash's lip curled briefly, but he smoothed his features. "She was in love once and was badly let down."

Jasper knew that, but the way Nash spoke made it seem somehow sordid. "Let down how?"

"A proposal was required and never came."

The duke blinked. "Required?"

Nash nodded curtly. "The indiscretion was hushed up by all concerned."

"Nash," the duke said slowly. "If you expect my support of this ridiculous union, you will have to provide me with all the details of this indiscretion of hers. Jasper and I both need to know now. You said nothing of any stain on her reputation when you hired the woman without references and brought her into our lives. I wish for no more surprises from my brothers."

"There is nothing to be concerned about." Nash pursed his lips a moment. "She met a rake and was charmed into his bed, and she expected a proposal that never came. The fellow abandoned her, and she was cast out of the orphanage where she still lived. I met her one night, many months later. I am quite sure impropriety is far in her past now."

The duke crossed his arms over his chest. "Continue."

But Jasper glared at Nash and willed him to shut his mouth. He had a feeling he knew what was coming next. The things Nash might say about Sophie were private and none of the duke's damn business. Nor his either.

Sophie had an extremely low opinion of rakes for a reason. She'd met the madam when she'd been ill...but that illness was never explained fully to him. She rarely spoke in any detail about her time before becoming a governess, and he had always been curious about why she remained silent.

Nash nodded. "She was fortunate a kind-hearted woman summoned me when difficulties arose," he said.

Jasper's heart stopped beating. "Difficulties?"

"She could have died if I'd not been there," Nash murmured. "She lost a child."

Jasper was appalled to hear that. Was it any wonder Sophie could not speak of such a past? Nash should have held his tongue. He had no respect at all for Sophie or her privacy.

Jasper was different from Nash in one essential respect. When it came to Sophie, there was *nothing* he wouldn't do to protect her and her reputation—even from his own brothers.

They were partners, or had been until guilt had gotten in the way of their friendship, romance, whatever it should be called. He deeply regretted what had happened to her and would change things if he could. If Nash had asked her to marry him today, she hadn't looked happy about it at all. For all Nash's certainty, Jasper could not believe Sophie would ever agree to such a cold match. The pair had nothing in common.

He stared at his brother...and realized the tiny fact Nash had forgotten to mention about his choice. Sophie would inherit all of Madam Clover's money and a thriving pleasure house one day, when she passed away.

He would pretend not to know any of that for

now. "Why would you choose to marry a penniless orphan?"

"I trust her," Nash murmured, looking slightly unconvincing.

Yes, Sophie could be trusted, but that wasn't the only reason Nash had picked her. Nash would marry Sophie for her eventual inheritance, too, and say nothing about it to anyone.

Jasper turned away, disgusted with his brother. He'd learned nothing since marrying Laura for the same reason. Jasper could not allow such a match to take place. He would not let Sophie commit her future to his brother's cold keeping.

Sophie should not live out her days in chaste misery when she didn't have to. She was much too passionate in nature for that fate.

Nash sighed. "She is the woman I want, brother. I brought her to be my children's governess and I like her. With her education and affectionate nature, she's perfectly fond of the children."

"So is Seymour," Jasper bit out, "and he would not require a ring should you ask him to watch over the children."

The duke smothered a laugh.

Jasper put his hands on his hips. "So why Sophie Radcliffe when any woman would do?"

"You've made no secret of your dislike for

her, Jasper," the duke noted. "I imagine that's why you cannot understand his decision. I admit, I'm struggling, too."

"Anyone can care for the boys," Jasper threw out. He wanted to give his brother one last chance. "But Nash, to marry a woman in your employ when the children will leave for proper schooling so soon? Why her, brother? Why now?"

"The offer has been made," Nash said as if that were final.

And to his mind, it probably was. Nash was stubborn, inflexible in his opinions, and his decision today was cruel to Sophie. He would not change his mind about her, now that he'd told them all what he'd decided. He had to give his brother reason to doubt himself. "Brother, tell me, when was the last time you attended a masquerade in London?"

"Really, Jasper," the duke cut in. "What does that matter now?"

"Oh, it matters." He caught Nash's eye. "Well?"

Although taken aback, Nash answered. "Last year, end of the season."

"Were you with a woman that night?"

Nash shuffled his feet. "Why do you ask that?"

"Answer the question. Were you ever unfaithful to Laura during your marriage?"

"Jasper?" the duke said quietly, "that is none of our..."

"Oh, but it will be, I suspect." He kept his gaze on Nash. "Were you with someone that night?"

"I might have been," he murmured, looking decidedly uncomfortable. "I was drinking a lot last year and my recollection of that night is hazy. I am ashamed of that."

"So you should be," Ravenswood cried out. "You swore to me there'd been no other woman in your life besides your wife. So much for your supposedly high morals. Taking me to task for keeping a mistress when I've no chance to marry her at all."

Jasper nodded, but his heart was heavy. Isabelle was not his daughter after all. She belonged to someone else. A man, his brother, that might never love her the way Jasper already did. "Rejoice brother. I am confident you were not unfaithful to your vows that night."

Nash's eyes snapped to his. "What do you mean?"

"You were not unfaithful because the woman *was* Laura." He drew in a deep breath and let it out slowly in the profound silence that followed his statement. The duke looked utterly shocked and Nash turned pale. He'd obviously had no idea about Laura or the pregnancy. "Laura had a child, a daughter, named Isabelle. The girl was delivered to the palace during your absence."

Nash collapsed to the floor, completely missing the seat of a chair, and the duke rushed to pull him up again in vain, calling his name.

But Nash could only shake his head. "It cannot be true."

Jasper stopped beside Nash, and pitied him for the first time in his entire life. "You will re-think your plans for divorce, brother. Laura *will* come home soon and you will have your family back though you've done nothing to deserve such a boon," Jasper hissed. "If you'll excuse me, your grace, there's something I need to look for."

CHAPTER TWENTY

"THERE YOU ARE," Jasper said, smiling broadly as he strode into the nursery.

Sophie straightened her spine and turned away from him. Today was not the day to deal with her favorite rake. Her mind was too much in a whirl to make any sense of her emotions. She could hardly concentrate on what the children were saying to her half the time since her meeting with their father.

She'd had a proposal from a man she did not love, and the one she *did* care for would never offer one instead. It was ridiculous to feel happy just for having Jasper near on such a troubling day.

He moved to stand at her side, watching the boys play their games together across the room with Isabelle. His presence made her feel less alone. But she pressed her lips together, fighting the longing to turn toward him, to have his arms wrapped about her body again. He made her feel good about herself without even trying.

And it was not easy to deal with her emotions when he was standing just inches away and yet so far out of reach.

He turned her around to face him. "My brothers will be busy for some time, and I'm afraid I have some news that might distress you."

Sophie nodded, glad that Lord Nash would be busy elsewhere. She would have a little more time alone with the children before she must say goodbye to everyone.

She had decided to leave. To return to London and her friends, who she missed desperately. She did not have to be a governess, or a proper lady if she didn't want to. Madam Clover had appreciated her company and work. It might not be respectable, but it was honest work and she was needed at the pleasure house, too.

"My brother told us about his intention to divorce Laura and marry you," Jasper told her bluntly.

Her face grew hot with embarrassment and she peeked at Jasper from the corner of her eye, frozen and uncertain of what to say. Lord Nash had *told* Jasper, and the duke, even though she'd denied him once already? Of course, he had. He never listened. "Oh."

Jasper moved to stand in front of her, blocking her from the children's view. "I love my brother. But he is the complete opposite of me. Once he sets his mind to something, it's impossible to change it."

Sophie hugged her chest. "You are alike in that."

"I would like to believe I learn from my mistakes," Jasper told her. "I have changed because of you. Getting to know Sophie Regina Radcliffe was not a mistake. We are alike. I had hoped we might remain close in the years to come, and we will, no matter what you decide about my brother."

Sophie turned her face away. She was in love with Jasper, and he didn't even know. "Friends?"

"Partners," he corrected. "Partners who put their trust in each other. Look out for each other's best interests. I'm going to trust you now with a truth my brother knows only half of yet."

She turned to face him, unable to hide her dread. "What is this great truth you share?"

He drew closer to whisper, "Laura has visited Ravenswood Palace. Just after Nash left, she found me out riding and demanded to see her children. I tried to bring her to Ravenswood, but she refused to come, and then, later, she tried to abduct her sons."

Sophie met his gaze, shocked. "Was that why Thomas went off alone?"

"Yes. She was not successful then, or since," Jasper whispered, capturing Sophie's hand and holding it tightly against his chest. "Thomas had almost reached her when I caught up with him the other day, and then she disappeared into the woods. He only saw her from a distance. I don't believe Thomas recognized her, but his curiosity remains strong."

At that very moment, Thomas left his brother and Isabelle and drifted toward the windows.

"He's looking out the windows more often, isn't he? I do the same thing."

"Yes, but I never imagined..." Sophie went to Thomas and suggested he show Isabelle his toy soldiers. She glanced out the windows now, herself. She'd wanted to meet Lady Laura Sweet for so long, but never imagined she'd already come home. She returned to Jasper. "Will she come back soon, do you think?"

"I believe so," Jasper warned. "We have something she wants. Her children. But she's like the wind. Swift and fleeting, not to mention as stubborn as Nash. Distrustful and bitter. I think she fears this place and my family."

Sophie closed her eyes. The poor woman. "Why did you not tell me you saw her before now?"

"I was not sure how you would feel about her. She had abandoned her children. I also didn't want you to worry about her trying to steal the children away from you. Together, we have kept them safe, but you need to know she distrusts you without even knowing you. She has learned where Nash met you, and Nash retired the last governess, her choice to watch over her children, against her wishes. She is suspicious of you. She suspects you and Nash have grown too close to be respectable."

Sophie grimaced. She would have to set the woman straight herself. Sophie would have encouraged the woman to reunite with her children, had she known she was near. But Sophie could understand Jasper's fears about a second abduction attempt, too, and did not blame him for keeping that quiet.

As much as she wished for a reunion, Sophie would not have allowed the children to be taken from their father while he was gone from the estate. She would have tried to stop Laura. Nash was back now, and he had responsibilities to his family, to keep them together. Yet he was downstairs, without a clue, imagining they would be married one day.

Jasper squeezed her hand but he was so very sad that she knew he had something painful to tell her. "There's something else I have to tell you about Isabelle."

Sophie gulped, but somehow she already knew what he was about to say. "She belongs to Nash, doesn't she?"

"Yes. She is his and Laura's offspring."

Sophie closed her eyes over the news. So much for her employer's supposed estrangement from his wife. "If that is true, he cannot be allowed to divorce Laura."

He exhaled loudly. "I am glad you agree with me on this."

Sophie put her hand on Jasper's chest, clutching his cravat. "What can we do to bring them together again?"

"I don't know," Jasper admitted with a shake of his head. "There are not two more stubborn individuals who ought never to have wed on this earth. I'd like to lock them in a dungeon until they make peace. Unfortunately, we don't have one at Ravenswood."

"Yes, that is a great pity," she agreed. "Their marriage is really none of our business though."

"Agreed but the children are."

Sophie bit her lip. Yes, the children were her reason for being at Ravenswood. Should they try for some sort of reconciliation or truce for their sake? She met Jasper's gaze. "It would not be easy getting them to stay together under this roof."

"No," Jasper replied, looking worried. "There would probably need to be some sort of calamity or bargain made to prevent them from going their separate ways immediately."

"Short of shackles or a locked bedchamber door, I've no suggestion," Sophie mused. "But His Grace might have a better idea? He knows his brother well."

"Yes, he might help with this. He's always been keen for a reconciliation. He does not want the scandal of a divorce."

"Or me as Nash's second bride either, I imagine, too," she said.

"It's not about you, Sophie."

"I know." She held fast to Jasper and marveled at how easy it was to talk to him still. They had changed so much over the summer. She had considered Jasper the worst sort of libertine and philanderer from nearly the first day they'd met. But over time, she had seen another side of him. A good man lurked beneath all his swagger and handsome features. Yes, he had his flaws, but then so did she.

She'd accused him of neglecting his responsibilities. Yet he cared about his family, his brothers, sister-in-law, and nephews happiness. He'd grown to love Isabelle. And he was helping her now figure things out as they went along together. She loved that Jasper confided in her, turned to her when he didn't know what to do.

She felt she could do the same with him as well.

"Getting that pair to admit they care about each other still would be a herculean feat," he said. "Nash never speaks of his feelings. He will also become angry if I meddle too much."

"If *we* meddle. *Partner*." She could not leave right now. Not until she knew Laura and her children had been reunited. Sophie moved away from Jasper, back toward the window and looked out. If she left, the children would have no governess.

The children would not have a governess but could have a mother instead.

Sophie smiled slowly. Laura was out there, somewhere. Biding her time. Waiting for a chance. An invitation of the right kind. Sophie saw movement and grinned when a shape emerged from the tree line some distance away. That was a woman on horseback.

Laura *was* out there now, hoping to see her children still.

They could have a mother if Sophie could just convince Laura to come back to take her rightful place. If that happened, Sophie could return to Madam Clover with an easy heart.

To begin, though, she needed to take the children to see their mother right now, before she disappeared once more. She did not know what the woman looked like, so she would need Jasper to accompany them as well.

She spun about—and found Jasper right behind her. "What answer you will give Nash?"

"The same one I already gave him. No."

Jasper dropped his head to touch hers, and Sophie found herself in his arms at last. "Did the idea that you could be a mother to my nephews tempt you at all?"

"No." She looked at him sharply. "Did you think it would?"

He smiled. "I hoped not. I had hoped you might prefer *me*, but rakes are universally considered lesser to supposedly proper men like my older brother."

"You're better than him in so many ways I cannot count them all." She laughed softly and kissed his cheek. "You took the time to know me. He never did."

Jasper held her hand tightly in his, and then kissed all her fingertips. "I hope I might be given a chance to know you even better one day. To prove I will always listen and consider your feelings."

"I'd like that, but something must be done about Nash and Laura today I'm afraid. We can't live under the threat of her stealing away her children when there is no reason for her to do so." She turned her gaze on him. "We need to find her and clear the air about me."

"How the devil do you propose we do that?"

She smiled at him and rushed away to snatch up her shawl. "I'll need your help and a proper introduction. Children we are going outside."

"But it's almost time for a story?" Thomas complained.

She moved to Thomas and ruffled his hair. "My dear boy, sometimes it's necessary to set your father's schedule aside."

Jasper followed her across the room and caught her hand. "I would be happy to accompany you, but not quite this very minute if you don't mind. There's something else I have to tell you."

"Yes?"

"Are you aware that Madam Clover plans to leave you the entirety of her fortune?"

Sophie frowned. "She mentioned something about leaving me some money once, before I came here to be a governess, but she's not mentioned it since. Why? How do you know about that, anyway?"

"Nash knew about the inheritance," Jasper whispered. "And he led Madam Clover to believe that he would marry you to see her wishes carried out."

"What wishes?"

"The continuation of her business," he said. "The care of her ladies. She's leaving it all to you."

Sophie shook her head. "I highly doubt your brother would have any interest in running a pleasure house."

"So do I," Jasper agreed. "And I suspect he never would have done it. But she believed you would make sure her ladies were cared for when she was gone, and I think that a fine idea."

"I would be honored to carry on her work," she promised, and narrowed her eyes suddenly. "Nash knew about my inheritance, you say?"

"Yes."

"Why that bounder."

"Well, that's far kinder than what I wanted to call him today," Jasper said. "I pilfered these from my brother's chamber just now. I found them stuffed into the back of a drawer. They are yours and open. I was not the one who did that."

Sophie took them from him, recognizing the items at once. "My letters! *Her* letters! Madam Clovers."

Jasper scowled. "Yes, it seems my brother did not care for you to keep the acquaintance of a madam after all and failed to mention that fact to anyone involved."

Sophie took them to the window and sorted

through them. A half dozen letters she'd written to Madam Clover was here. And more of Madam Clover's letters, besides, including one that was very thick and looked to be important. She unfolded all the letters and scanned them quickly.

She nearly cried at the contents of the thickest one. "This is about her last will and testament, naming me as sole heir."

"Congratulations," he murmured.

Sophie stomped her foot, trying not to weep over the matter. "She might have said something while she was here! I don't deserve this."

"Madam Clover believes in you, as do I Sophie. She told me to take care of you. She knew, suspected, my brother was using you ill and tasked me to fix things. Life is short, Sophie. You should be with people who care about you, not someone who will ignore your needs."

Sophie gulped, looking at him and still trying not to cry. "This changes everything."

"Yes, I'm sure it does. You have better options than remaining here as a governess. You can do anything your heart desires. You always could though."

Sophie hurried to Jasper, caught his face in her hands, and pulled him down until his lips were inches from hers. He looked surprised. "Thank you, partner," she whispered.

She could be Jasper's mistress and continue their affair now.

He grinned back at her and then kissed the tip of her nose. "You are very welcome, Sophie Regina Radcliffe," he promised, settling his hands on her hips. "Now, I find myself in need of your wise counsel again. There is yet another thorny issue that I desperately need a solution for. I'm certain you will know what I should do."

She smiled at him. How far they'd come from those months when they'd disliked each other so much that they couldn't have a civil conversation. They were truly becoming the best of friends. A pity that would change, with her return to London even more pressing now. But she could go back to London and hope to see him sometimes and still help Jasper build his fortune, and madam's, too. "Anything? What can I do to help you now?"

Jasper took up her hand again. "I am not sure of how to proceed about a matter of great delicacy." There was a hint of a bashful smile on his face now, and he threaded her fingers through his and squeezed her hands tightly. "Tell me what a rake must do to discover if the woman he admires, loves, most in the world might consider marrying him one day?"

CHAPTER TWENTY-ONE

FOR A MOMENT, Jasper feared Sophie might faint. She must not have imagined what had been growing in his heart for some time because of her influence and friendship. He had not believed himself capable of such love, either, until it had almost been too late to declare himself her man. But he did not want Sophie to marry anyone other than him. Jasper wanted Sophie to be his forever, and not as his secret lover or mistress while she tended other people's children or the business of the brothel. He wanted her to have her own children and career. And he wanted to be there to support her in every endeavor.

"I... I..." she stammered.

"Too much of a surprise?"

"Well, yes," she said, and then rushed away to pick up Isabelle, who had started to complain that no one paid her any notice.

Jasper wanted Sophie to belong with him here at the palace or anywhere else she cared to live. As long as he could be somewhere nearby, he thought he could be happy with just the crumbs of her attention, too. It had nothing to do with the money she would inherit from Madam Clover. That would not come for years and years, if he had any say. Money hadn't influenced his decision one bit. But falling in love had.

Even if she said no today, he would stand by her decision and ensure she saw her London friends and complied with the old madam's last wishes in the end. He would not let her responsibilities be stolen away from her, as Nash must surely have intended to do all along. Why else hide correspondence discussing an inheritance? Was it any wonder Madam Clover had been concerned enough to come looking for Sophie, too?

He took Isabelle from her. "What *do* you want in a man, Sophie?"

"I have it," she promised, tickling the little girl under the chin, and leaning into him. "What more do you want, Jasper?"

So, so much, but something remarkably simple, too. He caught her eye. "Everything, but what I want most amounts to two things—you and us."

"Us?"

"Just as we are, with a little more *us*, perhaps." He nodded and decided there was no point dithering over the right wording or waiting for a better time. "Marry me, Sophie. Become a doting aunt, but be my partner in all things forevermore. Travel to London with me or without me to visit your friends. They are your family. I respect you *and* them. Ravenswood will never be your prison again."

Sophie grew still, and then her breath rushed out of her. "I thought you were set against marriage."

"I just hadn't spent enough time with the right woman. There is no one better suited to giving me all this than you," he said, sweeping his hand out to encompass her and the children nearby.

This was everything. Family, responsibilities, and the passion of a surprising love that had come out of nowhere. Caught him so much by surprise that he had not known what to do about it soon enough.

"I never knew I needed this before you showed me what was missing from my life. I will, of course, maintain some rakish tendencies, but be warned, I plan to divert them entirely to your seduction. I will steal you away from your responsibilities to have fun with me alone often, I suspect. We will follow your rules or none at all. I leave the choice entirely for you."

A pair of small hands landed on his thigh, and he found his nephew Liam asking to be picked up. Jasper lifted him and deposited him on his hip, so the boy was face to face with them all. Thomas arrived next, standing close but a little apart. He'd not quite recovered his composure from when Jasper had given him a stern talking to. He gestured the boy closer and was gratified when he was hugged by the child. "What do you say, Sophie? Care to take a long walk with me and see where we end up together?"

"We are going to the woods," Liam reminded him. "Thomas would really like to go with us, too."

Laura could be there at this time of day, too. He's spotted her at the edge of the woods again yesterday, but she'd ridden off before he could have a hope of reaching her. If the children were with him, and they were on foot, she might just come out at last.

He glanced at Sophie. "I don't know. You'll have to ask Sophie if she could bear the long walk today."

He arched a brow, waiting for her response to taking a trip to the woods and to the prospect of marrying him one day as well. She still seemed a little shocked that he'd offered, to be honest. He would give her as much time as she required to decide. She had been the recipient of two proposals in one day. Only one of them had come from a place of love. She'd been disappointed in love before, and he could understand her hesitation to commit herself to another rake. Marriage had never been his priority, but Sophie was now. He would let her come to her decision in her own good time.

He dropped Liam to his feet and adjusted Isabelle in his arms. The little girl was such an amusing bundle of joy, but became heavy after a while. He'd like to hold her as long as he could until he had his own. A child who represented the best of him and all of Sophie, because to him, there was no better woman to be found anywhere.

Jasper presented his arm to Sophie, and after a moment, she hooked hers through it. Her grip grew tighter as they proceeded downstairs together and stepped outside into the sunshine without encountering his brothers. When they started moving away from the palace, she did not release him, but held fast and stayed close.

Glancing at her face, he saw tears standing in her eyes now. He looked away lest she become embarrassed and waited patiently while she composed herself. It occurred to him that Sophie was very much like Nash in that one small way. She hadn't ever been at ease revealing her emotions or her desires to him. It would be his greatest delight to draw her out in the future.

Today, however, he just hoped to hear a response of any sort. He wasn't a truly patient man when he saw something he wanted, and that was Sophie and only Sophie would do for him now. "Jasper, there's something I have to tell you about my past first."

"No, there is not," he said quickly, wishing to spare her the painful confession.

She looked up at him, and her smile slowly slipped from her face. "You know. Nash told you."

"You were ill," he said, and pulled her a little tighter against him. "What did you name the babe?"

"My boy," she whispered. "Alexander."

"I like it," he whispered. Jasper dropped a kiss to her brow. "I'd like to hear everything about him one day if you will tell me yourself."

A sob tore from her throat, and he stopped to let her bury her face in his shoulder. Her tears were brief and then she made an effort to compose herself for the children's sake. "I will. One day. I promise you."

Jasper nodded and handed her his handkerchief. "In your own time, as always, my dear."

Sophie sniffed. "Do you think the duke would mind very much if we returned to London as soon as Laura has settled into the palace? I should love to live there again. I miss the city."

Jasper laughed and put his arm about her shoulders, holding her close. "So do I. Ravenswood cannot hold us here if we want to go."

"Will you not miss them? Your family?" Sophie asked.

"My family is you. I never want to be without you," he promised. "I will always have my brother's."

Sophie suddenly stretched up and pressed her lips to his. "That was the most perfect proposal I've ever heard of. I love you, Jasper."

"And I love you more," he countered.

He kissed her properly, little caring that the children were staring and starting to snicker into their hands now. He had no need to hide his feeling for Sophie anymore. Everyone was going to know that the governess had stolen his heart by the end of today. This was only the beginning of their new and scandalous life together he suspected. He'd found the perfect bride and she actually returned his feelings in equal measure. "Later, we'll sneak away together and plan our great escape. I'm not going to wait until we're married to be alone with you by the way. Nash can look after his own children for a change at night."

"Or Laura will." Sophie frowned. "Look. Is that her?"

"Yes."

Sophie strode ahead of their little group without waiting as Laura emerged from the trees on foot now. Sophie went straight to her and dipped into a deep, respectful curtsy. "My lady, welcome home."

"You must be the governess I've heard so much about," Laura murmured, though she was scowling at him over Sophie's head. But then her gaze dipped to take in her sons and he saw her eyes fill with tears.

"Yes, my lady," Sophie said as she rose and stepped back. "It is an honor to finally meet you. Children, come and greet your mother."

Jasper stopped at Sophie's side. Thomas' eyes had grown wide, but he kept a distance from Laura for the moment. Liam did not remember her at all and hugged Sophie about the legs, but peeking at Laura shyly.

Sophie patted the boy's shoulder and winced. "He's too young to remember your face, I'm afraid. But Isabelle surely is no stranger to you."

Sophie took the child from his arms suddenly and thrust the girl at Laura.

Laura's arms went about the little girl, and both mother and child uttered a sob of relief.

Jasper grinned. "Sophie did the same when

she believed me the girl's father by mistake. But that was not the sound I made."

"I think it was more of a screech of 'help'?" Sophie teased. Yet a single tear rolled down her cheek. He put his arms about her waist and held her close as mother, sons and daughter stared at each other. "I love families reunited," she whispered to him.

"Wait until their father hears about this," he warned.

"Never mind him now. This is all that matters to me." Sophie wiped her face clear of tears and smiled at Laura again. "They are wonderful children, my lady. I am so proud to have had the privilege of looking after them while you were away. But they need more than I could ever give them. They need their mother again. You must come home, because I am leaving Ravenswood and I don't want them to be lonely."

Jasper was so proud of the way she spoke to Laura with such kindness and compassion and respect. Sophie had known loss and trouble in her life and could understand and sympathize with Laura's situation in a way he could not.

They would make wonderful sisters, united against Nash's rules and coldness, if Laura dared to trust her words and come back home with them.

Laura sniffed. "You must be tired from your

long walk carrying her." She backed toward a fallen log, holding Isabelle tight against her chest, and sat herself down.

"It's not that far to walk home again," Liam explained to Laura, releasing Sophie to follow his mother. "Are you really our mother?"

"Yes, I am," Laura admitted, and it was plain to see she was worried about his reaction. "I missed you."

"Sophie always said you would come back soon. Is that my sister?"

"Yes, she is," Laura admitted.

"That's good. She needs more than a governess, too. We need our mama," Thomas said, and then sat down close to Laura, allowing her to pull him into her embrace.

Jasper pressed his lips close to Sophie's ear. "Do you think they would notice if we slipped away now?"

"Possibly not, but we can't leave them out here alone. Laura comes home today or she might never. We'll be there by her side offering our support when Nash sees her again," Sophie said, her expression setting in determined lines. "We'll help her find her place in their lives again, and then we'll be married."

"If you think that would be best," Jasper whispered grinning at the way his life was being properly brought to order.

"I do," Sophie told him and smiled. "She needs her children as much as I need my favorite rake."

"You should call me your betrothed now, my dear," he replied, grinning and offered his arm. "I am a rake no longer," he vowed. "I am utterly yours."

CHAPTER TWENTY-TWO

SOPHIE WAS the first to catch sight of the duke standing at the foot of the garden, hands on his hips, watching them all with an inscrutable expression on his face. She moved past Jasper, and headed directly to him and curtsied. "Your grace, isn't it wonderful? Lady Laura has returned."

"Indeed, it is, Mrs. Radcliffe. Indeed it is."

"It is a day of celebration for the family, but I regret to inform you that Lord Nash no longer has a governess to tend his children. I resign my position immediately and will take my leave of the estate soon."

He appeared startled by her announcement. "Is that so?"

"Yes. The children have their mother back, so they will not be neglected."

"Ah, I thought perhaps Jasper might have

scared you off with his little party with his friends."

"No." A ghost of a smile touched his lips.

"Did you think I didn't know what he was up to and disapproved?"

She frowned. "Well, I suppose I did."

"These are difficult times, Mrs. Radcliffe, and we must all play to our strengths," the duke murmured. "Jasper excels at helping people give him their money and enjoy doing so. Excuse me, for now. We will talk again before you leave."

And then he walked past her to approach Laura who regarded him with deep suspicion. The pair greeted each other warily, and the duke lowered his head to whisper something to the woman.

Jasper left them, coming to stand by Sophie's side. "He's pleased."

"I'm sure he is. He's lost a governess and regained a sister," she said dryly.

"It's not about you," Jasper promised in a whisper. "You'll belong in the family too, I promise."

Sophie turned her attention back to the duke, who was taking a keen interest in Isabelle now, bending down to the child's level. Tickling her cheek and laughing when she tried to catch his finger with her mouth. "What a charming girl," he said, loud enough for all to hear. "She looks a great deal like our mama at that age. I must show you the portrait of her tonight, sister, so we can compare. She'll be a beauty when she's grown."

"She could never hold a candle to her own mother," Nash announced, surprising Sophie almost out of her skin because he was standing right behind her and heaping praise on his wife. Sophie had never heard him speak so warmly of Laura before. But there was an impatient edge, a huskiness, to his voice, too.

He barged past them, and Jasper pulled Sophie to one side. She held her breath as Nash advanced on his wife, wondering what he would do or say to the woman that had fled him and their marriage. There must have been something frightening in his expression because the boys fled the scene, rushing to Sophie for comfort.

Laura raised her chin. Eyes flashing defiance at her husband as he looked down on her without smiling or saying a single word of welcome.

That battle of wills might have gone on forever had the duke not begun coughing. That diverted Nash's attention immediately away from his wife. Sophie saw Laura gulp and take a deep breath to steady herself. Was she afraid of her husband's temper? She did not move away if she was, though. She kept her attention on him, not the duke.

Sophie glanced at Jasper. "What do we do now?"

He shrugged. "Offer tea?"

She nodded and called out. "My lady, would you care to come inside and take tea with the children?"

Laura met her gaze, and after a moment's consideration, inclined her head regally. "I would like that very much. You can tell me how long you and Jasper have been engaged?"

The duke paused his coughing, which may not have been genuine after all, and glanced their way. His eyes narrowed and his expression changed to one of utter bewilderment. "Engaged?"

Jasper brought Sophie's hand up to his lips to kiss. "Isn't it wonderful news, brother? I hadn't a chance to tell you about us with everything else going on."

The duke glanced sideways at Nash to see how he was taking the news, and then back at her. A slow smile spread across his face, and it seemed genuine. "Actually, it is wonderful news," he said eventually, straightening at last. "And it better explains your sudden resignation, too."

He laughed, but Lord Nash just stood there, immobilized by shock it seemed until Laura walked past him to place a kiss on Jasper's cheek and offered her congratulations. Then Nash twitched. His hand clenched at his side. His face slowly turned red.

Sophie grew alarmed that he was about to say something indelicate about the unexpected match they'd made. Yet he remained silent and finally looked away.

Laura turned her gaze on Jasper. "Be good to her, brother dear."

"Oh, I will be so, so good," he promised with a teasing wink for Sophie that made her laugh. She knew just how good he could be. He offered Laura his other arm. "Now about that tea, sister."

Laura nodded and linked arms with him. "Yes, tea and something for the children to eat, too."

"Of course," Jasper promised, and then looked at Ravenswood. "Your grace we will be in the morning room."

"The drawing room, if you please," he suggested instead. "We'll all go in together now."

"I'll join you all shortly," Sophie whispered, disengaging herself from Jasper.

She had a few words to say to Lord Nash in private first.

Lord Nash made a sound as Laura walked off toward the palace, carrying her daughter. The children rushed after them, offering to show her the way which, of course, she must already know. The duke did not immediately move to follow them but spoke to Lord Nash in a flurry of she whispers she didn't want to understand at all.

Sophie glanced over her shoulder to see Jasper and Laura disappear into the palace, and when she turned back, the duke was standing in front of her.

"Give him a minute," Ravensworth whispered. "Nash did not know about Isabelle."

But Sophie was done taking orders and strode to meet her former employer. "You had no right to keep my correspondence hidden from me. Those letters were precious to me and the only link I still had to my child."

Nash lowered his head. "I'm sorry. I thought to protect you."

"Oh I can easily guess what you thought. Marry me and your money worries might disappear one day, too."

His head jerked up then. "No. I liked you. I really, truly liked you. Laura and I were near strangers to each other until the day we married."

She wasn't sure she believed him, but it didn't matter anymore. "We will never speak of your proposal or the misplacement of my letters again, Nash. I am going to marry your brother and be happy. He suits me far better than you ever could."

Lord Nash winced. "I believe you."

"Good. Now, you will go inside to your wife

and children this very minute, my lord. Make peace with Laura and be a better father to your children, too."

He seemed taken about with her ordering him about for a moment and then his shoulders sagged. "How can I face her again?"

Sophie felt a moment of compassion for the man, but also exasperation. He had a long way to go if he wanted to be a better man or husband. "Go. To. Her. It is never too late to right a wrong."

He gulped and then wiped at his eyes before he walked toward the palace, his shoulder still slumped in defeat. Sophie followed more slowly and met Jasper at the doors.

"My brother was crying." Jasper looked astonished by that. "What did you say to him?"

"Only what needed to be said." She smiled. "That went better than expected."

"Yes, but that was the easy part. Getting them under the same roof. Keeping them there will be harder."

"They might disagree and argue, but Nash, Laura, and the children are together again as we hoped. They have to sort out the problems of their own marriage now. Keeping them together is a problem for the duke to sort out now, isn't it?"

"Indeed, yes," Jasper agreed. "Ravenswood is best at handling my brother. We'll stay the night, two at the most, then head to London to share our good news with Madam Clover and your friends there about our marriage."

"Maybe London could wait a few days longer," she suggested. "Laura might need a little help at first with managing all three children at once."

"As long as I have your love, I will be content to stay anywhere you want."

"Thank you for loving me." Sophie leaned into Jasper's arms and his fingers caressed the back of her neck, sending a shiver down her spine. She looked up at him and saw mischief in his eyes. "You know, I never stood a chance once you sat in my lap."

"We're taking that chair with us so you can sit in mine every night then." He laughed and kissed her soundly, sparking those restless feelings that only he could ever satisfy. She hoped he never stopped seducing her.

The End

WILD RANDALLS SERIES

Engaging the Enemy ~ Forsaking the Prize

Guarding the Spoils ~ Hunting the Hero

*

SAINTS AND SINNERS SERIES

The Duke and I ~ A Gentleman's Vow

An Earl of Her Own ~ The Lady Tamed

*

REBEL HEARTS SERIES

The Wedding Affair ~ An Affair of Honor

The Christmas Affair ~ An Affair so Right

*

MISS MAYHEM SERIES

Miss Watson's First Scandal

Miss George's Second Chance

Miss Radley's Third Dare

Miss Merton's Last Hope

ABOUT THE AUTHOR

USA Today Bestselling Author Heather Boyd believes every character she creates deserves their own happily-ever-after—no matter how much trouble she puts them through. With that goal in mind, she writes steamy romances that skirt the boundaries of propriety to keep readers enthralled until the wee hours of the morning. Heather has published over fifty regency romance novels and shorter works full of daring seductions and distinguished rogues. She lives north of Sydney, Australia, with her trio of rogues and a fluffy four-legged overlord.

Learn more about Heather at:
www.HeatherBoydBooks.com

www.ingramcontent.com/pod-product-compliance
Lightning Source LLC
Chambersburg PA
CBHW030800200726
48285CB00013B/309